Unexpected Visitors

On that almost mythical summer night, two of Emory's "friends"—whom we had brought to Georgia from the Amity Moon Base—approached the house from the cottage in back. Their mask-like "faces" and long mechanical strides unfortunately attracted the attention of Guest, who followed them right up to the door.

"We can't take them into the Urban Nucleaus!" he shouted. I told him now he could surely see why Emory and I were not ready to return to Atlanta; the city had to have time to adjust to what we had discovered. "I won't help you!" He whispered. "You can't expect me to help you. I'm dead against bringing them in!"

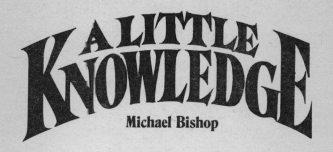

A LITTLE KNOWLEDGE

Michael Bishop

A BERKLEY MEDALLION BOOK
published by
BERKLEY PUBLISHING CORPORATION

Berkley Publishing Corporation
200 Madison Avenue
New York, New York 10016

SBN 425-03671-5

*BERKLEY MEDALLION BOOKS are published by
Berkley Publishing Corporation
200 Madison Avenue
New York, N.Y. 10016*

BERKLEY MEDALLION BOOK ® TM 757,375

Printed in the United States of America

Berkley Medallion Edition, MARCH, 1978

"Do you like science fiction?"
"No, my husband writes it."

Jeri, this book is for you. . . .

We have no ideology. We have no theology. We dance.

—perhaps-apocryphal remark of a Shinto priest

CONTENTS

A LITTLE KNOWLEDGE

PROLOGUE

The Introduction to *Out and Back Again: The Autobiography of Fiona Bitler* 2069

I am a citizen of Atlanta. In addition, I am a human being with even more compelling allegiances. After almost a third of a century in voluntary exile, I have been back in Atlanta only three New Calendar "seasonal" months. Even so, I continue to view my personal history as a comment on and a reflection of the latter-day history of this city. Although half my life has been spent under the unlidded skies of New Free Europe, I am Atlanta's child.

Unconsulted and, I imagine, loudly indignant at our removal from a dirt farm near Toombsboro, Georgia, I came into the city in 2001 with my parents, Amos and Candis Foe, during the Third Evacuation Lottery, sixty-eight years ago. This was three years before the vast honeycombing of our dome-in-progress was at last made rentless overhead. I was six months old. My infancy, childhood, adolescence, and young womanhood all belong to this city. Atlanta's institutions, my parents, and I worked sometimes together, sometimes at cross-purposes, to forge my personality and character (with which I am resignedly rather than smugly satisfied), and my one remaining ambition is, before I die, to Make My City a Better Place.

Often, like one who has contrived to keep himself off a battlefield, I have twinges of conscience. It hurts me that my thirty-two-year sabbatical with Emory Nettlinger in the Bavarian and Scandinavian Polities of New Free Europe has permitted me to escape the worst of Atlanta's religious, political, and social persecutions. For it was in the Autumn of 2034, five years after Carlo Bitler's assassination, that I smuggled the genius child of my husband's murderer out of the city, reached Savannah, and took him aboard a steam vessel whimsically christened the *Phoenix* to the

1

port of Bremerhaven, on the cloudy North Sea. From thence we journeyed to Salzburg, two years later to Vienna, three years after that to Munich, and finally to Scandipol, where Nils Caspersson's Light-Probe Institute soon became the focal point of Emory's life and work. It was in Scandipol, too, that I began to understand the cruel and estranging nature of my exile.

But in 2035, here in Atlanta, Carlo's assassination together with the civil disturbances resulting from it goaded the Urban Council and the Conclave of Ward Representatives into a flurry of secret joint sessions. During these meetings the Council/Conclave drew up, ratified, and took steps to implement that body of legislation known ever since as the "Retrenchment Edicts."

Herein were proscribed, upon penalty of imprisonment or loss of suffrage, the right of assembly; the possession and use of any variety of private duplicating machine; the funding of community concerts, street dances, under-strata festivals and flea markets, and "Chautauqua" evenings on the Level 4 Mall; the distribution of materials deemed by the First Councilor as obscene, irreligious, anticlerical, or seditious; and the right of the individual to worship, or not, as he pleased. Although the Edicts granted legal status and toleration to both the New Nation of Islam and the Federated Urban Society for Krishna Consciousness (or FUSKCONites), Ortho-Urbanism became the city's "offical faith." The days following the enactments of these repressive laws, in fact, have constituted a shameful Dark Age by Decree.

Having for three decades absented ourselves from the soul-destroying effects of this Dark Age, Emory and I have at last returned to the city. We have brought with us the emissaries of an as-yet-unrevealed new order, ambassadors of a harrowing but surely brilliantly unifying Light. With the rest of you, I, Fiona Bitler, await the revelation at hand.

In the meantime, several people have urged me to write the story of my life. An autobiography. A narrative, they seem to feel, in which I cannot help but star—even though, in recognition of talents larger than as well as fundamentally different in their thrust from my own, I have chosen to live out my life in the luminary presence of two great men: Carlo Bitler and Emory Nettlinger. One has been dead nearly forty years; the other is a quarter of a century younger than I. Still, the essence of who I am sings between the lives of these two men like a current alternating with a blinding fidelity of purpose and motion between two poles.

My existence, I hasten to explain, is a thing apart from Carlo and Emory, but it is bounded, and therefore partially defined, by their lives. If I am to be the protagonist of a book entitled after my name, then someone else will have to write that book. *This* one will principally depict me as a midwife of others' talents; and that, I think, is altogether in keeping with the outward-directed aims of both my travels and my resolves.

Perhaps I should add here that neither First Councilor Lesser nor the High Bishop Asbury Holman are among those who have urged me to undertake this project. They would infinitely prefer my silence. And until last Wednesday, the 18th Day of Winter 2068, I would have been content to oblige them. On that day, however, something happened to puncture my complacency and to install me at this console urgently keying out the most intimate details of my sixty-eight years. What happened? An insignificant thing, seemingly: I had a visit from a matronly Tower-dweller named Melanie Noble, whom I very nearly did not allow to come up to my suite.

I was afraid that an unexpected glimpse of one of our emissaries might prove a disastrous shock to her. I was afraid that she was one of those sad, deranged people who reassure themselves as to their personal worth by importuning the famous or the mighty, of whom I am at best a low-magnitude specimen. In truth, I was afraid of being manipulated and bored.

But the woman persisted, sending up her name three times, and finally I consented to see her. Carrying a bound sheaf of papers, she entered dowdy and abashed. Now and again, as she sat across from me in Emory's chair, she plucked nervously at the frayed netting of the apron she wore over her black quasi-sarong: an apron not for service but for show. I noticed that she wore cosmetics expertly, with a hint of controlled hysteria for the passing of her middle age. She looked to be about ten years younger than I, but fleshier and not quite so tall.

Nevertheless, something engaging in the woman's face, a youthful cast in her eyes, struck me as familiar—and then I recalled that her last name was the same as that of a young woman, a mere girl, who had come nearly two years ago as the third and least-experienced member of a "resources-reclamation" team to my cousin Jonah Trap's plantation outside Toombsboro. The girl's name was Clio Noble, and her team's ostensible mission had been to fetch Emory and me back into the city for our skills. But, only recently arrived from Scandipol, we were not yet ready to come, and it surprised us to learn that the Human Development Commission already had intelligence of our presence in the old Georgia countryside.

Clio Noble argued persuasively, but naively, that the authorities would welcome us home, an assumption we couldn't afford to share, and we successfully deflected the r.r. team's purpose only by a traumatic midnight confrontation in the stairwell and foyer of my cousin's trice-restored antebellum house. As I looked at the woman across from me, an older and less animated Clio, all these events flickered widly in my mind.

"Are you Clio Noble's mother?" I asked her.

Startled, she nodded an assent. Our small talk had not prepared her for so direct a question or so accurate a surmise. Then, somehow, I understood that Melanie Noble's daughter was dead. The woman plucked at the netting of her apron; her subtle, robin-egg-blue eyeliner stayed pencil sharp against a bright welling of tears. I waited.

"Toward the end of Autumn Clio disappeared from her cubicle on Level 9," she said finially. "After she came back from the Open the Summer before last, she resigned her job as a resources-reclamation specialist and the Public Housing Authority put her on Level 9 for failing to fulfill the requirements of her training. Clio called it the 'Last Circle.' I tried to get her to come live with Sanders and me in the Towers, but she wouldn't have it. Said she hadn't got out from under one obligation just so she could take on one she'd had before."

"Is she alive, do you think?"

"I don't think so. People get down that far, Mz Bitler, and they just disappear. You never find them again." She blinked away the moisture in her eyes, and I began to feel that Clio's mother could not decide which was the greater tragedy: her daughter's embarrassing consignment to the "Last Circle" or her ominous disappearance. "Like that other team member who came back with her," Melanie Noble hurried on, conscious of my gaze. "You know, that Indian fella." Here she opened the folder in her lap and turned to a page inside its front cover. "Alexander Guest, that's who I mean. He quit, too, after coming back from the mission, and Clio says in here," tapping the folder, "that she never saw him again. He just disappeared, you see, the same way Clio has. I think, Mz Bitler—I think the city's responsible, it's all their fault."

Melanie Noble had a crooked sort of courage. Her accusation was brave. Probably it was also just. For the first time in her life she had been moved to cry foul of an authority she had always deferred to, if not selfishly supported for the arbitrary favors it bestowed. And with a folder containing her daughter's account of our meeting near Toombsboro two Summers ago, she had come to me hoping that my heart would be filled with the same hunger for vengeance as her own. For, believing Clio dead, Melanie Noble was more bent on reinflicting her shame and hurt elsewhere than on determining beyond doubt the fate of her daughter. Only a direct assault on her own family had the power to stir her social conscience.

I said nothing. I was thinking of Alexander Guest, the full-blooded Cherokee Indian who had come out to Jonah's plantation with Clio and Newlyn Yates, the r. r. team's leader.

On that almost mythical summer night of fireflies and muted thunder, two of Emory's "friends"—whom we had brought to Georgia via Scandipol and the Amity Moon Base—approached the house from the servants' cottage in back. Their inhuman visages and their dreamlike, mechanical strides unfortunately attracted the attention of Guest, who had chosen to sleep not in the house with his comrades but beneath the oak trees on the wide front lawn. Catching sight of our emissaries, Guest followed them right up to the door and raised such a terrifying alarm of whoops and incoherent warnings that soon the entire household had gathered panic-stricken but curious on the stairs or in the classroom next to the foyer.

"*We can't take them into the Urban Nucleus!*" Guest was shouting at Clio and Yates, his immediate superior, above him on the stairs—as our alien visitors slipped from the hall into the parlor and the rest of us moved sluggishly to restore a sense of order and logic to the bewilderingly sundered night. Finally I led the big man back onto the lawn and told him that now he could surely see why Emory and I were as yet unready to return to Atlanta. The city had to have advance knowledge of our coming and time to adjust to the significance of that knowledge. "*I won't help you,*" Guest whispered at me beneath the Master's Oak. "*You can't expect me to help you. I'm dead against bringin' 'em in, Mz Bitler.*" Above the lawn, fireflies winked cryptically and thunder boomed like dying rockets in a distant sky. . .

"That fella who led the team—Yates, Newlyn Yates—he disappeared, too," Melanie Noble said, interrupting my thoughts. "But he never came back to the city at all. He defected, Clio wrote. What happened to him, Mz Bitler? Where is he now?"

"Somewhere in the Scandinavian Polity, I suppose. Emory saw to it that he was granted political asylum."

"Well, he was the smart one of the three, then. At least he *controlled* his disappearance, didn't he?" Mz Noble made it clear that she intended to leave Clio's journal at the Regency with me; she hoped it would provide us—her and me, partners in revenge—with the necessary ammunition to fell those responsible for her daughter's disgraceful banishment and death. Their defeat, she openly acknowledged, would be a vindication not only of Clio but of herself and her husband Sanders. Finally she stood and patted her lips self-consciously with the back of her hand.

"Please remember as you're reading my daughter's journal, Mz Bitler, that Clio was still little more than a girl when she wrote it. She says some sharp things about her father and me in here, and she confesses a loveless bit of bodyburning with that fella Yates when they were given the same room at your cousin's house—but I haven't changed a word of it, I haven't tried to make her look any better than she did herself. Anyway, when you get through, you'll know what a good person Clio really was at heart, in spite of all the changes she suffered these last few seasons. See if I'm not right, Mz Bitler.''

On this little challenge Melanie Noble's visit ended, and, later, I found that she was absolutely right. Her daughter—as the girl had so naturally revealed herself at the Phoenix Plantation—was an appealing combination of candor and naiveté. Reading her account of her resources-reclamation team's final mission, I experienced a strong sense of identity with Clio Noble and saw in her attitudes and stances a reflection of myself at twenty-one.

Thursday, the following day, I called upon officials in the Biomonitor Agency, the Missing Persons Bureau, the *Journal/Constitution* newstapes, and UrNu Waste Conversion to help me learn what might have happened to the girl. Dead, the word came back from a man in Waste Conversion (as I had somehow known it would): dead and disposed of a good five weeks ago, having ''O.D.'d'' on a solution consisting of one part thiopental sodium and two parts contaminated commercial Tetra Nabinol.

"Did this happen in her own cubicle?" I asked my informant over the telecom unit.

"No," he said. "She was found at two o'clock in the morning in a transit-tunnel. She was slumped against a wall. She'd just drawn a great big, off-center cross up on it behind her. The bad T-Nab, a lip-ice cylinder, and a used vein-tape were still on her person."

"Why weren't her parents notified of her death, then?"

"It took us a while to find out who she was. Fingerprints and cell slides had to be matched up. Nobody asked about her for at least a week, that was another thing."

"And when they did ask?"

"Somebody decided it was kinder to say she'd disappeared. That's what we usually say when they O.D. or suicide. It's policy, near about. We tell 'em the truth if their relatives persist, but this girl's parents didn't stay at us. They knew she hadn't just disappeared. They all do."

Where the exhortations of Emory and a few well-meaning friends have all failed, this incident, not yet a week old, has succeeded in laying on my brow and back the burden of autobiography. Was my first husband shot down that the disenfranchised might more easily fall victim to despair? Did Emory and I exile ourselves from the Dome out of cowardice rather than the conviction that our work in New Free Europe would be universally liberating?

I have to answer both these questions in the negative, but I must do so in such a way that my voice crying "No!" is heard from Scandipol to Toombsboro to the twenty-five nuclei of the Urban Federation. Transcribing my life and interpreting it, then, will be a labor not merely of self-justification but of faith—for I am sure that under the Retrenchment Edicts a book like mine will find it difficult, if not impossible, to secure the imprimatur of First Councilor Lesser. Only by faith—a faith as uncompromising as Clio Noble's before the undercity broke her—will I be able to persevere in this work and bring it to completion.

Perhaps by then, the emissaries who live down the hall from Emory and me will have chosen to disclose their purpose. The last words in Clio's journal, alluding directly to our visitors from 61 Cygni, go like this: "*Are we now, all of us, living in Bethlehem? And, if so, in whose tax books must we enroll ourselves?*" These are questions that haunt me, too.

But with a startling diversity of social programs in Atlanta's recent past (I think of the Glissador Corps, whose members were caught in a Level 9 assembly hall and gassed to death during their putative "revolt" in 2063, and of the geriatric septigamoklans begun by Dr. Leland Tanner and unwisely abandoned twenty-one years ago), I still believe that the New Jerusalem is realizable here and now. In this, my experience and my reason indict me as a Pollyanna, but my faith, hard pressed, will not concede the day.

If it's my portion to be damned, may God see fit to damn me as an unregenerate visionary.

—Winter the 25th, 2068
Regency Hyatt House

BOOK ONE

GENESIS

I

KNOWING nothing at all of what was in store for him, Julian Cawthon opened the door of his Level 9 cubicle and retreated before the advance of a young woman with bobbing curls and three members of the Federated Urban Society for Krishna Consciousness. It was Sunday evening, and Julian was clad only in red pajama bottoms and a bodyshirt inscribed with the name of Atlanta's last-place domediving team, the Meteors. Heavy of heart and bladder, he tried to recall where he had met this annoying, irrepressible girl who now had a hand on his stomach.

"Saba?" he ventured.

"Happy birthday, Julian. Brought some friends. You shouldn't be celebrating alone, you know."

Deftly Julian stepped aside, stuck his head out the door, and looked up and down the corridor. In its dim red light the paraplegic beggar/guard MeeJee Stone sat sleepily astride his rollerboard with a submachine gun in his lap. MeeJee raised the gun in weary salute, and Julian ducked back inside.

Saba Something-or-Other proceeded to introduce him to the three robed FUSKCONites clustering uncertainly about her. The two men, Swami Prabhupad and the much younger Gadahar, wore saffron linen and sandals made of twisted yellow plastic, while Radharani sported a sari of muted golds and browns and smiled self-effacingly at Julian. As for Saba, her hair was braided around each ear like a ram's horn. That was appropriate, Julian thought. Hadn't she just butted in?

"You all sit down," Julian said. "I'll be right back."

He'd done it, all right. That afternoon he had exchanged residence numbers with Saba in a pedestrian court off New Peachtree, right after losing his third straight chess match to old Dame Seedy. Saba Something-or-Other had stood behind him the whole time, kibitzing his every advance of pawn. . . .

Julian stalked into his bath-booth, relieved himself, and changed into a pair of khaki street shorts. Taped to the corner of his medicine cabinet was a photograph of two of the first sentient aliens humanity had ever encountered. Bent and yellowed, it had been on his mirror

11

for over four years now. As if for succor Julian glanced at the photograph.

Now there were *six* Cygnusians living on the top floor of the Regency. One more, Julian thought, and they'd have a regular septigamoklan of starfolk up there: a unit as close and self-supportive as the seven-person marriage groups the Human Development Commission had bound in civil matrimony back in the thirties and forties, when the problems of the aged had suddenly met with a host of innovative solutions from the city's social scientists. Now the only septigamoklan left in Atlanta—if you could call a unit of six a septigamoklan—had no human members at all and lived not in the Geriatrics Hostel of the HDC Tower but in the refrigerated penthouse of an ancient hotel. The human septigamoklanners who so long ago had married one another until inevitable death do them part; who had taken such whimsical and gutsy family names as Phoenix, Greypanther, and O'Possum; and who had striven to relume their lives when everyone but a few hard-headed Yea Sayers believed them in the smoky candle-end of their days—these old people had seen their "unnatural" marriages sacrificed on an altar of pungent theocratic incense and endlessly unraveling red tape. Today you had Cygnusians living at city expense in the Regency, tottering about like a family of wooden effigies; and Julian had a half-formed twinge of hostility toward them that this should be so, even as he was fascinated by their presence and the ambiguities of their relationship. A septigamoklan of aliens rather than of human beings. . . . But it wasn't six Cygnusians that Julian had to contend with tonight, it was this pushy girl Saba and three devotees of the ineffable Lord Krishna.

When he came back into the cubicle's main living area, Julian found the FUSKCONites seated cross-legged in front of his sofa. Annoyingly, he heard Saba rustling about in his sleeper-cove and workroom where she had absolutely no business.

"Saba has been coming to our center," Radharani volunteered after an uncomfortable silence. "We believe the *Bhagavad-Gita* in Swami Bhaktivedanta's translation has taken its hold on her."

"Do you have a copy?" Gadahar asked earnestly.

"No," Julian said. "Only a Bible and a cassette of the Koran." Did these people intend to proselytize him in his own cubicle?

The FUSKCONites were an UrNu-sanctioned sect, but they were supposed to confine their missionary efforts to three or four public courts, the walks in front of the *kirtan* centers, and the dwellings of people who had expressly asked to hear their message. The same held for the adherents of Ortho-Urbanism and Malcolm Muhammed's New Nation of Islam, at least technically; in practice the

Ortho-Urbanists took advantage of their status as the "Official Church" to suppress the activities of the two sanctioned minority religions and to root out utterly such inadmissible underground sects as the Christian Zionists, the American Hoodoo Criers, the Deist Devotees of Didigwari, the Primitive Baptists, the Spiritualist Elucidators of Dante, and whatever other odd boil of superstition and inspiration might be brewing both aboveground and in the undercity.

In his sleeper-cove Julian could hear paper being shuffled, pens and pencils moved, his visicom unit tampered with.

Radharani, saying that she and her friends had brought refreshments for the party, asked for and received a serving bowl. Into this she shook peanuts and apricots from an embroidered bag, and Gadahar fetched five cups of water from the kitchen-board. What a hot time we're going to have, Julian reflected. Knowing that Saba was gaily riffling through his work, he was fidgety and morose. For whose sins was he suffering this genteel invasion?

"Saba tells us you're a writer of fiction," said Gadahar when they were at last seated around the peanuts and apricots. He raised his eyebrows to the uppermost wrinkle in his shaven forehead. "Untruths, I believe that is."

"Ah, no," said his mentor, Swami Prabhupad, a brittle old man with not even hair enough for a scalp lock. "Truth revealed through artifice. In just this way, Gadahar, the *Mahabharata* itself is a fiction."

For courtesy's sake Julian told the FUSKCONites of his attempts to publish his work. In Atlanta, however, there was but one paying market, the Sunday fiction supplement to the *Journal/Constitution* newstapes. Although he had recently begun to submit his work through the transit tunnels to outlets in the Nuclei of Washington and Miami, still he had sold nothing. The Labor Placement Authority, he felt sure, was covertly monitoring his lack of progress and waiting for a chance to add his name to its placement rosters. "Tomorrow's really my birthday," he explained. "I'll be twenty-one and no longer exempt from the public-utility obligation, you see."

Saba interrupted their talk with a burst of raucous laughter. "Hey, Julie, you're writing about *them*, aren't you?" Her pretty ram's head appeared around the sleeper-cover's doorframe. "The Siggies, right?" Without waiting for a reply her head withdrew again.

"Your water's getting luke," Julian shouted after her.

In a moment, by a chain of transitions utterly lost to Julian, Swami Prabhupad was holding forth on palingenesis, the mayâvic world, and antimaterial oneness with the Lord Sri Krishna. "Don't worry about body, or matter, or that which gives rise to 'false ego,' " he was cautioning Julian. "The soul is amphibious, it lives on two planes . . . . Proteus, you may remember, was an amphibious sea god with the gift of prophecy, young man. But he would not reveal his truths to any but those who could hold fast to him while he changed shape under their hands. Oh, no. Well . . .so it is with our souls. We must hold fast to pure self in order to obtain the final truth outside the Wheel of Life and Death."

A moment later Prabhupad had extracted from him the intelligence that both Julian's father and mother were dead, dead at thirty-five, victims of what First Councilor Lesser had been pleased to call "The Glissador Revolt." Eight years dead, in fact. Mama Queequeg, as Julian had called his mother, and dear old clownish Papa Ty, both taken from him by an act of mass political murder. . . .

"The Wheel turns," Prabhupad was saying, "even when you're young. And the amphibious soul longs to escape the material world and journey to the plane of antimatter, which is not a planet such as our mysterious Regency starmen hail from, but instead a realm of spirit. . . . Spirit is the true antimatter, Mr Cawthon."

And then Saba came into the room carrying a sheaf of papers and moving her lips as if trying to decipher a set of hieroglyphics. Julian hopped up from the floor to intercept her, but she raised a hand to halt him, hoisted herself to the edge of the kitchen-board, and thumbed through his papers like an actress perusing an abstruse script.

"What's this, Julie? Tell me what it is."

"The first story I ever wrote. I keep it as a marker."

"A marker?"

"Like a pencil mark on a doorframe. To see how much I've grown. I wrote that story just after moving down here from Bondville."

" 'No Other Gods,' " Saba intoned, lifting an arm into the air. " 'A Short Story by J.T.L.Kosturko.' Is that you, Julie?"

"A pseudonym. One of my earlier incarnations. I thought it was sophisticated." He advanced on Saba again "Give it here, okay?"

"Uh-uh, Julie. I want to read it for Swami Prabhupad and his friends. I think everybody ought to get to hear it." And stumbling over the perverse spellings, busted syntax, and idiosyncratic punctuation of Julian's sixteen-year-old self, Saba began to read.

Why try to stop her? She was illustrating nobody's loutishness but her own. Even so, in the company of these serene, wide-eyed strangers it was hard for Julian to stand his ground, a merciless cruelty to have to listen to Saba read.

"No Other Gods" was terrible. It dealt with six aliens who had come to Earth to free mankind from religious superstition. The aliens' names were Lileplagak, Claxspkr, Podor, Elabelaberi, Snoke, and Yyrzstine; and Saba had so much trouble pronouncing them that Julian was forced to help her. He did so with exaggerated politeness and patience, as if to heighten the effect of her gaucherie . . . . Just after the climax of "No Other Gods," when the people of Earth renounced their barbarian faiths, the Cygnusians returned to their orbiting space vehicle, entered its High Throne Room, and there knelt before their god, the mighty Cygnusian sphinx, to give thanks for their victory over the heathen. The End.

"Did you really write that?" Radharani asked, obviously delighted. "It's very, very awful."

"Yessum. Five years ago I wrote it," Julian confessed. "Two years before Fiona Bitler and Emory Nettlinger brought the first two starmen into the city from the Scandinavian Polity. Don't ask me how I knew to call my aliens Cygnusians, though. I don't have any idea."

"Five years ago," Prabhupad said, excusing him, "you were another personality. What has remained constant, Mr Cawthon, is your questing consciousness."

"It's true," Saba said. "He don't write like that anymore."

She hopped down and slipped past Julian into his sleeper-cove again. "Here, I'll show you."

"*Saba!*" How could the Lord Krishna have a hold on this young woman? She had glommed onto Him as one more exotic, disposable commodity to use up and toss away. Poor Prabhupad, Gadahar, and Radharani, they were nothing to her but spiritual grist. Couldn't they see that?

"Saba, get your tight little ass out of my cove!" At once Julian regretted his choice of words, for Gadahar put his skinny hand on Radharani's wrist and Julian realized that they were married.

"What did you say?" Saba came out of his cove with another manuscript, his latest one, and glared at him tauntingly. She had heard him, all right.

"Saba, I didn't want a birthday party, okay? I thank you for thinking of it, but I've got work to do."

The girl smiled at him. "Okay, Julie. I missed your birthday by a day anyhow, didn't I?" Then her voice changed, her dimples disappeared, and her arm cocked back like a lever on a spring. "But I ain't gonna miss *you*, Julie!"

And she threw the story in his face. Nearly slipping on one of the drifting pages, Julian grabbed her arm, whirled her away from him as if reviving an outlawed dance, and, getting his bare right foot on her butt, propelled her across the room to the door. She hit it with the palms of her hands and slid to her knees. Again Julian slipped, but caught himself in the doorframe of his sleeper-cove.

Radharani rose gracefully, went to Saba, and tried to help her up.

"We'll go now, Mr Cawthon," Swami Prabhupad said.

Julian strode angrily to Saba, waved Radharani off, and took the haughty teenager aside. When she started to speak, he covered her mouth with his hand and pinched her lips outward so that she couldn't bite him. One of her ram's horns came undone and bobbed like a sofa spring over her breast. Julian activated his cubicle's door and shoved her into the hanging red fog of the concourse. He followed her out.

"Stinking mullet!" the girl cried. "Damn halfnhalf!"

"Saba, the next time you see me and Dame Seedy locked in combat, pass on by. Just pass on by."

Closing with him, Saba tried to tromp on his instep. Her arms flailed at him hysterically. As MeeJee Stone came cruising toward them on his rollerboard, Julian shoved Saba away from him and retreated in one long stride into his cubicle. The door whirred shut.

"You don't really want that one, do you?" he asked the FUSK-CONites, who stood facing him with expressions torn between outrage and sympathy, bewildered as to whom their sympathy should go.

"Saba," Prabhupad said, "is sixteen. As you were once."

"We must go with Saba," Radharani almost whispered. "We should not have come, Mr Cawthon—but I'm grateful that this disturbance didn't touch your cubicle-mate, if for nothing else. Goodnight."

Embarrassed, Julian inclined his head.

"Your terrible story was most thought-provoking," Gadahar told him in farewell. "Goodnight."

After the unearthly trio had joined Saba in the corridor, Julian surveyed the mess in his cubicle. No, they hadn't disturbed Menny, that was definitely something to be grateful for. In fact, he would commandeer Menny's sleeper-cove for the night. Because the big man had slept there only ten or twelve times in the last five years, his cove was always tidy, beautifully tidy, and Julian didn't feel like straightening up the mess Saba and her friends had left in their wake. He entered Menny's still, monkish room and stretched out on his bed.

An insane little ditty, of either his own or someone else's invention, came into Julian's head and taunted him with its rhythm. It wouldn't go away. He found himself compulsively repeating it.

You wouldn't give a fig,
Newton, To crown a Cygnusian.
So just drop an apple
Into Humanity's Chapel
And sin, sin, sin. *Amen.*

A masterpiece, whoever had written it. It was all there: physics
and physiognomy, science and religion, gravity and humor, cosmology and myth, paradise and fall, horticulture and whoredom,
puritanism and licentiousness, the commonplace and the far-out,
commercialism and . . . but you could go on like that all night.

Closing his eyes, Julian shut out the unpleasantness of the last
hour and struggled toward an uneasy sleep.

II

A MOTHER-OF-PEARL light suffusing the Dome as Weather Control
slowly bled dawn into the affairs of the city, Tonsured Billy came
down the steps of the West Peachtree rectormitory building and
hailed her across a sea of hurrying students.

"Margot!" Tonsured Billy called. "Hey, Margot, wait up!"

Amid the press of bodies in the quadrangle Margot Eastwin
halted and watched her classmate thread his way toward her. Everyone was off to Monday classes at the King Theological Complex on
North Avenue (once the campus of an institution popularly known as
Georgia Tech), and Margot was impatient to reach the transit
station. Come on, she thought at Billy, come on now. He approached her lumberingly, his hands empty of notes and instruction-
al packets.

"What's on today, Margot? I missed Thursday and Friday."

"I know. Why?"

"Because the fifth-year curriculum's nothing but eyewash!" His
Nordic face radiated resentment, agitation.

Margot laughed. "So you played hooky in protest?"

"I played hooky," Billy admitted. "Huckleberry Björkman."

In an asymmetrical sweep of glass and molded concrete the West Peachtree transit-terminal rose out of the pedestrian court ahead of them. They came under its transparent minaret as if entering a cathedral, and with hundreds of others jogged down its dank steps to the platform reserved for seminary students. The noise underground made conversation impossible. Margot put her fingers in her ears and grinned at Tonsured Billy. He was wearing an orange-and-blue sackshirt from Consolidated Rich's Contemporary Urban Leaders Series: the Asbury Holman physiognograph. The dome of Bill's skull sat like a pink island in the middle of his hanging blond tresses.

A good many of the fifth-year deacon-candidates were wearing tonsures nowadays, even some of the girls. It struck Margot as a subtly specious way of calling attention to oneself. The Ortho-Urbanist Church didn't sponsor a single monastic order, nor did it require its novices to shave their heads. She could hear old Steinfels saying, "If you want to go about bald, join the FUSKCONites. You halfhearted poseurs leave an unsightly fringe, but they get right down to a pigtail.".

The aero-train was coming. Students jostled for position as the *Tillich Carrier*, sighing like a streamlined vacuum cleaner, eased into the first station on the rectormitory-seminary line. Even though the trains were all glass, and acrylic ribbing, and amberplex shields, Margot always thought of Pound's haikuesque poem "In a Station of the Metro" when she had to get aboard during the morning rush: " '*Faces on a wet, black bough*,' " she recited, and nobody heard her. And now the train's dockside wall was curling down into its fuselage to permit onloading and bodies were surging over the gap between the platform and the open train.

Inside the last coach, human chatter and mechanical whooshing alike absorbed into the white noise of the *Tillich Carrier's* movement, it was quieter, and Margot told Tonsured Billy that Steinfels had gone to some sort of conference in the New Orleans Nucleus and that they were going to have a guest lecturer.

"What's it going to be this time?" Billy leaned his head against the padded seat back. " 'Then and Now: The Judeo-Christian Stance of Popular-Media Advice Columnists'?"

"Uh-hu, Billy, I don't think so."

With no prompting whatever, Billy went into a well-rehearsed spiel about their having been through all the "this-a-mologies" and "that-a-mologies" in the King Complex catalogue and the apparent desire of their professors to drive away deacon-candidates in bored-to-death hordes. "Conspiratorial ancient geezers," he concluded bitterly. "The old fools think they're protecting the purity of their calling. *Our* calling."

Tweaking the nose of his Asbury Holman physiognograph, Margot reminded Billy that the High Bishop was still in his early forties.

"Wyatt? The exception that proves the rule, Margot."

They rode for a while without saying anything. She would have liked to study a little, but Tonsured Billy's presence belayed that hope. She was four or five years older than most of her classmates, and Billy was the only one of them she had let intrude on her single-minded quest for a deaconry. Everyone else had given up on her, and he had become her transit-train and luncheon companion by virtue of his imperviousness to her shyness. To others, Margot knew, they were the Forthright Lummox and the Secretive Snob. All right. For all that, they still might make good deacons. . . .

"Who is it?" the Forthright Lummox asked. He leaned forward, and Holman's batik face was folded between moustache and nose. "Who's the guest lecturer? Did Steinfels tell you?"

"A Japanese American is all I remember." Margot consulted her notes. "Karl Tagomi."

"Aiii! . . . I've heard him talk. A sententious little Nip. At a comparative religion symposium he discussed the relationship of the Shinto 'god-shelf' to the Ortho-Urban use of statues and images. I think the man's secretly a devotee of some Oriental system. . . . What's his topic?"

"I don't know. It's all part of the Permutations of the Trinity seminar. Before you stone the man why don't you hear him out?"

Billy put his hands on his knees. "Okay. Christian forebearance. . . . I often pray for patience, Margot. I really do."

Covering his hand with her own, Margot wobbled Billy's kneecap fraternally. "Would you like me to pray for you, too?"

Tonsured Billy smiled a wan smile. "Please."

The aero-train's whooshing mutated into a gassy hiss as its computer system began applying the brakes. Like those of a gleaming, subterranean cavern, damply aglow, the walls of the North Avenue station solidified around the *Tillich Carrier*, and passengers struggled to their feet.

Billy sat rigid as a stone. "Do you know where I went when I played hooky? Nowhere at all on Thursday. But Friday, Margot, Friday afternoon I checked into the Regency Hyatt House and stayed there until two P.M. on Sunday. Blew a week's earnies."

"What for? Are you sixteen years old, Billy?"

The dockside wall of their coach pleated and curled back beneath the train's undercarriage, and Margot pulled Tonsured Billy to his feet by clutching at the sleeve of his sackshirt. Stragglers to the Feast of Learning, they climbed through the echoing North Avenue station behind a moving wall of their fellow seminarians.

As they walked, Billy told her an outlandish story. After ambling all over Five Points on Friday morning, he had strolled past the turreted Regency and talked himself into wandering inside. In the hotel's broad, open courtyard he walked by the New Kafe Köbenhavn and caught sight of Fiona Bitler and Emory Nettlinger at a table over wine. Standing by the cafe's wrought-iron railing, Billy heard the little physicist say, "Just one more, Fiona. They want us to bring one more in, to complete their 'family.' After that, I don't know." Tonsured Billy felt sure that Nettlinger was telling Mz Bitler that he had to make another trip to Scandipol, old Köbenhavn, to meet a seventh Cygnusian and escort it back to the city. At this point Billy had gone into the restaurant and taken up an adjacent table.

"Another Cygnusian?" Margot said. "What for?" They were now on one of the seminary's lower terrace levels, climbing toward the inflatable burgundy-colored superstructures making up the King Theological Complex. As the solar lamps overhead began to burn at full intensity and a breeze circulated gently through the dome, the morning took on a carnival gaudiness exactly suited to Billy's story.

"I don't know," he replied, his tresses lifting out behind him. "The only other thing I heard Nettlinger tell Mz Bitler was, 'It's time the populace got used to them, Fiona. Blank and Blank have been here nearly four years now.' He said two strange names, Margot, words full of glottals and liquids."

"Does Mz Bitler really look like Nettlinger's mother?" Margot asked, recalling that Fiona had once taught the future physicist in an old Van-Ed program. "She still looks handsome in the visicom tapes."

"Oh, she is. Dignified-looking, with a sad smile. But she's got to be nearly seventy, Margot."

Bumping shoulders and elbows with their classmates, they reached the terrace level on which trembled the wine red husk of Ogrodnik Hall, like a hot-air balloon tethered to a slab of concrete. The noise inside was a minor of that in the transit-stations, and the narrow domelight running the length of the superstructure admitted a grainy lambency that Margot half believed slowed their progress through the hall. A dimness seemed to congeal about them as they walked. . . .

When the "Bitlingers" left the New Kafe Köbenhavn, Billy checked into the Regency, asking for a room as close to the Cygnusians' penthouse as the desk clerk could give him. He ended up on the fourteenth floor and didn't set eyes on a starman the entire weekend.

"But why did you do it, Billy? What sense did it make?"

"No rational sense, I suppose. I did it . . . well, because something's happening, Margot. On Sunday morning I saw Nettlinger leave the Regency in a battery cart, carrying a clothes satchel."

"Going to Scandipol? To the Light-Probe Institute?"

"Righto, Margot. Where he'll greet an alien shuttled in from the NFE moon base and return to Atlanta with him. Something's happening, you see, something's happening!"

They entered the Permutations of the Trinity classroom and took a mimeographed handout from each of the two piles on Steinfels's modular desk. In the back of the room, their heads together like those of three choristers, Lewis Potter, Fredelle Fowles, and Alvar Caballero were moving their lips, trying to commit to memory the text on one of the handouts. His mind elsewhere, Tonsured Billy ignored them.

"We're due a communication from the angels," he cried. "Margot, I've got a feeling we're soon going to hear from On High."

"You and Billy Blake, Billy."

They took up desks near the trio working with Steinfels's mimeographed study sheets and, spreading hers out before her, Margot found herself reading a kakinki bit of doggerel.

I'm a ramblin' wreck from Georgia Tech
And a helluva engineer.
Like all jolly good fellows
I drink my whiskey clear:
I'm a ramblin' wreck from Georgia Tech
And a helluva engineer. . . .

There were additional stanzas below this one, and to Margot each one was as arcane as a chapter from Revelations.

"What's this?" Tonsured Billy asked, looking up.

Lewis Potter, an ascetic-looking black, said, "It's part of the commencement ceremony. We sing it. We sing it right after old Saganella Ruth gives us our diplomas."

"The reason it's included," said Fredelle Fowles, clacking three turquoise pendants together in front of her breasts, "is that there are a pair of doddering old souls on the Urban Council who're alumni of the engineering school that used to be here."

Margot, lowering her head to her desk, had difficulty holding back her laughter. Ramblin' Wrecks and Cygnusians. Jenny-O, Margot's adoptive mother, would have enjoyed living in such times. Just that old sweetheart's luck to die before the introduction of space critters into the cyclorama of Human Events. Fight songs and aliens. Poor Jenny-O, so untimely taken . . .

"Transcendental idiocy," Tonsured Billy mumbled. "What's on the other sheet?"

"The title of Tagomi's talk this morning." Alvar Caballero read it for the others. " 'Analogies Among the Three Points of the Formal Bonsai Display and the Persons of the Christian Trinity.' "

"Oh boy," said Billy.

In the mote-shot corridor outside their classroom Margot saw a tall figure go gliding past. She started. She glanced self-consciously at the rumpled physiognograph on Billy's sackshirt, and Billy, noticing her sudden flinch, lifted his eyebrows questioningly.

"I saw someone," Margot said. "He was—" She stopped. "He was wearing buckskin. . . ."

III

FROM a long way off there came an insistent thudding, like sounds muffled by water or the beery fog of a hangover. Feeling about blindly, Julian levered himself upright and heard the *bam-bam-bam* take on a distincter, more frightening reality. The computer-keyed clock above his kitchen-board said nine forty-three. He'd slept ten hours. The thudding continued.

"Hole yo' hosses," Julian whispered, conscious of Mama Queequeg rising through his words. At his cubicle's door he hesitated a moment before activating the communicator there. "Enough pounding okay?"

"Julie," a thin voice replied, "it's MeeJee." That explained the pounding: MeeJee couldn't reach the chimes. He had lost his legs and suffered a dislocation of the lower spine in a demolition accident with the McAlpine Company. "Got a message from that gal what was here last night, that Saba Dearborn gal."

Something-or-Other = Dearborn. A mistake getting involved with little Saba, a mistake exchanging residence numbers with her. Among the FUSKCONites, Julian remembered, there circulated the story of an otherwise devout man who at the moment of his death thought of a stag rather than of the Lord Krishna; thus he achieved not bliss but reincarnation as a stag. Deer born. That was the sort of sanctimonial story that had probably attracted Saba to the movement, not the spiritual dialectic of the *Bhagavad-Gita*. . . .

"MeeJee, I don't think I want that message."

"It jes' a note, Julie. She say to give it to you."

Wearily he let the door slide back, and as he did, MeeJee, there below him, used the butt of his submachine gun and his left hand to oar himself out into the middle of the corridor. His face betrayed terror and apology, but Julian had no time to study it. From opposite sides of his door, where they had concealed themselves, two men pushed into Julian's cubicle and forced him backwards toward the sofa. One was a huge Caucasian wearing a pair of light-amplification glasses for the Basement and a tentlike, sweetly perfumed herringbone tunic. The other intruder was a dainty deep-purple clad all in off-white gabardine, a man so small and neat it seemed he ought to be employed in delicate tasks like threading needles or polishing the insides of thimbles. An invasion force of two. Driven across the room to a sofa cushion, Julian listened to the *bam-bam-bam* of his heart and stared up into their set, uncompromising faces.

"I'm Elias Sand," the deep-purple said. "That's Gideon Clever."

Gideon Clever nodded and sat down in front of the sofa, next to the bowl that Radharani had filled with peanuts and apricots; he appeared genuinely disappointed that the bowl was empty. But for a pupil-sized opening in each lens, his light-amp glasses were dark, glinting blue, and with the empty bowl before him Mr Clever was more beggarlike than the paraplegic MeeJee.

"And you're Julian Cawthon," Elias Sand went on. "Twenty-one today." Whereas Mr Clever was probably an indifferent Ortho-Urbanist, Julian felt sure that Sand was an ardent New Moslem, one of Malcolm Muhammed's modern "reconcilers." His conventional dress, his neatness, his close-cropped hair, all pointed to the affiliation. When he spoke he made distracting use of his chin, swinging it back and forth like a tiny wrecking ball. "We're here to discuss parasitism with you. That's why we've come, Mr Cawthon."

"Parasitism?" A word that hadn't come into use, in a political sense, until the Retrenchment Edicts of two or three decades past.

"Parasitism," Gideon Clever affirmed.

"The failure to fulfill one's public-utility obligation."

"Uselessness," said Mr Clever by way of clarification.

"Mr Clever and I," said Elias Sand, "are research agents for the LPA, Mr Cawthon. Ernest Dearborn, our director, told us to anticipate antisocial behavior on your part. Violence, perhaps. His daughter informed him last night of her rude expulsion from this cubicle, you see.''

A mistake getting involved with little Saba. . . . Don't be a smart son, Julian warned himself; take it slow and easy. If this weren't all part of an elaborate show, Sand and Clever would already have shiv-gutted you or torn your head off with a squishcap cartridge. But Saba, little Saba, that gal has been working for her daddy, monitoring your progress toward "public utility." How often enlightenment was a function of being disillusioned. . . . Julian, gripping the left-hand sofa arm, tried to clear his throat.

Aloud, he told his interrogators that he had been searching for markets for his work in Atlanta and other Urban Nuclei. To mitigate their idea that he was an idler he even volunteered that he was almost entirely self-educated, that for three full years after obtaining his Level 9 cubicle he had spent eight hours a day in the public library up on Carnegie Boulevard. This was an exaggeration, a panic-induced lie. Even if it hadn't been, he could not have escaped the sleazy clamminess settling upon him for telling the LPA henchmen anything at all. Silence was much, much cleaner.

"But you haven't placed any of your work," said Elias Sand, ignoring most of this commentary. "And until you do, you're technically guilty of parasitism.''

Mr Clever, taking off his glasses, revealed eyes miraculously small and squinty, like those in a bleached hydroponic potato. "You have until next Monday to register with the offices on Decatur Street. Usually the grace period's a little longer, but Director Dearborn feels it'll be more . . . well, more—'' He stalled out and rubbed his eyes.

"Beneficial,'' Elias Sand prompted.

"More *beneficial* if somebody of your antisociable tenacies is on the job as pronto as possible.''

"Because I showed Daughter Saba to the door?''

"With your foot,'' Mr Clever admonished. His glasses went back on, and the dark blue lenses tilted reflectingly up at Julian.

Elias Sand smiled at his partner's qualification, then frowned to blot out his smile. Glancing at the sleeper-cove in which Julian had slept, he asked, "Your cubicle-mate at work, Mr Cawthon?''

"He's out. His shift doesn't begin until two.'' There was no need to tell them that Menny had been out for five years.

"Ah. We wanted to inform him, too. We wanted him to know you might be moving out. . . . Because if you don't sign the LPA roster by Monday you'll be dumped into the corridor, gang-pressed for street duty or the morgue-to-converter run, and transferred to a com-flop until one of our agents deems you fit for reevaluation.''

"All this for showing Saba to the door? With my foot?"

Sand liked that line. He smiled again. As if this smile were a cue to be helpful, Mr Clever rose and carried Radharani's bowl through the mess of the main living area to the kitchen-board. Sand followed him, nudging at papers with his toe.

"Can I offer you some breakfast?" Julian asked them.

Mr Clever, visibly brightening, wanted to know what was available. Hopeful of placating the agents with food, Julian crossed to the kitchen-board and knelt between them in order to look over his larder. The freezer unit of the icebox contained a single pigeon pot pie.

"No thanks," said Gideon Clever. "Had one last night."

Pie in hand, Julian straightened up and looked bemusedly from Clever to Sand, neither of whom so much as blinked. The pigeon pot pie was designed to self-heat when vigorously shaken, and, wary of his visitors' nearness, Julian vigorously shook the package. Then he put it on a hotpad, and a moment later they could all hear the pie bubbling . . . cooing . . . preening in its own juices.

Without warning the LPA agents each lifted a foot and in excruciating synchrony stomped on Julian's naked insteps. Julian, crumpling to his knees, heard lift above his cooing pot pie a ferocious whine, like the noise of a missile hurtling heavenward at an ungodly speed. When he grasped his ankles and rolled against the icebox, the whine finally died.

"May Allah be blessed," said Elias Sand somewhere above him. "I wish I were a better man."

And he and Mr Clever quietly let themselves out.

IV

"THE bonsai," said Mr Karl Tagomi, "is a tree that has been purposely dwarfed and coaxed into a graceful and beautiful shape. The tree you see here, despite its small size, is almost eighty years old."

Margot leaned forward to focus on the potted willow on Steinfels's desk.

"Before the construction of the Dome," Mr Tagomi continued, hooking his lapels and revealing the spash-pattern waistcoat under his tunic, "Atlanta had a society devoted to the arts of bonsai and miniature landscaping. No more, I regret to say; no more."

"That's all very good," Tonsured Billy said, speaking without raising his hand, "but what has all this to do with Christian theology?"

"Not an unfair question. But since I have only just begun, please hear my remarks of introduction." Mr Tagomi unrolled a scroll he'd been holding and hung it from a clip at the top of the chalkboard. Then he took a statuette of a bearded Oriental fisherman from a slipperbox and aligned the figurine with the potted bonsai and the scroll so that the three objects formed an equilateral triangle. "I would hope," Mr Tagomi said, "that this arrangement jogs the memory of some studious person who recalls his comparative-religion courses."

"The formal bonsai display," Margot finally responded, since her classmates showed no readiness to answer.

"Good. And in the Shinto prescription what do the three points of the display represent?"

Tonsured Billy, extending his legs and folding his arms, spoke at the ceiling: "The scroll means Heaven. . . ."

"Yes?"

"The tree means Earth, and the carving of the fisherman stands for Humanity. The three comprise Creation, each one possessing *kami*—god spirits or mystical essences—pertinent to its own sphere." Then, as if to show his contempt for the catalogue he'd just run through, Billy said, "It all boils down to a primitive polytheism without any accompanying awareness of human sin."

"Human sin," said Mr Tagomi reflectively. "There is no other kind, I believe. Still, in many ways, sin is a peculiarly Western concept, and to impute a failure to know it to Shinto is to judge that religion outside the context in which it was formulated. Please remember—" Tagomi consulted a roster. "—please remember, Mr Björkman, that Shinto is typical of Oriental religions in that it assumes—perhaps on a more *primitive* level than Buddhism or Taoism—an identification of God and Man. Most Western religions, you see, regard God and Man as distinct and not always reconcilable entities, creator and created, so that the principal goal of the created one is to establish a balanced individual *relationship* with his God, not an absolute *identity* with Him. In the Occident and the Levant this goal has led to an active pursuit of God's favor and of salvation through Him."

Head down, Tagomi explained that the theological goals of the Orient had led to an alternative psychology and a wholly different temperament. Seeking oneness with the Godhead of which he was originally a part, the Eastern devotee turned to such things as meditation and yoga to achieve his goal, with the result that Westerners adjudged his quest as an essentially passive one. Free will gave way to serene acquiescence in the immutably recurring Order of Creation, and one took a seat on the Great Mandala and went for a ride that inevitably ended where it had begun. God was immanent in the wholeness of Creation; he was not merely a Father to whom one might appeal on the historical as well as the spiritual plane. Margot's classmates sat stonily through this lecture.

"Therefore," Mr Tagomi concluded, sensing their impatience, "it is inappropriate to fault Shinto for failing to possess an elaborate doctrine of," nodding at Billy, "human sin."

Fondling her turquoise pendants, Fredelle Fowles asked if it wasn't true that there were Occidental religions that regarded God as immanent rather than as . . . "well, just sort of Fatherlike."

Tagomi said yes and mentioned the religions of a great many American Indian peoples. "But to call these systems 'Western,' " he added, "might not be truth-serving, since our Amerinds have their oh-so-distant origins in the East. . . . Do you suppose the Catholic explorer Columbus had an *inspiration* when he said of the people in the New World, 'Surely you are Indians'? Do you suppose?"

"Are you expressing a preference for the Eastern view?" Mz Fowles asked. "The Eastern psychology?"

"I am trying to answer your questions as you ask them. Both approaches have virtues, both failings. As for me, you see, I am an Ortho-Urbanist who believes." He abruptly unclipped the scroll from the chalkboard and faced the class again. "What do I have hereon, please?"

Tonsured Billy looked up. "The scroll representing Heaven traditionally is inscribed with a poem, sometimes a haiku."

"Correct, Mr Björkman"—and reading from the scroll, Tagomi chalked a haiku on the board to the right of the bonsai display.

> Off the rainy shore
>   he opens a slate grey shell;
>   in its mouth, fierce light.

"This haiku, people, is a fine example of how Shinto develops in its followers a deep respect for the numinous in the world order."

"Sir," said Lewis Potter, "since the man in the poem has found a pearl in the oyster—you know, 'fierce light'—couldn't his respect for the numinous actually be delight at the prospect of getting rich?''

The class laughed, and Margot with them. Out in the dark Pacific she envisioned a poor Shinto fisherman oystering with a look of mad, distorted greed on his face: *Cough up your pearls, you little molluscan swine, come on now, cough 'em up! . . .*

"Well, in the West and perhaps in the Japan of the years after World War Two," said Mr Tagomi, smiling, "such a reading might be appropriate. . . . But I am not wholly sure. The poem, you will notice, records only the empirical fact of the discovery, but the fact *suggests* awe and surprise and wonder, you see. And these responses to the world are typically Shinto. . . . It may be interesting to you to learn that the man who developed the Japanese pearl industry held a funeral service for the oysters who had died so that he and his nation might prosper."

Snickers all around. Aloud Margot said, " '*The Walrus and the Carpenter/Were walking close at hand.*' " The words slipped out.

"I beg your pardon."

"Excuse me, sir. Sanctimonious tears for the deaths of others, is what I meant. A requiem for oysters, in the circumstances you describe, smacks to me—to all of us, I suppose—of hypocrisy."

"Well, it's the attitude behind the action we must judge, is it not? Okay, then. In this case of Mr Mikimoto of the pearl industry most evidence would confirm his sincerity. Even if it did not, this one instance would not disprove the sincerity of other Shintoists in their respect for the *kami* in the things of Creation. Okay?"

"Analogies to the Trinity?" Billy said pointedly.

Mr Tagomi glanced at the boy with no surprise, no irritation. "We began with the scroll and the poem. We will continue now." He went to the board again, erased the haiku, and chalked up a set of odd equations, *tuppa-tuppa, tup-tup, tuppa-tup.* "Okay," said Mr Tagomi, turning back to them with a final *scccrr-ick* of chalk, "that is the whole of your lesson. As you may easily deduce from the chart, each Person of the Trinity may correspond to each one of the points of the formal bonsai display." And with that he fell silent.

BONSAI DISPLAY	CORR.	TRINITY[1]	TR.[2]	TR.[3]
Scroll	Heaven	Father	Christ	H.G.
Figurine	Man	Christ	H.G.	Father
Tree	Earth	Holy Ghost	Father	Christ

"Sir, is that all?" Mz Fowles asked after a moment. "Aren't you going to explain why?"

"Because there are three points in the display," Billy said, too loudly, "and *three* Persons in the Trinity. Tomorrow we'll discuss the profound relationships between the Holy Trinity and the first Roman Triumvirate, on Wednesday those between the Trini—"

"Doubtless you could go on wittily all day, Mr Björkman, and I would not hinder you, except for my duty to present this material."

Speaking in lackluster tones, as if the material were of someone else's devising, Karl Tagomi said that the scroll, standing for Heaven, of course had affinities with *all* the Persons of the Trinity, because each Person had His spiritual residence in Heaven. The scroll bore a poem, he said, because "*In the beginning was the Word, and the Word was with God, and the Word was God.*" As for the Paraclete, He inhered in the tree (Earth) and the figurine (Man) as well as in the scroll (Heaven) because it was His spirit's suffusing of the things of Nature that imparted to them the numinous qualities venerated as *kami* by Shintoists, and because it was the Holy Ghost's working through men that made manifest their possession of souls.

"That brings us to the Son," Tagomi said more enthusiastically. "You will notice—" he picked up the figurine "—that this statue is of a fisherman. A man. Humanity. Christ was God made flesh, and He said to Simon and Andrew, '*Follow me and I will make you fishers of men.*' He is the divinity in each of us, the flesh made God whose potential we all share. Is that not beautiful?" Now Tagomi's face seemed to shine from some internal source.

"How do we draw an analogy," Alvar Caballero asked, "between Christ and the bonsai tree itself, as the third column says we can?"

"The bonsai is an analogue of the Cross, upon which the Son died, having come to Earth—which the tree represents, you see— for that express purpose. In the Western view the tree becomes a *living* mediator of our Salvation, whereas in the East it is associated with the Bodhi-tree, the tree of the Awakening of the Buddha."

Margot saw Tonsured Billy straighten and rouse himself. "Sir," he interjected, "couldn't the bonsai be associated with Yggdrasil, too, the mythic ash tree that grows through all Creation, its trunk and branches representing Earth and Heaven, its roots in Hell?"

"I am not an expert on this," Mr Tagomi said, his forehead betraying a degree of surprise, "but my feeling is yes, yes, it could. Please note, however, that in the Norse system we must substitute Hell for the corner of the bonsai triangle now occupied by Man."

"Because," said Tonsured Billy, excited, "Christianity is a humanistic religion offering the hope of salvation, not just the threat of Hell." The orange-and-blue Asbury Holman on his shirt was smiling toothily.

"Yes," said Tagomi. "That, I believe, is why we are all here. . . . And in Shinto, of course, Man is viewed as an integral part of both Earth and Heaven, who carries in him the *kiyoki kokoro*, or pure heart, that is essentially divine, as Christ was both divine and human, as we are both human and divine. You see?"

"But what's the point," said Mz Fowles, gesturing at the board, "of bringing in a bonsai display to—"

She stopped. A man wearing fringed moccasins and a jacket with Buffalo Bill trim had appeared in the doorway. . . .

V

THE frozen, hovering interior of the Peachtree lift-terminal always reminded Julian of a church, a Gothic cathedral. In many ways it seemed both a holier and a colder place than the geodesic Worship Center erected a decade ago on the sites of the old Roman Catholic Church of the Conception and the Central Presbyterian Church. You could hear a faint, liturgical murmuring among the passengers disembarking from their capsules, and an odor of uneasy sanctity was exuded from the buttresses and walls.

It was a long walk to the Atlanta Newstapes Building from the lift-terminal, but Julian whirled into its foyer in fifteen minutes.

Five floors up, he emerged into a typer-clackety hallway partitioned into cubbyholes and niches full of communications equipment, bustling people, and a smell like machine oil laid over human sweat.

"Get out of the fucking hall," a dogfaced man in one of the niches advised him. "You'll get run over." The man had a work area but no privacy. Behind his desk Julian could see several large photographs on display and an old-fashioned hat-tree loaded down with cameras.

Julian sat down in an austere metal chair beside the desk.

"Nicholas Tybourn," the dogfaced man said without looking up. "Who are you looking for?"

"Mz Cixous. Josie Cixous, the fiction editor."

"Not in. And your name?" Julian told him, and Tybourn raised his watery, cornflower eyes. "Ah, J.T.L. Kosturko in the flesh. . . . I recall your old pen name, Mr Cawthon, because a man named J.L. Kosturko—no T, mind you—used to be a ward rep a few years back, and briefly Josie and I thought it was him submitting to us in his dotage. Then the same sort of stories started coming in as by . . . well, as by Julian Cawthon."

"Kosturko was my grandfather," Julian said coldly. "The establishment part of my heritage. I was an idiot to use his name." Offended, he stood up and twisted his latest story in his hands. "*Jour/Con*, jour/coff. You get your thricks going through the fiction-supplement slush heap?"

"A way with words," Tybourn said wearily, "Josie's a reporter as well as an editor. I'm one of her principal slush shovelers. I'll read that, if you sit down."

Staring at the photographs behind the newsman's desk, Julian felt like a man on trial: six aged faces regarded him with expressions ranging from senile self-satisfaction to beatific pity.

"Like 'em?" Tybourn asked. "Members of one of the experimental septigamoklans sanctioned by the UrNu Human Development Commission several years back. All dead now, every one."

"Where's the seventh member?" And using this question as a kind of camouflage, Julian sat down again.

"She took the pictures, Julian. Her name was Zoe Breedlove, one of the best photographers the combine ever employed and one of the last two septigamoklanners to die. I bought the photographs from her estate. . . . Are you going to let me read that story or not?"

"Okay. It's not finished, though." Tybourn's work niche became Julian's confessional, the dogfaced newsman his priest, as he told Tybourn all about Saba Dearborn and the agents of the LPA.

"So it's either glory in the newstapes or working out a conviction for parasitism, is that it?"

"Yes, sir. Or registering for arbitrary placement."

"No matter. I have to judge this," backhanding the manuscript, "on its merits, not your personal circumstances. . . . Tell me what this one's about."

"It's an interior monologue," Julian began.

"Acch. Not really? I'll bet it's from the viewpoint of a Cygnusian, too. Lord, Julian."

Chargrined and resentful, Julian said nothing. Why didn't the man simply read what he had brought him? Why this paternal taking-to-task, as if Julian had somehow disgraced the name of a mutual ancestor?

Finally Tybourn spread the manuscript out and read the first few lines aloud:

On the topmost floor of the Regency Hyatt House, in that suite of darkened, foggily cool, vinegar-scented rooms given over to the visitors from 61 Cygni, an alien moves with an outward clumsiness and an inscaping grace to the blessedly boomvoiced mediator between—

"*'Blessedly boomvoiced mediator,'* for Crissake!" Then he shook his head and continued reading in silence. When he was finished, Julian took the story from the newsman's hands and Tybourn relinquished it with a gesture of apology. "Henry James is dead, and the interior monologue's an awfully rusty old spike, Julian, even when you're trying to wedge it into a Cygnusian's head. You need to polish its point. There's no ending here, only a tapering off."

"Maybe I'll go over to Decatur Street." As Julian stood up, fighting back a resentment he knew to be misdirected, a troop of children came in disorganized double files down the aisle from the elevator. Wearing either the drab grey uniforms of Urban Scouts, with phoenix armbands, or bright, eye-maiming mufti, the kids carried note pads, cameras, portable printout machines, and dictaphone units. The woman leading them was Josie Cixous, and her children's crusade spun past toward a door at the far end of the hall.

One kid didn't go by. A black girl wearing a butterfly gown and a modified Turkana hairstyle, of a sort that only males had once strutted, paused beside Tybourn's desk and laid a manila envelope atop the clutter there.

"Hey, Yetunde," Tybourn said. "Meet Julian Cawthon."

"Hey, Mistah Cah Thawn," Yetunde said. She showed Julian a crescent of white in her left eye, then lowered her head so that her mock-Turkana mudpack threatened to make a pattylike dropping on the desk. Somehow it stayed in place. Somehow it wasn't unattractive on the girl. Yetunde's arms flashed out of her sleeves, and in one motion she emptied the manila packet on the desk. "New uns, Mistah Nick. We jes' developed 'em."

Even upside down the subjects of the photographs were recognizable as Cygnusians: close-ups, long shots, group portraits. And Julian thought instantly of the yellowed picture taped to his bathbooth mirror.

"Very nice," Tybourn said, looking through them. "We'll run these two in the dailies, these two in the Sunday supplement."

"Lovely shit," Yetunde said. "That's lovely shit, Mistah Nick."

Before the girl could gather up her work and leave, Mz Cixous's stormtrooping protégés burst from the door at the end of the hall and came marching back down the aisle. This time, smiling blithely, the fiction editor trailed them.

"We're off to the Level 4 Mall," she informed Tybourn, going past, "to see 'Cygnor the Cygnusian' at the Dixie-Apple Autumn Savings Sale. Since Yetunde had a hand in arranging this event, Idhe's letting the kids cover it." Idhe, Julian knew, was the general editor of the *Jour/Con* newstapes.

"Yeah," Yetunde confirmed. "My great-aunt say it okay for one of the Cygni people to meet the public."

And then the group was gone, fled toward the elevator. In response to Julian's puzzled look Tybourn explained that Yetunde was a niece or cousin of Fiona Bitler's. Her last name was Trap, and she was living with the "Bitlingers" in the Regency. As for the children with Mz Cixous, they were participants in a Van-Ed Witness-and-Work program inaugurated by Yetunde's "great-aunt."

"The idea's to get the kids out of care centers so they can see what grownups do when they go off to work. Then the kids go to work, too. A kind of bridge between generations," Tybourn concluded dubiously. He transposed two piles of paper on his desk. Absently he opened and closed a semistuck drawer.

Julian hesitated, his weight on one foot.

"Nine years ago," Tybourn suddenly volunteered, without looking up, "my only son went hoisterjack. Violently, though, the way they never used to. I haven't seen him since, Julian. Sometimes I pray he fell down a lift-shaft and got thrown anonymously into the waste-converters . . . you know, before he murdered some old soul tottering home from a game of checkers. That's what I sometimes pray, God forgive me."

Embarrassed again, Julian kept what he hoped was a respectful silence. What could he say? Tybourn had opened a door he hadn't knocked on.

But unslinging a camera from his hat-tree Tybourn said, "Got an assignment," and left Julian staring at the portrait of an emaciated-looking black woman, one of Zoe Breedlove's six geriatric "spouses." The old woman's eyes were merry, disturbingly alive, and it took Julian a moment or two to pull away from her and follow Tybourn to the elevators.

"Where you going?"

"Yesterday Nettlinger left for Scandipol. Today, the first public appearance of a Cygnusian since the brief one after their arrival.

Later this week, an even more important debut. I'll take my pick."

"What's the more important debut?" Descending, the elevator seemed to lift Julian's stomach into the knot of his Adam's apple.

Tybourn spoke as if reading a memo to himself: "On the twenty-first there's going to be a special service in the Worship Center. One of the Cygnusians asked permission to attend and, *voilà* they've arranged a Saturday service, Bishop Holman presiding, so the city's bigwigs can go without having to rub shoulders with the hoi polloi."

"Saggy Nelly's doing." Julian dogged Tybourn's heels through the foyer of the Newstapes Building. "Get me a ticket. Get me in."

Nicholas Tybourn barked as if he'd been kicked. He halted and looked at Julian. "This interest of yours is almost pathological. And you're skying it if you think *I* can get you in. I don't assign the people to cover these events. I don't give out free tickets." The ghosts of Grady, Gulliver, and McGill whirling with him, he whirled through the revolving doors into a p-court alive with artificial flowers and tumbling fountain water. Hydrangeas. Loops of liquid crystal.

Julian struggled through the doors after Tybourn, catching up with him and consciously trying to intimidate him with his persistence and his greater height. "Save me from Director Dearborn's dirty-laundry lists, that's all I'm asking. Take me on as a copyboy and shit-runner."

Halting abruptly and tilting his head back, Tybourn stared into the gold concavity of the Dome. A squat little girder-car was negotiating a rail high above Peachtree Center. "Jesus," he said quietly. "Okay, I'll try. Give me that story fragment and I'll telecom you if there's an extra ticket. Maybe Idhe'll let you do a story of some kind."

"Dat fine," Julian said, shuffling. "Dat A-OK. Mistah Nick."

"Swallow the patois, Julian, Don't make this harder than it is."

The Black Sambo routine had been a mistake. Partly to redeem himself, partly because he wanted to know, Julian asked Tybourn what his assignment was, where he was off to.

But Tybourn waved his hand ill-temperedly and stalked forward through the monstrous blue hydrangeas of the p-court. In his camera straps and rumpled clothes he resembled an old-timey biplane pilot. Julian tried to imagine him at an audience with Saganella Ruth Lesser, Atlanta's First Councilor, maneuvering to take her photograph. . . .

All at once the face of the old black woman in the photograph on Tybourn's wall asserted itself in Julian's consciousness, and he realized that he knew that old woman! Parthena Cawthon, he told himself, just short of dumbfounded; my great-grandmother, my

mama's paternal grandmama. And he recalled that once upon a time
Parthena had indeed been a member of a septigamoklan. Lordy,
yes, hadn't his Mama Queequeg told him with wit and pride of old
Parthena's indomitable spirit? It was a shame he had never had the
chance to meet her.

Died the year I was born, Julian thought. And there in broad
lamplight he had the uncanny sensation that across the barrier of her
death his great-grandmother Parthena Cawthon had reached out and
touched him. . . .

VI

ALTHOUGH Margot hadn't heard him coming down the hall, she was
looking at the doorway before he appeared in it . . . so that the man,
indeed wearing moccasins, fawncolored leggings, and a fringed
jacket with tiny crosses stitched into the synthasuede of each breast
pocket, took on substance as if between eye blinks.

"Sir," Mr Tagomi said, "you must come in."

Margot and her classmates were out of their seats automatically
as the High Bishop, Asbury Holman, came smiling into the room,
hunching his shoulders as if that would make him invisible. She had
seen Holman at close range before, but never in a costume other
than the clerical, and certainly not with his hair free and flowing like
that of a film or holovision frontiersman.

"Please," Holman said, "go ahead with your discussion."

When he seated himself across the room from Margot and Billy,
his hair and jacket fringe cascaded over the desk's back and sides
like tinsel on a Christmas tree. Everyone else sat down, too.

"I just wanted to know," Fredelle Fowles resumed, "why it's
necessary to find these correspondences between the bonsai display
and the Trinity. It seems—"

"Contrived," Tonsured Billy said, reverting to cynicism.

He's reverting for Holman, Margot thought, in order to spotlight his own disillusionment with the fifth-year curriculum. Although he had been cheerfully cooperating with Tagomi only a moment past, he now seemed ready to take an ax to both the bonsai representing Earth and his beloved Yggdrasil. Please stop before you get to the Cross, Billy. . . .

But Mr Tagomi said, "Oh, I share your dismay in the face of contrivance. I am not one who believes, as a malapropian character in a fine twentieth-century novel seems to, that genius is the ability to perceive analogies where none exist."

Across the room Bishop Holman chuckled appreciatively, and several of Margot's classmates eyed him with wary expressions.

"What is it," Mr Tagomi continued, "that I have wanted this lecture to demonstrate? Not the potential cleverness each of us may possess, nor intellectual elasticity, nor merely our knowledge of religions other than our own. What, then?"

Because the class sat sullenly unresponsive in spite of Holman's presence, Margot ventured an answer: "The universal idea of the latent divinity of our human nature?" How awkward that sounded. . . .

"Good," Mr Tagomi said charitably. "But in my mind is an answer perhaps more *secular* than what you are anticipating. . . . What could it be that I have sought to lead you toward?"

"Is this a guessing game?" Billy wondered aloud.

"Only if you do not know the answer." Then, as if to soften this rebuke, Tagomi said, "Interconnectedness. . . . Maybe it is almost too obvious to say aloud. But that is the point of my table here and of the correlations we have made. . . . Bonsai as Earth, as Cross, as Bodhi-tree, as the wholeness signified by Yggdrasil. And as each of these religio-mythic formulations contain a message of both the human and the natural realms, the similarity of the formulations, I say, suggests the interconnectedness of the minds and souls of the formulators."

The little man glanced at his digital implant, saw the time, and, after bowing quaintly, perched himself on the edge of Steinfels's desk. Margot found herself staring at his slippered feet, which didn't even touch the floor.

"Very fine, Mr Tagomi, very fine. I apologize if I've disrupted things." That said, the High Bishop rose from his desk, went forward, and assumed a stance almost gunfighterish. Spreading his arms as if to embrace everyone in the room, he effectively curtained off Mr Tagomi behind a fall of fringe. "I'm here for two reasons, candidates. First, to scotch a rumor before it gets started by confirming it in advance. And second, to bestow an honor." His buckskin wings slapped back down.

Pacing, Holman told the class that on the previous Saturday

morning the physicist Emory Nettlinger had approached him to ask
if a lone Cygnusian might attend "a typical Ortho-Urban service."
Certainly, Holman had replied, promising to make arrangements
for the very next weekend. . . . This news, Margot saw, glancing
about the room, was sinking into her classmates' consciousness
slowly, very slowly, like a libation poured on hard ground. Only
Tonsured Billy seemed to be completely aware what it meant.

"Your Holiness," he cried, as if in spite of himself. "Your
Holiness, isn't that a rather *bizarre* permission to grant?"

"I don't deny it, Mr Björkman—" (Holman made a point of
knowing all the fifth-year candidates' surnames, and Margot recalled that he had come to the cloth by an indirect route and from an
unexpected quarter; it was something she had in common with the
man.) "—but I've purposely dismissed all theological complica-
tions in this matter. My yes to Nettlinger was given spontaneously,
you see. And even on subsequent consideration I have no real
qualms about my decision."

Then, sauntering forward thoughtfully, he told the class of the
special Saturday service he had planned and of Fiona Bitler's
intention to accompany her guest from 61 Cygni to that service.
It would be, he said, a service unique in the history of humanity.

"Saturday," Billy whispered at Margot, "as if we were recidi-
vist Jews or Seventh-Day Adventists." Although crazy enough to
spend a week's earnies trying to catch a glimpse of a Cygnusian,
now that Holman had proposed introducing one to an Ortho-Urban
congregation Billy had grown argumentative and abusive. Why?
The boy was afraid of the Something That Was Happening in
Atlanta, without knowing exactly what it was; his uncertainty, in
fact, contributed to his fear. . . .

"Your Holiness," he insisted (and Margot was amazed by the
tenacity of his craziness), "aren't we sponsoring a spectacle if we
permit an alien to visit the Bitler Memorial Chapel during a service?"

"All religion is a smidgen spectacle, Mr Björkman, ours included." Holman's innocent-outlaw eyes coruscated above his
moustaches. "Whosoever truly wishes to worship, will worship."

Reluctantly Tonsured Billy subsided, and through a slit-window
in the balloon wall Margot saw a servo-janitor come choogling
around the corner of Ogrodnik Hall, blowing clean the already
immaculate terrace.

"The second reason I've come to your classroom," Holman was
saying as the machine whuffled by, "is to announce the name of the
deacon-candidate who'll perform the service-assist this Saturday. A
computer selection, you see. Academics, religious commitment,

personal maturity . . . all weighed and counterweighed. And that selection is—*Margot Eastwin!*''

Hearing her name announced so exuberantly, Margot turned blushing from the slit-window and found Tonsured Billy's moist hand covering her own dry one. Her classmates were looking at her curiously. Mr Tagomi's expression, she could see, was sympathetic. She could think of nothing to say, nothing at all. The syllables of a strange concept slipped in and out of her mind as she tried to think how to respond. Inter. Connected. Ness. There ought to be a way to make her thoughts cohere, a way to discover some meaning in what had just happened. Inter. Connected. Ness. The High Bishop was preparing to leave.

"Mr Björkman," he said suddenly, directing the class's attention away from her.

"Your Holiness?"

"I like that shirt." And Asbury Holman was gone before Margot could draw together the syllables of Mr Tagomi's haunting word.

VII

ON the semicircular steps of the First Ortho-Urban Worship Center, Julian stood beside Nicholas Tybourn and waited for the hammered aluminum doors to swing open. Weather Control was coaxing the city into twilight, and Tybourn, his tunic crisscrossed with camera straps, grimaced at the gaily bedecked ticket-holders on the tiers of Cherokee marble above them. Uptown, a Coca-Cola sign flicked on and off and contributed somehow to Julian's excitement. And across from the Worship Center the old state capitol building, now called UrNu House, seemed to attend to everything that was happening. For several decades that remodeled building had been the home of joint sessions of the City Council and the Conclave of Ward Representatives.

"Is Saggy Nelly coming this evening?" Julian asked.

"Shhh," Tybourn said. "No. No, she isn't. She'll have a closed-circuit hookup, though. She doesn't miss any of Holman's sermons."

In the pedestrian court across Hunter Street a group of curious onlookers huddled behind a police cordon, staring at the bigwig ticket-holders and the stained-glass triangles comprising the upper quarter of the Worship Center's exterior. Julian didn't begrudge these people their curiosity: that's where *he* would have been if he hadn't somehow finagled a ticket from the unhappy Tybourn. Now and again people shoved each other for a better view, and after a while a police van arrived and stood off Central Avenue to observe and control the crowd.

"They oughta just go home," Tybourn said. "They're not going to see what they came to see."

"Is he here already?" Julian asked. (He supposed "he" was the proper pronoun; the point *had* been argued.)

"More than likely. Mz Bitler was supposed to sneak him into the Worship Center through the ecclesiastic day-care school and nursery underneath it. He's probably been here all day." (Tybourn was using "he" too. Okay, then. So be it.)

Come on, Julian thought, rocking on his heels, open the door.

With a hellish clang, obeying Julian's wish, someone set the doors in motion. Street slippers and paper hems shush-shushed up the steps toward the opening, beyond which lay the amber and gold magnificence of the sanctuary, and a crude sort of line took shape. From the sanctuary loft the voice of the Worship Center's grand orpianoogla spilled down upon the congregation like an harmonic waterfall. Torrents of doomcracking music, terrifying in the power with which they fell and rang. Julian could not help shrinking back from this music.

Between the two huge doors a young woman in a virginal deacon's alb was taking tickets and punching attendance cards. Even though it was three weeks into Autumn, Julian would have to show her an unpunched card. Unless he made eleven more services before the year was out, the city would computer-deduct from his monitored inheritance a penalty for "spiritual dereliction." And, seeing the unpunched card, the girl would probably give him a churchly dirty look.

As it happened, Julian came in behind Tybourn at the rear of the procession, and the girl didn't even look at him. Instead she closed the monstrous doors with a touch, pivoted about, and walked to the head of the queued-up dignitaries in the church's central aisle.

All Julian got of her was a smell like milky lime: Lime Mime, a commercial powder recycled from converter ash and then artificially scented. It didn't last long, this taste of her. The notes of the grand orpianoogla seemed almost to rinse it away as they deafened him, overpowering every other sensation.

Julian looked up. The woman in the loft was playing "Upward for Aye on Wings," a hymn he had learned not from his Mama Queequeg, who hadn't been religious, but from Gramma Mary, her mama, who had. The roar of the hymn reverberated in the very marrow of his bones.

He was being left. The others were turning at the altar rail and filing into the Carlo Bitler Memorial Chapel, Tybourn with them. It didn't matter. He was seeing his mama again, and Papa Ty, and his dead grandmother too. Upward for aye. . . . That's what churches did for you, they yanked out your guts by means of some kind of powerful external stimulus and then called the gastric disturbances in your soul "mystery." Stalled there, Julian was close to tears, bitter ones. This sort of thing always made him adolescently bitter. He wondered how he was going to follow through on his intention to ogle some goofy-looking starman when kaleidoscopic portraits of his own parents were tinkling inside his head like broken glass.

I can't, he thought. I can't go in there. The surgings of the grand orpianoogla came and went in time with the beatings of his heart, with the retreats and advances of his own private Armageddon. . . .

Then the scent of Lime Mime came back to him. "What's the matter?" the deacon asked him, raising her voice to be heard.

"The music," Julian said. He gestured vaguely.

"Come into the chapel. It's this loud in the sanctuary because of the amplifiers." And she led him down the central aisle, past the altar rail, and into the Bitler Memorial Chapel, whose namesake, Fiona's first husband, had been murdered, twice as many years ago as Julian was old, at a joint session of the Council/Conclave. . . . He sat down in the last pew and looked over the heads of the seated bigwigs at a gold and purple mosaic behind the chapel's pulpit.

A mahogany effigy of Christ hung by nearly invisible wires above the pulpit and drew Julian's eyes upward. Arms outspread, feet gracefully pointed, the sculpture looked remarkably serene in its familiar agony.

> Serene in my agony
> I am carved in mahogany. . . .

A nice start, but he couldn't take it any further. The orp' in the sanctuary shifted out of "Upward for Aye on Wings" into a processional. A flashbulb exploded in the aisle, and the people in front of Julian clambered to their feet.

Tybourn, who was backing down the chapel aisle from the door, caught sight of Julian and said, "Here they come." His camera flared three more times as he passed out of sight, and an incenselike smoke—*blip, blip, blip*—drifted away above the congregation.

In the wake of this came the deacon who had led Julian from the sanctuary, bearing in her hands a huge white Bible. Behind her marched two preadolescent children wearing Urban Scout uniforms and holding aloft the Ortho-Urban and Atlanta Nucleus banners. After them came seven elderly choir members in gold and purple robes, their blue-grey heads erect and their eyes deadly serious.

The High Bishop Asbury Holman followed these people, smiling amiably and nodding at his acquaintances. For Julian this man's most distinguishing feature, excepting his starched canonicals and beribboned miter, was his Wyatt Earp moustache. Looking at the High Bishop was somehow exhilarating, even though Julian had never really had much traffic with the things Holman stood for.

After the flags were set and the choir seated, the young deacon led the two Urban Scouts back up the aisle to the rear of the chapel. As she went by, Julian noticed that she seemed to be talking to herself.

The processional music broke off in mid-note.

His arms mirroring those of the effigy above him, Asbury Holman motioned everyone to sit. As he began his introductory remarks Tybourn slid into the pew beside Julian.

"Well," Julian said, "where's our starman?"

With a wobble of his jowls Tybourn pointed to a booth in the gallery circling the chapel's interior. Julian peered. Although the chancel area was brightly lit, a gloom hovered about the elevated gallery, and it was only with difficulty that Julian made out the profile of Fiona Bitler and, partially obscured beside her, the masklike head of The Visitor. Then, distracting him, the lime-scented deacon returned from the sanctuary and took up a seat at the end of Julian and Tybourn's pew. She folded her hands and sat just out of reach like a mournful pietà.

"And now," Bishop Holman was saying, "we encourage those new to the First Ortho-Urban Worship Center to rise in order that we may recognize and greet you. You'll find a visitor's card and button—"

"He's got to be kidding," Tybourn whispered.

"—on the pew in front of you. So, if you'll—"

The deacon glanced at Julian and gave him a faraway smile. Her attention returned at once to Holman. A haunted, pretty face, Julian thought, with a mind most likely fogged out in Lime Mime and incense . . .

Tybourn elbowed him. In the chapel's gallery booth The Visitor from 61 Cygni levered himself upright and faced back toward the congregation. His forearms were like prosthetic devices . . . cloth-wrapped metal poles, frighteningly long. His face, and the halo of bone or cartilage behind it, resembled the finished product of a fine computerized lathe, but for the fact that the starman's mouth parts moved in a distinctly unwooden way, altogether silently.

"By all means," Tybourn grumbled. "Give him a visitor's button."

"Shhh. I thought you'd be taking pictures."

"Not during. Later."

It was a disappointment not to be able to see the Cygnusian's eyes. Photographs showed the creatures to have pupils like tiny hourglasses laid on their sides, so that in reality a Cygnusian had *four* pupils, two thinly joined bulbs per eye. The better to see you with. And these hourglass pupils were set in their rigid faces against a patchlike ground having the texture, or at least the appearance, of canvas.

Asbury Holman, smiling, briefly joined in and then stilled the congregation's polite applause, and The Visitor sat.

"Thank you, everyone," said Fiona Bitler, half rising from her chair. "We're here, in this chapel dedicated in memory of my late husband, because our visitor wished to come and because we were graciously given permission to attend. We hope the remainder of this service will go forward as if nothing at all were out of the ordinary about our presence here." She seemed to nod at everyone and immediately took up her chair again.

The service followed. Just to abide it, Julian had to curtain off any recollection of the storefront church where Gramma Mary had made him sit straight and starched for Sunday school. Nevertheless, he remembered ecstatic shouts, talking in tongues, disquieting calls to repentance. . . .

" '*What has been is what will be*,' " Bishop Holman was reading, " ' *and what has been done is what will be done; and there is nothing new under the sun. Is there a thing of which it is said, "See, this is new"? It has been already, in the ages before us.*

" '*There is no remembrance of former things, nor will there be any remembrance of later things yet to happen among those who come after.*' That's from Ecclesiastes, the Preacher."

The Bishop turned the pages of his unwieldy white Bible. "And this is from Matthew in the New Testament: '*Now when Jesus came into the district of Caesarea Philippi, he asked his disciples, "Who do men say that the Son of man is?" And they said, "Some say John the Baptist, others say Elijah, and others Jeremiah or one of the prophets."* ' . . . But the fact is, He wasn't John the Baptist, or Elijah, or Jeremiah, or even Isaiah crying in the wilderness. He was the Messiah, a Person altogether new under the sun. Paradoxically,

He was also as ancient as the Father. And this, people, is the heart of my message to you this day. . . ."

After the reading of the two Biblical texts Julian survived a recitation of the Urban Creed, the choir's rendition of "In Christ There Is No East or West," the taking of the collection, and the sermon itself, which developed into both a refutation of Ecclesiastes's gloomy fatalism and a glorification of Christ's redeeming and rejuvenating newness.

At the end of his sermon Bishop Holman said, "I now invite any of you who wish to pledge your lives to Our Savior, or to reaffirm your commitment to Him to come to the altar." The orpianoogla began playing "Come to the Church in the Wild Wood," and the moustachioed Bishop descended from his pulpit and spread wide his arms as if to receive into them all the citizens of the dome.

"Nobody's moving," Julian whispered to Tybourn.

"It's always like this. He'll stand there a few minutes, the choir'll sing a closing hymn, and that'll be it."

"Where you going?"

"Pictures." Tybourn hefted a camera, slid out of the pew, and crept forward down the wall under the chapel's gallery.

To Julian's right the dark-haired deacon was also sliding away from him, preparing for the recessional. She didn't get quite so far as Tybourn had.

Fiona Bitler's guest was coming down a helical stairway from the elevated booth. His body flowed, with an occasional hiccup at one of his many conspicuous joints. Once down, the Cygnusian proceeded to the altar railing and knelt there in front of Bishop Holman, directly under the suspended effigy of the Savior. The hinged body of the starman, Julian noted, gave every evidence of having been made for sackcloth and ashes, prayer and penance. Not at all nonplussed, Holman extended his hand and said,

"In response to our visitor's public commitment we do hereby accept him into the fellowship of Christ."

There was a commotion in the main aisle. Tybourn, fighting to position himself, began popping off the evanescent haloes of his profession: *blip, blip, blip*. A murmuring of astonishment blew back and forth; people stood up, spilled into the aisles, jousted with each other for a better view of what they had already witnessed. Julian, also on his feet, caught the deacon's eye while the grand orpianoogla kept inviting people to come to the church in the wild wood. She was stalled as he had earlier been stalled, her expression heartrending.

Thinking *turnabout's fair play*, he made his way down the empty pew to the young woman and offered her a gentle reminder of her duties. "The recessional," he said. "Don't forget it."

"I won't," she said, half smiling. "It's going to take a few minutes for things to get sorted out, though. I'm waiting."

Julian waited with her. A little bit later the recessional ceremony did take place, but amid a singularly unreligious hubbub and confusion as counter-flows of people clogged the aisles. Crazy, he thought, standing aloof from the jostling. Absolutely crazy. . . .

VIII

AN hour later, perched in pipestem slacks and ponchocape on the top rungs of the monkey bars outside the Worship Center, Margot saw him approaching from the church. Beneath her, his shadowy arms reached up and encircled a pair of the cage's outer bars.

"Do you always head for the playground after a service-assist?"

She couldn't see his face, but he sounded well-meaning rather than derisive. "Ape, man, angel," she finally responded. "You can feel like all three out here."

"In which category does a Cygnusian fall?"

What could she answer? She had no more idea than he did. He was probably a newsman, and he was out here intruding on her bewildered reverie because he wanted to do an interview with a participant in The Event. Okay. It was his job, after all, and everyone had a calling.

"You're an agno," Margot declared, "aren't you?"

"I'm not really anything." He put his entire weight on his arms so that he swayed to one side. "I've been through everything, nearly, and now I'm back to the beginning: out-and-out ignorance."

"That's agnosticism, isn't it?"

"Maybe. The agno's 'I don't know' is a stance. When I say out-and-out ignorance, I mean that I absolutely *don't know*—not even enough to say, 'Hey, that means I'm an agno.' Do you see?''

"I think I do. But for some people that'd be an awfully fine distinction to draw." Margot gave a short, shy laugh. What an intimate discussion to strike up with a stranger. What had induced her boldness?

The young man below her shifted his weight and slumped to the other side of the monkey bars. There he hung, a playground companion. Together they watched an acetylenic star flare out from a welding torch on the northwest quadrant of the dome. The pedestrian court across Hunter Street had emptied long ago.

"Does Bishop Holman ever play out here?" he asked after a while, so deadpan Margot wondered if he really thought that likely.

"This equipment's for the children in the center under the church. . . . The Littlest Angel Ecclesiastical Nursery School and Around-the-Clock Care Center, it's called."

"Not really?"

"Really. The High Bishop Andrew Ogrodnik named it that, Bishop Holman's predecessor." She told him her name, and he told her that his was Julian Cawthon and that one of the interesting things about him was that his great-grandmother had belonged to one of the city's first and last septigamoklans years ago. From this off-the-wall bit of intelligence he jumped to his relationship with the *Jour/Con* combine, and Margot asked him if he was supposed to write up The Event.

"Well, I'm supposed to write up *something*, I think. I'm trying to find a sidelight to The Event."

"Me?"

"Is that all right?" He stopped swinging and wedged himself into one of the squares of metal below her. All she could see was the soft ball of his head, his hands spread on his knees. "I'm asking your permission, Mz Eastwin, so there won't be any question of a violation of rights."

"Okay. But what was that business about your great-grandmother?"

"I don't know. A means of introduction, I guess. . . . And she's been on my mind ever since I saw her picture. Three nights out of the last five I've dreamed about her. In my dreams she speaks Plantation Patois."

Margot climbed down through the center of the monkey bars and left them through an opening next to Julian's. Rearranging her cape with her arms she said, "Well, thanks for asking my permission. I guess you have it. . . . Are you hungry, Mr Cawthon?"

"Call me Julian. But I am indeed."

"Then let's go to Latrobes's."

"Each for each? And some talk?"

"Each for each, Julian." She was frightened and hungry at once. Her body floated beneath her like an ague, all because of The Event. It would be good to get away from both the Worship Center and the rectormitory for a time. Beside Julian Cawthon, she walked to the transit-station under the twin-tower buildings.

In spite of the beggar/guards on duty at the old MARTA station, its walls had been beautifully, hideously, everywhere bedizened with graffiti: philosophy, poetry, obscenity, humor. Margot always read the messages scribbled or swirled on the poured masonry, and always tried to see *through* them into the heart of the artist. The ones with religious or cosmological themes, if you had a small empathetic talent, were often the easiest to decipher. She glanced at a graffito with a political as well as a spiritual malaise behind it:

Jesus Bear
Allah Bear
Little Krishna Bear

"I read them too," Julian admitted. "I've even written them."

"I think I understand the impulse."

"But you don't indulge?"

She shook her head. "An image of myself established *against* Jenny-O's liberal model for me, I guess." She explained that Jenny-O was her foster mother, her *only* mother, an old woman with a Rabelaisian spirit. She asked Julian what his own background was.

The train was running late, and a few Saturday-night Hill folk were gathering for the ride downtown. Margot felt sure that Julian viewed all these people as "surfacesiders," herself among them, even though she and Jenny-O had lived in a Level 7 cubicle the entirety of their lives together. But Julian . . . well, he had the hive-dweller's habitual glower and etiolated, searching hands.

"Me?" he answered. "I'm an unreformed writer of underground verse. A poet with tunnel vision." He touched her hand and led her behind a number of people to a section of wall discolored by water marks and stress faultings. He pointed at a pair of stanzas scratched into the concrete at ankle level.

"Did you do these? You must have had to lie on your stomach."

"Not me. A kid I knew in Bondville. He occasionally re-inks the stanzas, always in red, always on his stomach. Today's Michelangelo ain't supine, he's prone. That we create on our bellies is probably part of the message." Julian read it aloud for her.

Simple Simon met a pieman
　　On route to a bazaar.
Simple Simon halved the pieman
　　With his scimitar.

"Zounds and fie, man!" said the pieman:
　　"Why so quick to make me wince, sweet?"
Said Bloody Simon to the pieman,
　　"I'm awfully fond of mincemeat."

"What, exactly does that illustrate?"

"Well," said Julian, walking her back to the main platform, "it shows us that evil is like a pie with a poison meringue. Opened, it's full of blackbirds. When life shoves such a pie in our faces the blackbirds scatter. But what do we do? We wipe our eyes and try not to absentmindedly lick our lips while the cyanide sweetness of unignorable evil is drying on our jaws. We are the mincemeat of our own apprehensions, slapstick scarecrows foolishly bedight, with—"

"Don't keep this up all night, okay?"

"Okay. Just about to fall on my arse, anyhow."

The aero-train arrived, and they went to Latrobe's. In the restaurant's window, beyond their own reflections, they saw an aquarium. Inside it there scrambled a veritable armada of lobsters.

"That's what I want," Margot said "Lobster."

The eatery was jammed. The sawdust on the floor had been smooched around into tiny dunes and flowers, and the butter-colored booths of Latrobe's seemed almost to be sweating from the heat of the people packed into them. The smells of beer and Mediterranean gage mingled with the tang of shrimp, and shrimp husks littered the floor. The music pouring out of the wall mounts just barely qualified as "borderline allowable" under the old Retrenchment Edict specifications.

"He fuckin' well accepted Jesus for his savior," a man in one of the booths said, but before Margot could hear any more of this conversation, the maître d' gestured them into a further room and the words that trailed after them were strange references to Saganella Ruth Lesser and the Council/Conclave. Margot found herself thinking, Is The Event just a political trick? Is there no likelihood at all of its being legitimate? At the back of her mind was another question, a curiously disconcerting one. . . . Did the conversion of a starman to the miracle of Christ's grace really count?

Margot ordered her lobster, and Julian asked for the spaghetti with shrimp sauce. These seafood items came into the city from the

Open. With other marine and agricultrual products fish was taken into Atlanta through one of several "receiving points" on the circumference of the Dome. These receiving points were off-limits to everyone but the unenfranchised laborers who did the heavy stevedoring there and a few supervisory officials. They were still off-limits four years *after* Fiona Bitler and Emory Nettlinger, with their starmen, had demolished the lie that the Open was a wasteland of kudzu and poisonous, endlessly replicating plasmas. . . .

Into the back room the maître d' pushed a cart equipped with a hotplate and a glass boiling pot. From a large waxen container beside the pot, using a pair of tongs, he extracted a lobster and turned it menacingly in the air. Margot looked at Julian, then nodded her approval. The maître d' drooped the lobster into the pot, where it flailed dreamily.

"Their nervous systems are different from ours," the maître d' said to Julian, whose expression was one of astonishment. "They feel no pain."

"Oh," Julian said. He looked unconvinced.

"Does that bother you?" Margot asked him. The lobster had begun to flush an intimidating crimson.

"Dat what us cannibal folk uster do to Chris-chun preachers," Julian said humorlessly. "Now dey doin' it to ole Brer Spinyback."

Margot exchanged a glance with the maître d', who nodded and with no trace of pique returned the cart to the kitchen.

"Thanks," Julian said. "I can't watch that sort of thing, even if they don't feel any pain. Since I probably wouldn't quail at *eating* lobster, I suppose it's a form of hypocrisy."

Sanctimonious tears for the deaths of others, Margot thought without a great deal of focus. . . . But she couldn't picture Julian holding a funeral service for the soul of her entrée. And as their meal progressed, she found herself opening up to him. With very little warning, in fact, she sprung on Julian the details of an experience that she still believed revelatory, and he listened attentively, occasionally asking questions.

"I was late entering the seminary because I spent the last years of my foster mother's life taking care of her. When Jenny-O died I was twenty-one, and I put my name on the LPA placement rosters, went to all the interviews they posted me to, and tried to dispel the murk Jenny-O's death had created around me. . . . One Friday morning, the sixth of Spring, I was in the transit-tunnels at five A.M. to get a headstart on the other harassed-looking applicants I'd been running into every day. I hadn't been able to sleep, and I was so early there was nobody else on the platform; I felt as if the fluoros in the ceiling had materialized me down there.

"After a while I heard a sound like a cat mewing. I turned around, but the mewing didn't come again, at least not right then. When it did happen again, I followed the mewing to a row of parcel lockers in a recessed area off the main platform. The tin faces of the lockers reflected me over and over again as I walked down the row, and then the mewing came again, much louder than the previous times. Instead of running away I started pulling the handles of the lockers and throwing open the ones that weren't keyed shut. The crying got louder as the doors banged back, and just as I wrenched open the final locker I was saying to myself, 'It's a baby, Margot; it's a baby.' And it was, Julian, an infant in a receiving blanket, not more than two or three weeks old.''

"A baby?" Julian pushed his plate aside.

"It'd probably been there most of that night, and for me it was like finding Moses in the bullrushes. A child to lead me out of my bondage to sloth and aimlessness and self-pity.''

Embarrassed, Margot stopped. She had never recounted this incident for anyone before and here she was spilling for a stranger the story of her . . . her spiritual rebirth. Maybe it was her week for talk. How had she ever gained a reputation for close-mouthed shyness?

Softly Julian said, "What did you do?"

"I carried him out of there, Julian. I went surfaceside and walked through four or five p-courts to the HDC buildings. The baby's hands and face were marbled with worrisome blue areas over a pallor like . . . you know, like jaundice, and I was afraid he might die in my arms. At the Agency, though, they took Little Moses with next to no red tape and no bullying insinuations that *I* was really the mother. Maybe old Mz Gaddis at the desk remembered me from my own tenure there, more than sixteen years before, or at least recognized my name. . . . Anyhow, they took him, and he was registered as Moses Eastwin—the Moses for me, and the Eastwin for poor old Jenny-O.''

"Are you sure the Eastwin wasn't a little for you, too?"

"I don't think so. It was a homage to Jenny-O given to me by Providence to perform, and so I joyfully performed it. . . . Finding the baby and recognizing that its beginnings mirrored my own, that was what triggered my revelation and turned me to the King Theological Complex. I've always believed, Julian, but I had to see my life as a continuation of Jenny-O's stewardship of me before I could *forget* Jenny-O, in a positive sense, and become myself. That's what little Moses let me do and why I decided to enter the seminary.''

Now Julian seemed to be studying her with a kind of neutral disbelief. "What happened to the little boy?"

"I visited him his first two years at the Agency center. Then they placed him, his name was changed, and I wasn't permitted to know into whose family he'd gone. That's the rule."

The maître d' returned, and Julian asked for a writing stub and a sheet or two of paper. "I'll write my 'sidelight' right here, Margot, so you can read the article and approve it."

"You don't need my approval. Besides, I've got to go."

"Wait now. This revelation of yours. Wasn't finding a baby in a parcel locker an awfully drastic way of coming to the cloth?"

"No more than some others. How'd you get to be a newsman?"

This question stilled him, and as a busboy cleared away Julian's dinnerware and gave him writing materials, Margot continued to eat, savoring not only the last delicate white flakes of her lobster but the rare quiet into which Latrobe's had just fallen.

" 'Upward for Aye on Wings,' " Julian said. "That's what I hear when there's nothing else to override it. I heard it on the monkey bars."

"Maybe that's *your* 'Voice out of the Whirlwind,' Julian."

"Not likely. An auditory afterimage is all. 'Voices' are either hallucinations or deceits of the physical world. Joan of Arc probably had a tooth tuned in to a pulsar."

"But *most* revelatory experiences are subjective, Julian; that's what gives them their impact. I don't mean to generalize my own experience or interpret it to have universal significance. I just know what it means for me."

"Well, let's see if what happened tonight doesn't get generalized, if it doesn't have a great deal of 'revelatory' value placed on it. All in the name of Ultimate Truth, too."

Margot finished eating, refused to let Julian walk from Latrobe's to West Peachtree with her, and after saying goodbye went forward to sign her prom-for. Julian didn't reproach her for wanting to go, but released her to the city with a skeptical squint. She held his face in her mind in spite of the chaotic images crowding forward for recognition and reached home well ahead of the rain.

IX

WHEN the two men ascended from the transit-station, the smaller man, a walleyed Negro with long hands, was trying to support his companion and lead him homeward through the ruins of a deserted neighborhood. His efforts were complicated by a pasteboard box that the larger man insisted on balancing unsteadily on his paunch.

"Nessim," the man with the box said. "Nessim, go on home."

"Soon's we got you safe to yours, Menny." Nessim Charles, an unenfranchised Muslim, had just watched Menny down five shots of wine-laced gin at an establishment called Steve & Dory's, and he feared that the big man would be murdered before he reached home. Nessim's bulging eyes seemed to take in and then recoil from the inward-leaning buildings of Coweta Town, whose official name was Urban Re-Renewal Area No. 9. Huggermuggers relished such places, and if the city's inescapable and sinister Watchers in the Dark caught sight of Menny and him, Nessim reflected, their conspicuous helplessness would invite attack.

"Nessim, there's nobody around but kitty cats." Menny leaned forward and spoke over the top of his box. "Miaow. Greetings, kitty cats."

The skinny lurkers and skulkers following along behind them, Nessim knew, did so because Menny's box contained several packages of flounder, now at thaw, that a teamster had given them for unloading his carrier so quickly. The box also contained a single live lobster to which Menny had tied a long piece of string at Steve & Dory's; now he set the box down and put the lobster on the crumbling street. It began to move off, and Menny pulled it up with a jerk of the string.

"*Menny!*"

"Shhh. I'm trying to figure things out, Nessim." He peered nearsightedly up the street. "Miaow. Miaow?"

51

"Figger out what? Why that Cygnusian 'cepted Ortho-Urbanism? Because it all a goddamn polit'cal trick, Menny."

"*Cygnuisances*," Menny corrected his friend, lazily unwrapping flounder while holding the lobster taut at tether's end. "We've got to feed these cats. They're starving."

In self-defense Nessim too began unwrapping the soggy packages of flounder. When Menny began throwing the unwrapped fish toward the sidewalks and building stoops, they landed as noisily as boards. Cats hurried forward on stiff legs, their tails kinking and unkinking above bungholes puckered in anticipation. The smell of the founder was a smell as of salt marshes, ocean silt, and expelled placentas; it drew the cats from blocks and neighborhoods away.

"I'm responsible for what happened tonight," Menny said.

"*How*, goddamn it? *How* you responsible?"

"Nessim, everything's going to happen again, did you know that? It's called Eternal Return. The smallest gnat you smush against the inside of your nose is gonna be raised up in some future creation so that some resurrected you will have to smush it again. Eternal Return." Menny tossed a fish at an advancing cat and almost decapitated the animal. "I don't believe that, Nessim. But history *is* cyclical, maybe—different people doing the same stupid things other people did years ago. And I'm responsible because I'm one of the stupid people who's repeated some of the stupid stuff other stupid people have done before me."

Maybe Menny wasn't as drunk as he, Nessim, had believed. Walking a lobster through Coweta Town and throwing out frozen flounder for a hundred mangy cats weren't acts of pure sobriety, but Menny did seem to have a crazy sort of grip on himself. The conversion of a "Bitlinger" starman had set him off, though, and ever since quitting time he had engaged in an insane monologue of self-recrimination. Now, leaving the empty box in the middle of the street, he lurched homeward again. His lobster clicked along behind the two of them like a child's pull toy, somehow keeping up.

"Look," Menny said, waving his string-free hand, "in 1734 General Oglethorpe took a whole crew of Indians back to England with him. What I'm trying to figure out is if our aliens are Indians or Englishmen. So far it's pretty clear to me they're exploiters, not noble savages."

"They ain' Indians," Nessim said patiently. "And they ain' Englishmen, neither."

"They're one or the other, Nessim. And they're not Indians. I'm a Cherokee, damn it, and I know they're not Indians."

" 'F you already know, how come you mullin' this so hard?"

"Because I *don't* know, you walleyed nigger!" He jerked the lobster forward with an angry gesture. "No goddamn certainty."

Behind them Nessim saw that a pair of lank, moth-eaten cats were stalking Menny's lobster, which was now holding up its pincers like four clumsy scimitars. "Shoo!" Nessim shouted, throwing his arms up and threatening the cats. And they were sent scuttling back into the dark.

Prodding and cajoling, Nessim got Menny to the Kudzu Shop, a dilapidated florist's establishment that the big man had on lease or loan from Julian Cawthon, his official cubicle-mate. The UrNu Housing Authority still believed Menny living with young Cawthon; had it known otherwise, both men would be subject to fines, loss of lodging, and confiscation of property—but it didn't know.

"First there was a man here named Simon Hadaka Fowler," said Menny, trying to get his key into the door. "Next came the Kosturkos, who ran this place on weekends right up to the time Saggy Nelly had 'em gassed. Then it was vacant three years till Julie let me come up here. All in the books, Nessim, every bit of it."

Since the lobster was hanging off the last step, Nessim lifted it free and swung it up to them. Inside he saw that the Kudzu Shop consisted of three discrete but connected units—a walk-in area for customers, a greenhouse, and, beyond these, a tiny patio court. Even though the panes in the roof of the greenhouse had long since been knocked out or shaken loose, the steam of photosynthesis still seemed to be present in the Kudzu Shop; the air was horribly muggy.

Menny deposited his lobster in the middle of an empty display fountain in the customer area, where it clambered weakly, seeking purchase. Menny then led Nessim into the greenhouse.

"Where I sleep," he said, waving an arm at the flower trays huddled under the windowless grid of the hothouse. The trays resembled coffins or capsized dinghies.

They proceeded to the patio, where the air was less close. Nessim was made to sit down at a work table in the center of the smooth flagstone court, where the adjacent buildings seemed to lean over him like eroding cliffs. Dome-glow gave them light to see by, and Menny picked up a long porcelain pot from a wooden shelf against the patio's back wall and placed it in front of Nessim. The pot contained a miniature tree. Then Menny put a second tree on the table and introduced the two of them as Aoyagi (Green Willow) and Zakura (Cherry Tree). He explained that they were bonsai, dwarf trees that he tended in lieu of paying rent to his absentee landlord. There had been four bonsai in the Kudzu Shop when Menny first moved in, but one had died and another he had sold to a little Japanese man who had known the shop's first owner.

"You sol' a tree you s'posed to be takin' care of?"

"Julie said it was okay, Nessim. We split the money." Then,

absentmindedly, he said, "The rule with bonsai is, once they reach a pretty size and shape, keep them living but don't let them grow." He repeated this rule as if to himself and then shook his head.

That done, Menny sat down beside Nessim, put an arm over his shoulder, and unsolicitedly told him a recurring dream he had been having. The dream concerned Menny's rounding up and herding right down Peachtree Street the six "Bitlinger" starmen now living in the Regency. As crowds gathered in the streets or hung out of windows to watch, on a little spotted pony Menny drove the aliens to the I-20 receiving point. Here he maneuvered them through the locks into the Open and then followed them out.

In his dream the Open resembled the surface of another planet, not the loblolly-studded and kudzu-enveloped landscape he remembered from his duty as a resources-reclamation specialist six years earlier. A hellishly red and a sick green sun burned gassily in the sky, and cinders and the caved-in husks of fallen trees were obstacles to easy movement. As Menny herded the Cygnusians across the ashes, the starmen began to weep and complain of their treatment. They wept hard little white pearls, several of which embedded themselves in the hooves of his pony; others lay glittering in the cinders like tiny stars.

"Weird," Nessim put in, trying to be agreeable.

Menny had no truck with the complaints of the Cygnusians, however, and in spite of his pony's partial lameness drove them to a corral made of cattle bones, with wagon wheels on the gate halves. A sign over the corral said CYGNUSIAN RESERVATION. . . .

At this point in his story there sounded a warning crash of thunder, CRAAA-ACK!, and a breeze rushed through the patio.

"Menny," Nessim said, "I gotta go."

But Menny continued his recitation, explaining that the Cygnusians begged him not to leave them there. "Is it my fault there's a Daughters of the Confederacy convention at the Regency this week?" Menny invariably taunted them. "You should have planned for that." And he bridled his pony about and returned through the cinders to the Urban Nucleus, where he was always greeted by streamers of ticker tape and showers of confetti, just as if he were a twentieth-century astronaut home from the moon. Running the starmen out of town had made him an urban celebrity, and the pearls in his pony's hooves, extracted, were worth a small but elegant fortune. Rich and famous, Alexander "Menewa" Guest was universally recognized as a patriot and hero. . . .

"Menny!" The honeycombing of the dome had suddenly thrown down at them a flash of greenish, stormlike light. Nessim glanced back through the greenhouse; the customer area in front was the only place likely to give them much shelter once the rain began. With an elbow Nessim gouged Menny out of his fantasy and led the big man in a dash through the Kudzu Shop.

Rain began to needle through the grid in the roof in several loud, terrifying barrages. Companionably dripping, Nessim and Menny stood side by side in the customer area trying to catch their breath.

"Unpredictable, that's the key to it," Nessim managed after a moment. " 'F you got a 'ratic personality, the city puts you in Weather Control. To play God in Atlanta unpredictableness is the only thing you need."

Menny crossed to the display fountain and lifted his lobster out of the empty basin. Then, unmindful of the water crashing down on his head, he carried it into the greenhouse and placed it tenderly in the corner of a broken tray, where water had already begun to collect. All at once the rain stopped, and steam rolled off the concrete floor in blinding gusts.

"That ain' gonna help it," Nessim told Menny. "They live in the ocean, lobsters do. In the ocean, Menny."

Understanding what was needed, Menny came into the customer area and found a round container on one of the shelves of the service counter. He broke away its top and went back to his enfeebled lobster.

In pity and silence Nessim Charles watched Menny sprinkle the poor beast's water with iodized salt.

X

WHEN Julian came out of Latrobe's, he heard the eerie, relayed ululations with which the New Islamites were called to prayer and saw a swarm of men in loose half-jacket burnooses. Julian knew that this swarm of men was rushing toward "Mosque Block," a section near Five Points given over in recent years to the masjid of the Atlantan Caliphate and the decorated courts surrounding it.

Intending to walk to the Newstapes Building, he was instead pulled along in eddies of unquestioning purpose toward the masjid on Pryor Street. Finally, he asserted himself and raced ahead, giddy with the way his body felt moving at such nimble speed through so many people.

On Mosque Block the walls were floodlit from street level, and the designs upon them, glorifying Allah by their percision rather than by any representational idolatry, were tricolor replicas of the majolica-tile patterns at the Alhambra in Spain: burgundy, blue, brown. No graven images for the Muslims, Julian thought, dazzled by the symmetry of the patterns and the porcelain brightness of the walls.

Then he was floating in the lights raying up from the circumference of the court in front of the New Islam mosque.

If you ignored the spirelike minaret beside it, the mosque resembled both the dome over Atlanta and the Worship Center on Capitol Hill. But you couldn't ignore the minaret, for on its lowest balcony a man was gesticulating, singing out the long, amelodic vowels of his summons. Julian recognized him as Ammon Aslama, one of Malcolm Muhammed's company-grade officers, whom the lights raying up from the patio seemed to project in two dimensions against the curve of the tower. In a few minutes Aslama left off crying the faithful to court and began haranguing them.

Julian lost himself in the crowd below the minaret and listened to the angry, self-confident mullah.

"In direct defiance of the exemption granted us over three decades ago," Aslama began, referring to the Retrenchment Edicts, "the Atlanta Nucleus has systematically sought to curtail our right to assemble. Tonight, however, we have had discovered to us a pretext for the denial of our rights unlike any the city has yet had the audacity to contrive."

Faces either slablike or sinewy, black or pale, surrounded Julian and lifted apprehensive eyes to the man on the minaret's balcony. The Edicts had exempted the small but perfervid Hare Krishna sect and the Black Muslims from the otherwise universal requirement of membership in the Ortho-Urban Church, but the Black Muslims had since mutated into a movement of Islamic reconciliation and now included a good many Caucasians under a new, nonracial banner.

"What pretext, Honorable Aslama?" a man beside Julian shouted.

"Tell us!" other voices cried.

Ammon Aslama, his black face glistening under a snowy headgear, stalked the balcony as he spoke. "On the pretext that a creature from another star has accepted Jesus Christ, a mere *human* forerunner of Muhammed, as its God! That's the flimsy scaffold on which they hope to pillory us, and we must now take up the weapon of knowledge to dismantle this scaffold of lies.!''

Before Julian could stop himself, he had shouted, ''It isn't a lie, Ammon Aslama! I was there! It happened!''

And immediately he could feel the agitated community of the New Islamites give way to hostility; heads turned toward him and eyes sought him out. Julian kept his own eyes riveted on Aslama.

''An Ortho-Urban comrade is among our number tonight,'' the man on the balcony called down, looking for and not finding Julian. ''We welcome him. And the point he raises is a valid one, which I will demonstrate is even *more* of a lie than he may realize. Our esteemed councilors lie not only to the people of New Islam, brothers, but to the adherents of their own so-called 'official' faith!''

Grudgingly, the men in the court turned away from Julian and gave their whole attention to the commanding black archangel on the tower. He had lifted his arms, making wings of the sleeves of his burnoose.

''It's no lie at all,'' Aslama shouted, ''that earlier this evening a creature represented to us for almost five years as being from 61 Cygni did in fact kneel at the altar of the 'official' Church. We don't question the authenticity of this simply *physical* occurrence.'' The mullah lowered his arms and stared down where he believed Julian to be. ''Nor do I question the veracity of our honorable Christian witness. . . . Know this, though: *That alien creature is an artificial construct!* It's a starman disney'd out of wood, wire, metal, and devilish deceit, and it took our Ortho-Urban hierarchy over four years to bring this monstrosity to a level of performance they hoped would wooleye us into rushing to their bankrupt creed!''

No, Julian thought, as the crowd shifted about him excitedly, that's wrong. Maybe the trip to the altar was a carefully calculated ruse, part of a program of deceit—but the Cygnusian himself isn't a lie, he's a living entity. . . .

Impiously someone cursed and spat on the patio tiles. Julian could feel the energy of reprisal surging, collecting itself, in the hair-taut postures of these men. Aslama's allegation seemed to them all too plausible, all too typical of the Nucleus's ruling cadre.

Was it possible that the Cygnusians were really aliens, but that the one who'd knelt before Holman was a construct programmed for converting? . . . Was it possible that the aliens were all machines, but that this one had *sincerely* converted? . . . Stop it, Julian, stop it. Whether they're born, or they hatch, or they're partially assembled out there those cold eleven lights, you know they're living intelligences. Ammon Aslama's ''answer'' grows out of paranoia and painful ignorance of what The Event actually signifies. And what that may be, nobody knows. . . .

Now Aslama was urging his people not to submit to the harassments of the police and agents-provocateurs of the UrNu B.I. He proclaimed that no tyranny may triumph unless those whom it desires to unman abet its cause by their own surrender; he preached resistance and manliness, and Julian couldn't help contrasting Aslama's appeal to the *machismo* of these men to the almost militant gentleness of the FUSKCONites. Malcolm Muhammed's followers, against the prevailing tide of UrNu society, generally preferred their women veiled and isolated, their men protectively aggressive. Most New Islamites were Levantine warriors, and as shouts went up, shouts and fisted hands, it appeared that soon there would be a march of Muslims on UrNu House, throng upon throng of men in burnooses demanding that First Councilor Lesser appear before them to denounce a host of her closest advisors as schemers and sowers of discord.

But before this could happen a crash of warning thunder clanged overhead—*CRAAA-ACK!*—and a breeze funneled out of the aisleway of majolica tiles and rippled the hoods and sleeves of the Muslims in the court.

Aslama glanced up at the dome, sidled hurriedly along his balcony railing, and found a door into the minaret. Soon the lights raying up from the court were picking out and nimbusing the first drops of rain that Weather Control, most likely on command, had begun to lob at them. As Julian pushed his way through the cursing, half-panicked men toward shelter, he laughed mirthlessly and tried to protect the limp roll of paper in his hands. No use. Torrents were bombarding the streets and courtways with such clatter and fury that the crowds evaporated from around him and he was hurtling headlong over slippery pavement toward the overhang of an old saving-and-loan building across Edgewood Avenue.

Here he unfolded his manuscript and found it to be legible, though a bit smeared and sodden. Then the rain stopped. The night was steamy with it, and he left the shelter of the overhang and made his way to the Newstapes Building through a vapor reminiscent of the smoke drifting away from a battlefield.

Gone with the wind, sweet Scarlett . . .

Upstairs, Tybourn had gone into a computer layout room to check the plates onto which his photographs from the Worship Center had been automatically telemetered, and Julian had a little trouble finding him. When he did, the newsman was in such ill humor, so fatigued and snappish, that Julian followed him to his work niche virtually on tiptoes, hoping somehow to pacify him. The old folks on the wall behind Tybourn's desk looked serene and benevolent,

more glad to see him than was anyone else in the building, and
Julian, on impulse, tried to tell Tybourn that one of the old women
was his great-grandmother, Parthena Cawthon, who—

"Enough, Julian! What have you got?"

He handed Tybourn his story, smeared as it was. "What's
wrong?"

"The news is already out, out on radio a couple of hours ago—
even though WUNA didn't have anybody at the Worship Center.
You didn't squeeze this one to them, did you?"

"Yeah," Julian said derisively, surprised. "That's exactly what
I did." Down the hall, esoteric machines softly purred and rattled.

Tybourn, ignoring Julian's testiness to concentrate on his own,
read throught the boy's story and then looked up. "Christ! This is all
about how a divinity student found a baby in a transit-station
locker."

"Sure it is. How many stories do you have on The Event itself?"

"Three. Doobie's, Truesalt's, and mine. . . . I've done a short
piece myself."

"Okay. There you go. This is a sidelight, Mr Tybourn, a story
about the deacon-candidate who assisted Holman."

"Yeah. But why?"

Julian raised his eyebrows. "Human interest?"

"The focus of The Event isn't human at all, Julian. I'm not
saying that the human ramifications aren't important or interesting,
just that this . . . this isn't going to trip Idhe's trip-hammer. And *I*
don't hire, Julian, I've told you that."

Acting a bit, pleading for an opportunity, Julian told Tybourn that
he had just been over on Mosque Block and that he could also write
up the reaction of the Muslim community to The Event.

"I'm in a cul-de-sac," Tybourn protested wearily. "It's my fault
that I allowed you to infer the authority to hire in me, but I don't—
repeat, *don't*—have that authority."

"No openings?"

"Go over to the LPA Monday morning, that's all I can advise
you."

Julian looked at the rising grey tide of the floor and waited to be
drowned by it. Oh, hell, he wasn't that terribly upset, not really. He
had turned to the combine out of mild desperation and a promise to
himself to try even the unlikely. And he'd got to see The Event,
hadn't he? How many others had been so lucky? He very nearly felt
sorry for Tybourn, who was now beginning to feel sorry for him.

As the newsman started to speak, down the corridor toward them
rolled a heavyset individual in a white suit and beige slippers. Male
or female, Julian couldn't tell.

In a voice of ambiguous gender this person said, "The Miami

Nucleus—its Oceanarium, anyhow—reports that it's got a whale ready to calve. Or foal. You know, have a baby.''

"Hello, Doobie," Tybourn said absently.

"It's a beluga . . . they're sometimes known as 'white whales.' When it calves, or foals, or whatever, there'll be seventy-eight of 'em in the whole world. Seventy-eight belugas!''

"That's great," Julian said sincerely.

"It's power and joy coming back into the world," Doobie went on. "Consciousness and celebration given back to us from the biosphere. Maybe the seas are forgiving us.''

"I hope so," Tybourn said. "I hate it they've been pissed."

Doobie was oblivious, joyful. The Event at the Worship Center might as well have not occurred, for this blessed one superseded it. Like people in a maternity-ward waiting room, hands clasped, heads almost bowed, the three of them stood together in the corridor. How long would the labor endure? What would they name the baby? . . .

XI

FOUR hours later Abu-Bakr descended to the streets and put his hands in the pockets of the short-waisted striped burnoose his wife had given him during Muharram, his birth-month. With the gutters running and the eaves dripping in the neighborhoods where he plied his trade, he had received Mz Bitler's permission to go home early. By utter accident he had caught Ammon Aslama's harangue on Mosque Block and knew that he would have to carry its warning, wrong-headed as he knew it to be, into the bosom of his family. Most nights he slept at the Regency and thus saw Zada and the children only during the day or on his nights off, and he wondered what the starman's sudden conversion was going to mean to them, the family of a Muslim playing "gopher" for his enemies. How would they react, knowing what they knew of his work? Though it was good to go home tonight, it was also unsettling. Some strange things had happened.

Abu-Bakr entered the lift-terminal off New Peachtree. Tonight, alone under its groined ceiling, this became for him the basilica of Hagia Sophia in Constantinople. After the great Turkish victory of 1453, Mohammed II had ridden his horse into the cathedral and ordered the infidel mosaics painted over so that it could be converted into a mosque.

What would it be like to ride a horse into the lift-terminal? What would people do?

Wistfully, Abu-Bakr smiled. The only horses in the city belonged to the Ortho-Urban cowboy bishop and his cassock-wearing cowhands—horses which they quartered in stables under Grand Field. What did they do with them? For what purpose did they keep horses? . . . Ah, if only Malcolm Muhammed had but one half of the power of the Ottoman sultan who had turned the most beautiful cathedral in Christendom into the most fabulous mosque in all Islam. . . .

Alone, Abu-Bakr entered a descent-capsule. "Level 6," he said, and he rode into the catacombs. Glowing with the anticipation of surprising his family, he was a piece of filament in an outsized light bulb.

In spite of his command, on Level 4 the descent-capsule stopped. You could usually expect someone to get on or off on this level because of the Mall. But no one approached, and in a moment the whirr of renewed descent began hissing in Abu's ears.

Then, out of the shadows beyond the waiting area, two frantically garbed men came rushing. They jumped for the running board at the base of the capsule and pressed their faces against the plastic tube as if to terrify the man inside. With these new passengers clinging to the capsule, it sank away from the Level 4 station like a slow-motion bomb.

Hoisterjacks. . .

Precious Allah, Abu-Bakr thought, retreating from the gargoyles staring in at him; let them be tickleheeling, nothing more. Skeptically he pushed the police call-button inside the capsule. Level 5 was already gone, and in a matter of seconds he would have to confront the aitchjays with no glass intervening. . . .

The man on the left wore a nylon stocking which had been daubed with paint so that crude red hourglasses enclosed his eye hollows. The other hoisterjack wore a latex hood from Consolidated Rich's; its resemblance to the physiognomies of the "Bitlinger" starmen was intentional, and Abu recalled having seen children wearing such masks. . . . Now the thugster on the left was laying spittle into the hosiery's mesh with his tongue, and Abu saw a

Crusader's Cross tattooed into the skin at his throat. The spittle and the tattoo were both the insignia of a mindless antagonism.

As they came down, Abu-Bakr could see that the Level 6 platform was unoccupied. "Level 7," he said desperately, "Level 7," but the capsule's instrumentation was programmed to obey commands in sequence and its panel skinned back automatically as the hoisterjacks jumped backwards into the corridor. Mindless, everything mindless. . .

"All ashore, Omar," the one in the latex hood said.

"That's right," the stocking-head added. "Us Cygnusians are hungry for infidels." And he drew a crescent-shaped knife from a sheath beside his red-and-white-checkered clown's pants.

"Of course, you could spit on the blade," said the other insinuatively. "It's the sword of Allah, you know. You could spit on it and come over to the True Way like us Cygnusians have done."

With a calm he didn't feel, Abu-Bakr stepped out of the tube and moved gingerly away to the left of the hoisterjacks. He moved toward the auxiliary corridor leading to his own cubicle; homing, instinctively homing. As he moved, the hoisterjacks tracked him with crouching bodies and arms extended into hoops. To escape them he would have to break through the barrier of their arms like a child playing Red Rover. He thought of Gebrail, his favorite, and imagined his children crying distantly in the concourses, "*Red Rover, Red Rover, let Gebrail come over*. . . ."

What if these two men aren't hoisterjacks at all? What if they're concourse trolls, the very police I've tried to summon to protect me, pawns of the Ortho-Urban establishment, hirelings of those who would intimidate us with the spurious conversion in their church? . . .

"Spit on the blade, Omar."

What had Ammon Aslama counseled? Not to abet the tyranny of the city with needless surrenders or accommodating weaknesses. Exactly.So Malcolm's lieutenant had charged them all from the tower on Mosque Block.

"I spit only on you!" Abu-Bakr cried, and somehow, out of the dryness of his mouth, he found saliva enough to wet each hoisterjack in turn. Giving them no time to react he sprang forward with a howl piteous and piercing, and his tormentors, dumbfounded, fell back briefly in a terror of their own.

An hour later Zada found her husband arranged outside their cubicle in the traditional Islamic posture of prayer, his genitals in his mouth.

XII

On Monday morning Steinfels (Old Turtle, as Margot's classmates called him) was back, after Tagomi had substituted for him for a week, and Tonsured Billy was probably ecstatic that the Master himself had returned to save them any more disquisitions on the Formal Bonsai Display.

"What a week you had," said Old Turtle, his green eyes murky behind butyrate-plastic contacts, after chattering a time about his visit to the Tulane Divinity School; "indeed, what a week. Lessoned in religious matters by a Japanese gardener, and one of you a witness to the most compelling event in human history since men walked on the moon. Eh, Margot?"

She felt everyone's eyes upon her again. No one had yet been able to grill her for particulars (she had come late to class on purpose), and she could sense the general need. Old Turtle's delay in asking her outright had been a sleazy sort of tact. . . . But why 'sleazy'? she asked herself. Wouldn't you be curious if you were in their position? Still, the taste in her mouth was a sour one. In a single day the symptoms of a "conversion hysteria" had begun to show themselves in Atlanta, and in yesterday's newstapes. . . . No, that was too horrible to think about.

"Mz Eastwin?" Old Turtle was saying. "Are you there?"

"Yes, sir." She found herself staring at the wag of his tortoiselike throat. "And, sir, I think Mr Tagomi proved himself considerably more than a 'Japanese gardener' last week."

"Of course, of course." His throat quivered as if it might draw his head down into his natty Madras overshirt. "Only joking. Tagomi's a dear friend. Had he been present in the Garden of Eden, you can be sure there'd have been no serpent in the well-tended grass to tempt our primal forebears."

Har de har har . . . except that no one laughed.

Pathetically Steinfels retreated. He told them how at Tulane he had lectured on the three B's of Early Twentieth-Century (Revised and Accepted) Theology: Barth, Brunner, and Bonhoefer. This was a subject he was dotty on, and his embarrassment disappeared as his enthusiasm for his topic inexorably overtook him. Tonsured Billy said that on the last day of class Old Turtle would reveal that Karl Barth was actually God, Dietrich Bonhoefer the Son, and good old Emil the ravening Paraclete. . . . And Billy *liked* Steinfels.

Even so, in one of Old Turtle's rare pauses, Billy interjected, "Did you tell the Tulies about Martin Buber, sir?"

"That . . . that *Jew*?" Steinfels managed as his murky eyes blinked. "Of course not. Why would I so much as raise his name, Mr Björkman?"

"A fourth B, sir. And didn't those other Bs, or at least the theology they represent, co-opt Buber's I-Thou principle?"

"Buber the Bullyragger! Blind interpersonal relationships with no relevancy at all to surviving in an environment as heartless as the Urban Nucleus. For help there, Mr Björkman, you've got to turn to Brunner."

"Yes, sir. But—"

"Think! Think, Mr Björkman! Buber gave serious attention to Polish Hasidism. The Cabala. Isaac Luria and the transmigration of souls. Metemphychosis. All that mystical Jewish tommyrot." Old Turtle was clearly delighted that he had been "provoked," but Margot knew that in a few moments they would be back to her and her part in The Event. She might as well resign herself and give them a good-natured account of it.

" 'Scuse me, sir," a thin voice said.

All eyes turned toward the door. This time Margot had had no hint at all that anyone might appear there. She saw a small boy of indeterminate age and race framed by the doorjambs. His face was free of guile, free of innocence, his most distinguishing feature being a head of rioting, multicolored hair. Like a nest of yarn.

The boy came in, gave Old Turtle an envelope, and stood beside the desk with his face screwed up as if in pain or distaste. No, neither of these: he was intimidated by the people staring at him. Then Margot noticed that he smelled. His compact little body seemed to be giving off an acetate made up of odorants of animal sweat. Was he wrinkling his face at himself?

"Mz Eastwin," Steinfels finally said, "you're to accompany this young syce to Grand Field."

Syce? What was that? Aloud she said, "Sir?"

"An invitation. Permission to miss class, too. Pity." And when Margot went forward, Old Turtle handed her another envelope and waved her on with a palsied hand.

In the corridor Margot dug out of the envelope a monogrammed card addressed to her and spoke to the little boy. "Hi. What's your name?"

"Eddie."

"Hey, Eddie." And she read the note, which was from Asbury Holman; he was inviting her to one of his "recreational matches," he wrote, in appreciation of her exemplary service at the Worship Center. He assured her that his invitation wasn't a decree, that she could come or not come as she liked, and that missing Steinfels's class wouldn't be fatal.

Swaggering, little Eddie led Margot through Ogrodnik Hall to the terrace outside. Here, a lean, long-maned, piebald gelding, with nothing to graze on and its reins hanging down like fallen suspenders, gave them a wide skeptical eye as they approached.

"This is Cherokee," Eddie said. "Bishop Holman's horse."

"He lets you ride it?"

Eddie tapped lightly on the horse's nose, and as if it were a camel, Cherokee bent its forelegs and went down on its knees, then brought its hind quarters to the pavement, too.

"Are we both going to ride?"

"I don't weigh much," Eddie said. "He c'n do it, ole Cherokee."

And with Eddie in front of her, Margot allowed the gelding to transport her from the wine-red balloon of Ogrodnik Hall, down the many staggered platforms of the Complex, to the recently remodeled grandstands of Grant Field. They trotted through the tunnel from which the stables projected right and left under the stadium's highest seats and sauntered lazily out into the lampshine coating the electric-green turf of the playing field.

On the runway in front of the bleachers Asbury Holman was waiting for them in his Buffalo Bill outfit, a .22 automatic rifle in his hands. The sight of the rifle jogged Margot's memory, but only fleetingly. . . . .

"Good to see you, Mz Eastwin. The others should be along in thirty minutes or so. Like to watch me shoot some skeet?"

They dismounted as they had mounted, Cherokee playing camel.

"Yes, Your Holiness." That would be as exciting as listening to Old Turtle's strained puns and anemic bons mots.

"We somehow started a ruckus Saturday night, Mz Eastwin. A few in the hierarchy believe I overstepped my rights in accepting our visitor's confession of faith. What do you think?"

"No, sir. I'm sure you did what you felt best."

"That's what I told an interviewer from the *Jour/Con* combine yesterday. That I acted as (quote) one sentient creature of good will toward another, with no hasty deliberation about the scriptural pros and cons (unquote). What do you think of that?''

"I don't think you have to defend yourself. You acted out of intuition rather than dogma."

Holman was pleased, but he hefted his rifle and tried not to let her see. "Ammo?" he asked Eddie. The boy said he had an eight-clip in the rifle and another one in the reservoir in its butt. "Okay, Eddie. Let's go shooting."

Margot took up a seat about eight rows up in the stadium's A-section, and Eddie trotted across the turf to the traphouse next to the goal posts in the northern end zone. His hair fluttered widly as he ran.

Astride Cherokee, Asbury Holman rode up and down in front of the traphouse while Eddie flicked out clay pigeons in response to each rifle report and the Bishop's simultaneous cry of "Ready!" Cherokee danced and pranced, and the pigeons shattered, falling to the track on the opposite side of the stadium. The rifle shots echoed under the dome's honeycombing like coins rattling in a collection plate.

"Bravo!" Margot called. Alone in the stands she applauded.

Then she recalled that over two decades ago, while still a teenager, Holman had been a special-assignments marksman for the Atlanta police force. A sniper. A sniper for justice. But after cutting down a dozen rapists, holdup artists, hostage-takers, and nickel-and-dime terrorists, he hadn't been able to stand it any longer. And so, as the old joke had it, he quit the police department and got himself a steady job. . . . Well, not a job, perhaps; a calling. He'd become a seminarian right here at the King Theological Complex. For services rendered, the city footed the expense of young Asbury's schooling, and he soon learned to make substantive distinctions between animate and inanimate clay, distinctions he'd already been hurtfully aware of. . . .

Down on the field Holman replaced his spent clip with the fresh one from the butt and began again.

Margot marveled at the way he broke one, two, three, four, five pigeons just like that. Jesus, he was a graceful man. Mr Death's blue-eyed boy, the boy in blue who'd once served Death and Justice by picking off enemies of the Nucleus. Now he was a Christian soldier, galloping as to war. His second clip gone, Holman twirled his rifle on one finger, carried it across his pommel, and in one unbroken motion holstered it.

"Gonna exercise Cherokee a bit," he called to Eddie and took the horse off around the track, waving at Margot as he went by.

Other off-duty clergy began arriving. Eddie disappeared into the tunnel with them to get their horses, and when they reappeared on the track, Margot recognized among them two lieutenant bishops, three priests, and two quite privileged deacons. . . . Five years ago, at Andrew Ogrodnik's death, Holman had been elected to the High Episcopacy by a College of the Clergy consisting of some of these same people. At the time Holman had been the youngest lieutenant bishop in the Church. Why Asbury Holman, then?

Well, his piety for one thing. Second, the optional but supposedly outdated vows of poverty, obedience, and chastity he had taken while still in divinity school. And, finally, the lingering aura of his old special-assignments reputation. . . . Or maybe his elevation had resulted in order to break a deadlock in the voting. . . .

Holman canted Cherokee silken and proud to the track where his colleagues had assembled. He handed his rifle down to Eddie, took from him a polo mallet and helmet, and trotted with the others out onto that heady green expanse. Eddie came up into the stands and sat beside Margot, as silent and inscrutable as an egg.

At play in the fields of the Lord, Margot thought.

The teams took their positions, and soon she was watching horses of all shapes and colors churn over the turf in pursuit of a small, skittering white ball. Mallets looped in the air beside the horses' soapy flanks, and clicked, or failed to click, as the mallet head went through the bottom of its arc, stirrup-supported bodies straining to make the epiphaniac connection between ball and mallet head. It was exciting to watch, a release from the prison of Steinfels's wit; a release from thoughts about all that had happened, was happening, and might happen tomorrow. Motion and color and animal grace as purgatives of the spirit.

Each team scored a goal, and during a rest period Bishop Holman called up to her, "How're you doing, Mz Eastwin?"

"Fine. I'd like to see the tie broken, though." Then she realized that there was something incongruously courtly about this exchange and wondered if Holman saw it too. Maiden to champion. No, his arena of expertise was metaphysical and administrative; interpersonal relationships weren't his strong suit. . . .

A few minutes into the resumed match Bishop Holman, in front of the opposition's goal, urged Cherokee forward to intercept a pass. The ball sped over the turf toward him, and Margot leaned forward as Holman lifted himself in his stirrups to strike it, his body canting out to the right of his horse. She saw the mallet flash through its underhanded backswing. . . .

Lieutenant Bishop Coryea, a strongly built woman of fifty-five or so, came pounding up from Holman's left rear on a palomino filly. Before she could pull up the reins the filly struck Cherokee's flank and bounced off Holman's leatherstockinged leg. Unable to control the downswing of his mallet, the High Bishop drove it shatteringly into his horse's right fetlock. Suddenly the horse had no legs under it at all, and Margot saw it rolling amid a commotion of neighings and snorts.

Eddie was on his feet beside Margot. "The old bitch!" he cried. "The old cunt!" Alarmingly, the boy was still holding Holman's .22, his face between rage and tears.

Margot also stood. Looking quickly to the field she saw that the Bishop had managed to get free of Cherokee before it crushed him beneath its rolling piebald body. Then he stood helplessly by as one of the defender's horses kicked Cherokee in the head and tore away the gelding's wide, liquid eye. The animal's scream reverberated in the stadium like a distillation of old cheers, run backwards at the wrong speed, and Eddie sprinted down from the A-section's main aisle with the rifle in front of him.

By necessity Margot had to follow. For a moment the lampshine turned everything before her white, as if snow blanketed all of Grant Field and the polo players were grey statues caught in a blizzard of light. This passed, and soon she and Eddie were walking onto the disaster of horses and ecclesiastics at whose center they found Asbury Holman crouched over the thrashing, bloody head of his gelding.

"Please," he said to the people staring down at him from horseback, "give me a moment or two with Cherokee."

The others obediently departed, Bishop Coryea's palomino leading the procession, and Holman whispered into Cherokee's ear. Eddie took another eight-clip from his pants pocket and inserted it in the .22. He cast a reproachful backward glance at the woman who had caused the collision, but his eyes no longer gleamed with murder; reproach, only. Then Eddie handed the .22 down to Holman.

Holman's buckskins were stained. HIs face was splotchy, as if it had been scraped along one jaw, dyed brown on the other. "I can't, Eddie. I just can't." Animated clay, inanimate clay, human being, beast. Margot saw that he was impotent to deal with these sudden alternatives, and she wanted to tie back his hair, wash his face, wake him up.

At the same time she was ashamed for him. She was ashamed for him because in his impotence he permitted Eddie, now quite clearly crying, to point the barrel of the little .22 three or four centimeters from the blind right eye of his, Holman's, horse and then fire a bullet into its head, one last coin rattling into the plate.

Afterwards Margot caught Eddie to her and held him as he sobbed into her jacket, while the High Bishop Asbury Holman squatted over Cherokee repeating again and again, "*Forgive me, forgive us; forgive me, forgive us; forgive me, forgive us. . . .*"

XIII

SCANDIPOL lay under a mantle of new-fallen snow. The Tivoli Gardens had been closed for over an old-style month, and the young king Christian had just returned from summering on the tennis courts of Stockholm and Oslo to the familiar immensities of Amalienborg Palace.

Winter, Emory Nettlinger thought, riding past Kongens Nytorv in a hearselike solar car. The true winter. He had just paid his respects to the young monarch and could now see the snow-furred equestrian statue of Christian V out his passenger window. Acch. What weather to be sitting a horse, especially a bone-cold metal one. . . . Everything had taken longer than he had expected. No one at the Light-Probe Institute had thought he would be returning from the Urban Nucleus to request another starman of them, and the shuttle from the Amity Moon Base still required four days, even if NFE probeships could whittle light-years into chronoscopic splinters. . . .

For reasons Emory didn't yet understand, Anna Eldh, his driver, was taking him to the Glyptotek to see a piece of contemporary statuary (which ought by rights to have been on display in the Vesterport building); and Oskar Lavard, old Nils Caspersson's son-in-law, was fiddling with his meerschaum pipe, putting his thumb into its empty bowl and then drawing it out again.

"Stop raping your pipe, Oskar. What are you two up to?"

"It's a piece of Just Dragsted's work," Oskar explained. "He insisted on its being displayed at the Glyptotek before presenting it to you to take back to Atlanta."

Emory leaned his head against the cold glass of the car window. Sunlight cartwheeled off the snow. Just Dragsted, he knew, was the son of Peter Dragsted, one of the three principal politmarshals of the Scandinavian Polity.

"There are many precedents, Dr Nettlinger," Anna Eldh said, her yellow-green eyes twinkling at him in the rearview mirror. "The French once gave the old United States its Statue of Liberty."

"Just's piece isn't so large as that," said Oskar, grinning warily. "You're supposed to fly it back with you, after all."

They rode for a time without saying anything, listening to the seethe and crunch of snow in the boulevards. The Light-Probe Institute lay in a southwesterly direction, off Vesterbrogade, but because of Just Dragsted and his influential father they would have to detour down Andersens Boulevard to the museum of sculptures, even with a freshly arrived Cygnusian waiting for them at the Institute.

Why can't I relax? Emory asked himself. A haunting sense of mission had plagued him since boyhood, and he wondered how many years he would be driven to compensate for his father's crimes. . . . Forty-six years ago Gerard Nettlinger, a pathologically racist doctor of dentistry, had conceived him. But Carlo Bitler, the man his real father had assassinated, was Emory's spiritual father, and the debt of his wife's first husband's martyrdom still had to be paid. Emory had helped deliver up the stars to mankind as a part of this payment, but the "nuclei" of the Urban Federation, his birth-city among them, had autistically refused delivery. . . .

Anna caught Emory's eyes in the mirror. "Sir, why do you choose to take another starman back with you? That makes seven, no?"

Oskar winced for him; everybody had asked that question, but of course Anna had a curiosity of her own. "It's what they themselves want," Emory told her. "Since a good many still remain at the moon base exchanging information, encoding communication methods, what harm in taking one more from their number?" They were on Hans Christian Andersens, and he could see a corner of the Tivoli Gardens.

Anna said, "Why did you take the *first* Cygnusians back to Atlanta with you, sir?"

"Frankly, I wanted them as exhibits toward the end of waking up the city. But it took a year and a half just to get them inside the Dome, and by then our visitors had indicated they didn't wish immediate contact."

Off to the right, the obelisk commemorating 1788; a rocket in the snow. How time—past, present, and future—collapsed upon itself in this city under a coverlet of white.

Anna parked the car a few minutes later in front of the Glyptotek, and out his window Emory could see Just Dragsted waiting for him, barefoot, a royal-purple cloak draped over his thin ascetic's shoulders. Even from several meters away the young man's eyes showed up to bizarre effect: orbs of pale glass magnifying the vacuity behind them. His pretended indifference to the cold disgusted Emory.

"Dr Nettlinger," the young Dragsted said a moment later, his glassy eyes swiveling like gun turrets. "Come see it, sir. My magnum opus, my Pietà. And I've done it only to bequeath it."

They went inside, and there it was, right inside the door, Just Dragsted's *Amity IntraGalaktika*.

"Just to develop the program, Dr Nettlinger, required a feverish two days. A scan of photographs, the measurement of my model, the preparation of the computer-lathe. Believe me, sir, this was an outpouring of concentration usually beyond my powers, and there—*there* is the result!"

Although Dragsted swept his arm and cloak sleeve toward the statue, Emory found himself staring at the man's feet: they were blue.

"Splendid," Anna cried. "It's splendid, Just," and Emory lifted his eyes to the work to see if she was right. At first glance the statue *was* splendid, a towering starman cut from mahogany and fitted with burnished chromium arms which, outspread, had a span of nearly three meters in spite of their being cocked at the elbows. The starman's halo-crest and body gleamed with mahogany-red highlights, and Emory's first reaction was that the politmarshal's idiot son had literally outdone himself. Then he paused and looked at the human figure seated in front of the starman, its head tilted back as if to gaze up fondly at her archangelic protector.

"The woman?" Emory said. "Is that supposed to be . . . Fiona?"

"The very one," Dragsted said. "Morphologically twinned from photographic feed-in and my own recollections of Mz Bitler from several years ago, sir." The turrets of his eyes seemed to revolve suicidally inward.

Anna and Oskar had been overawed by Dragsted's Cygnusian, for the carving of Fiona was an utter botch; it might have been shaped by another console-sculptor altogether, a novice, a hack, a bumpkin. In short, Emory decided, this figure is typical of every other piece of Just Dragsted's work I've ever seen. He said so aloud.

Dragsted recoiled. "Sir, then we must see a different woman—"

"Evidently."

"*This* is how she seems to me. A woman in full possession of herself, a maturity equal to her years, a sensuality firmly controlled—"

"Good. Which is also how she seems to me. But this—" Emory brusquely indicated the statue. "—this isn't how she *looks.*"

"Ah, Dr Nettlinger, perhaps it's all owing to the inadequacy of the photos at my disposal. I had a live model only for the starman.''

''Or the inadequacy of your recollections and your—'' Emory started to say ''talent,'' but tact and a sudden realization stayed him. ''You had a *live* model for the alien? A Cygnusian from the Amity Moon Base? And you began and completed this work all in the last week?''

''Of course.''

Oskar had his pipe out again, and Anna was all at once wandering off to one of the display rooms. Emory clicked his heels together and exhaled a painfully pent breath.

''Oskar, Oskar, that means that this blue-footed dilettante, who survives by nepotism and knuckleheadedness, has had a starman at his disposal since the first word of my return to Scandipol. You've made me wait a week when I might have left several days ago—and all for the sake of this amateur Rodin's grandiose whim!''

''Not so grandiose, Emory,'' Oskar said conciliatorily. ''A gift for your Nucleus. The motive might have been worse.''

''That's all right, Dr Lavard,'' young Dragsted said. ''Scientists often have little aesthetic aptitude. I forgive him.''

''Thank you, Just.'' Emory turned to Oskar. ''I'm going to have to go look at the Egyptian statuary before we return to the Institute. That's what I need, I think.'' Soon, soon he would be back with Fiona; his wife, his mother, his sister. Fiona. The real one. Hands clasped at the small of his back, he walked away from Oskar Levard and Just Dragsted.

Anna Eldh returned warily to them from the opposite wing.

''Mz Eldh,'' Dragsted said, ''look at my feet.''

Obligingly Anna looked down at the young man's unshod feet, with their milky nails and free-standing veins.

''Are they blue, Mz Eldh? Are They?''

''No. Not anymore.''

The console-sculptor lifted his eyebrows and hands at the same time, appealing to both Mz Eldh and Dr Lavard. ''There, you see. It's just as I say. No aesthetic sense.''

XIV

A BUZZING called him from his bed. " 'Lo," he said into the telecom unit. "Flophouse for Uselessly Indentured Debtors. FLUID's our acronym, fluid's our biggest sin."

"That you, Julian?"

"That's me."

"Tybourn here. You interested in interviewing for a job? More intriguing work you may not be able to find. Nothing to do with writing, though."

Julian said that he was interested, and Tybourn told him to meet him in the Regency courtyard as soon as he could get away. Surfaceside, Julian hurled himself ballistically through the p-courts until the blue saucer of the hotel loomed like a portent over Peachtree Center and he had to stop beneath it like a meteor peeled of its inessential layers of nickel rind and rarefied gas. He had burnt himself out getting to the Regency, and inside he found Tybourn near the Kafe Köbehavn.

"Here," the man said, pressing a piece of paper on him. "A recommendation. Take it upstairs to the saucer, the Sojourner Room as they're calling it now, and give it to Yetunde. Tell her you met her briefly at the *Jour/Con* building a week ago. I've primed her some already, of course."

"Yetunde?"

"Right. Do good. I've got work a-brewin'."

Alone, Julian rode an elevator-capsule up to the rooftop saucer. In the opalescent shell of the Sojourner Room he found Yetunde Trap seated in a leather booth ringed about by baroquely carven room-dividers. Totemic African faces stared out of the dividers at him, and Yetunde, in a straight-hanging Cleopatra wig, accepted the recommendation he handed across the table to her. Beside her were a camera and a pink-skinned, dark-haired doll as large as a year-old child, a Bella Donna Babykins from Consolidated Rich's child development department. Perplexingly, the doll reminded Julian of an infant version of Margot Eastwin.

"Hey, Mistah Caw Thawm," Yetunde said. "I remember you, all right. Please sit down."

As he did, the girl picked up the Bella Donna Babykins and began bouncing it affectionately in her lap. On each bounce the doll's eyes opened and closed, radiant cornflowers.

"You in good shape, Mistah Julian." *Blink-blink.*

"Passable, I suppose. I ran all the way here."

"Good reflexes?" *Blink.*

"I believe so."

"You frustrate easy?" *Blink-blink.*

"No, I really don't." Julian tried to avoid the eyes of the bouncing doll. "If something's outside my capabilities, I try to get help."

"Whad'd you do befo'?" *Blink.*

"Self-employed. I guess I've laid myself off, though."

"How long you know Mistah Nick?" *Blink-blink.*

"Since last Monday."

"All right, Mistah Julian, these questions I gonna ask now are ones we're deep innersted in how you answer 'em, okay?"

"Okay," I'm pretty interested in that myself, he thought.

Yetunde set her doll on the inlaid marble surface of the table and disrobed it. Overslip, blouse, halter-skirt, petticoats, slippers, stockings, panties—a wardrobe from plantation days. And lo! Bella Donna's limbs and posterior and baby paunch were as pleasantly dimpled as thumb-kneaded dough. Vulnerable.

"How you feel about the Cygnostikoi, Mistah Julian?" As she asked this, the girl removed Bella Donna's stomach panel, a curved section of plastic containing the umbilical, and Julian shifted uncomfortably. By popping the umbilical through the panel with her thumb Yetunde converted the doll to an "outy." Then she unscrewed the belly button and set it on the table like a little pink thimble.

"The what?" Julian rubbed his jaw.

"The Cygnostikoi. You prolly think of 'em as Cygnusians. But since Em's been gone they asked us to call them Cygnostikoi. What I'm askin' is, how you feel about the starmen?"

"Curious. Very curious. More so than most. I want to know about them. That's why I finagled my way into the Worship Center."

"All right, then. Do you *resent* the Cygnostikoi?" Yetunde peeled the doll's hair off its head and then removed the top of its skull. She put these items on the table next to the stomach panel and belly button. Julian could now see the doll's realistic internal organs and the grey convolutions of its "brain," a walnut in its shell.

"Only if I get to thinking about where I live and where they live. It's fairly likely that people in the Basement will resent surfacesiders, particularly non-people living in a penthouse. I suppose I do too, some."

"You *hate* 'em then?" The girl opened out the doll's chest panels, revealing a plastic ribcage. Inside this, the heart and lungs.

"Uh-uh. No, I don't."

Yetunde took off the doll's plump vinyl arms and legs. Like monstrous sausages they lay there, terrifyingly cute. "How you know you don't?"

"I just don't, Yetunde. I really don't."

The girl gave him a toothsome grin. "Lovely shit, Mistah Julian." And she detached the ribs and lay them atop the doll's wig. (Julian could not help imagining that they had just dined on ineptly skinned alley cat.) "How you feel about a Cygnostik 'ceptin' Ortho-Urbanism?"

"Ambivalent. Unless it's good for them—which it usually isn't—I'm not ecstatic about *anyone* accepting Ortho-Urbanism."

Next came the liver, spleen, stomach, kidneys, pancreas, and intestines, both large and small. "Why you think he did it?" Yetunde asked.

"I'm an agno on that, Yetunde. . . . Can anyone who isn't a Cygnusian—a Cygnostik, I mean—know that? I just hope it wasn't a politically motivated performance, an exploitation."

"Okay, Mistah Julian." To the bone heap and organ bank Yetunde added the winged lungs and the diaphanously veined heart. "Here it is: You think you could work for the Cygnostikoi and live around 'em too?"

"Well," he said cautiously, "I don't have any religious scruples against it, Yetunde."

"What kind you got, then?" The girl lifted the brain out of its case, separated the right and left hemispheres, performed a series of small lobotomies, laid out all the pieces. Lobes, brain stem, limbric system.

"Is fear a scruple?"

"Fear o' what? The Cygnostikoi or the people who'd be upset knowin' you was workin' for 'em?" She picked up the husk of her doll and peered into the cavities she had cleared as if looking for something.

"The starmen. I can usually accommodate myself to people."

"Well, this job come open 'cause the fella in it befo' got sliced up by aitchjays. Maybe you read about it?" Yetunde turned the limbless doll upside down and shook it. "Anyhow, most of what you do, you got to do at night.'' She righted Bella Donna Babykins and took from its mouth an infant's incomplete dental plate. She probed the oral cavity with a finger. ''Abu got kilt 'cause he was a New Islamite, though, not 'cause he worked at night; no more reason than that.''

''The aitchjays probably thought The Event gave them an excuse for a religious vendetta.''

''A excuse was all it was, Mistah Julian. Jes's viciousness, sorry-soul meanness.'' She tried to insert her fingernails behind the left eyeball, but the vinyl eyelid kept falling into place, winking with mindless good humor.

Men love the darkness for their deeds are evil, Julian was thinking abstractedly.

''Could you live in the Regency while you're doin' this Cygnostikoi work, Mistah Julian, and keep it all secret?''

Could he? Probably. It was ironic, though, that the very employment that would save his Level 9 cubicle made that cubicle's availability a matter of small consequence to him. . . . ''Yessum,'' Julian said. ''I could.''

The eyeball popped. Yetunde peered into the socket as if it were a keyhole, shook her head, then set to work on the other eye. ''Well, Mistah Julian, you gonna be a errand runner, a private eye, and a domessick, all at once.''

''A domestic. You mean a house nigger?''

Yetunde looked up. ''No. But you ain' gonna be a zeckative, either. This is a job, Cousin Em say, where you start at the top and the bottom at the same time. It's work to it.''

''Okay. No white gloves and coat, though.''

''Uh-uh.'' The eyeball popped. Yetunde extracted a tiny metal crab from its socket. ''Look, Mistah Julian. It's Cancer.'' To the doll she said, ''Hey, Olivia, you okay fo' one mo' day, ole lovely Livvie.'' Olivia was a nice name; Julian was grateful Yetunde didn't call the doll Bella Donna Babykins, or Margot. . . .

''One of the Cygnostikoi,'' the girl was saying, ''he hides Cancer, then gives me my baby, and I got to save her. Man, I uz startin' to get worried. That eye 'bout the las' place I could look.''

Yetunde began to reassemble the doll. Brain, skull cap, hair. Lungs and heart, ribcage, chest panels. Intestinal organs, stomach panel, navel. And, finally, the cheerful eyeballs. On went the clothes, too. Cancer, however, remained in the middle of the table, a chigger-red mite.

''You want this job, Mistah Julian?'' He said he did. ''You hired, then. You begin tonight, if that's okay with you. . . . Now I got to take your pitcher.'' The girl put Olivia down, took up her camera, and before Julian could grin, twitch, grimace, or even blink, exploded an A-bomb of light in his eyes. The proof was ready instantaneously, and Yetunde showed it to him.

In it, Julian looked like a man who had just been informed of his having either a fatal disease or a secret too complicated for him to grasp without outside aid.

"Now you're aboard. Tonight I'll tell you what you got to do."

BOOK TWO

PSALMS

XV

AND on the topmost floor of the Regency Hyatt House, in that suite of darkened, foggily cool, vinegar-scented rooms given over to the visitors from 61 Cygni, an alien moves with an outward clumsiness and an inscaping grace to the blessedly boomvoiced mediator between his reality and theirs that these people have provided the Cygnostikoi: an orpianoogla, portable variety, at which, arranging his limbs, psiphoning power out of the air, clambering over sustained cords and ascending orotund runs into the "noosphere"(as some of them call it) above the heartaches and hungers, Lileplagak taps a vein of incredible singing richness, and the Regency Hotel, even unto the blue revolving saucer of the Sojourner Room, reverberates with a paean not so much unearthly as unheavenly, as if the Cygnostik orpianooglist had struck through the apocryphal march on the "Omega Point" to the God-as-Being behind the God-as-Process evolving with the biosystems to which the abiding God-as-Being remains evermore external and above: for the music that Lileplagak draws from both his rumblybumbly machine and his articulate fingers coursing with forces both organic and mechanical is a chorale monstrously narcissistic in its adulation of the eternally still Pulse of Godhead which has not beat once during the entire giga-giga-millennial unraveling of these supposedly converging consciousnesses: narcissistic because this adulation is for that aspect of the Pulse of Godhead (or the God Beyond the World) which has given of itself, tragically, an in-process consciousness incarnate in both thisplace Humanity and the thereborn/therebuilt Cygnostikoi, i.e., a reverence of the *kami*, or the *pneuma*, or the godhood of all the particular selves broken from the devolutionarily frangible Godhead entirely transcendent to Creation, whose highest manifestation for a significant proportion of Humanity is the historical enfleshing of the Second Person of the Trinity, but for the Cygnostikoi is the algebraic equivalency *God* = *I* and its subtly different converse corollary *I* = *God*: notions hateful to almost all the votaries of thisplace religious systems except for those conceiving of a celebratory worship involving submergent identification rather than right relationship, and consequently different from Lileplagak's cosmologic metaphysics in which the shard is not merely a part but paradoxically the All, for the destruction of a single *pneuma* is the destruction of that cosmic Deity whose passion has entrapped rather than released the many consciousnesses *returning to* instead of *evolving toward* It; yes, notions hateful to most, although accepted in superficial adolescent guises by many thisplace dissidents whose major sin against the Cygnostik equivalency is the wholly nonliteral implementation in their lives of the axiom, The Shard Is All; through all of which rumblybumbly-intimated praise, a boomvoiced rendition of "Upward for Aye on Wings," the phantomesque man from 61 Cygni regales his compatriots and hosts with his own acquiescence, musically phrased, in regarding the Second Person of the Trinity as a suitable proxy for the devotional impulses traditionally reserved on his world for the deity resident in the complex gestalt of The Shard That Is All, his planet's population therefore united in the veneration of rotating divinities in a self-serving, septigamically organized pantheon of worshipper-gods; while he simultaneously keeps his B-sun pupils, the outermost bulbs of each horizontal hourglass of an eye, peeled on the one side for the fog-parting entrance of child, woman, or man, and on the other side for the feline consciousness whom he has earlier frightened by too jittery-jabbery an approach, surprised in flagrant delicto out of its litter box, inadvertently chased between his own lower extremities, and *treed*, so to speak, in the involute metal branches and tripartite mattress folds of a Regency hide-a-bed; wherefrom, at too frequent intervals, the material correspondent of the feline consciousness protests its incarceration by lifting up an atonal caterwaul or a piteous miaow in purely fortuitous accompaniment of Lileplagak's orpianoogla performance; at the end of which, drained of the impulse for adulation, Lileplagak frankensteinmonsters across the carpet, his polelike arms purring with microminiaturized pulleys and winches, delicate wires going up and down in lubricating gells of erythrocytes and leukocytes, until he attains—lumbedy lumbedy, lump lump lump—the hide-a-bed containing the kitty cat, lowers himself to the cushions overcapping the convolute guts of this paradigmatically *human* furnishing, and there rests himself as the beast beneath his alien glutei cowers aghast, Lileplagak himself no longer intent on the hymning of eulogistic ditties nor on the quest of *Felis catus*—facilitated eupepsia, but instead on the goodness of death and on the means whereby

one of his genus and species can most easily terminate into the
noncognitive areality of this goodness, knowing that even if the
death is of the irreversible variety rather than the short-term sort by
which in countless excarnations he has survived the touristic tedium
of these terrestrially measured years, it would matter nothing to the
thisplace Humanity among whom he has wonderingly come; but
realizing with a negation of self not often ascribed to candidates for
godhood that this hypothetical but intensely probable indifference
to his own long-term demise would be not only prophesiable and
sure but fitting and proper for thisplace persons to feel, particularly
in the light of the barbarism, depravity, hatred, contempt, revul-
sion, and divisive parochialism exhibited in *one another's*
presences and in that of the less well integrated material systems not
yet possessing consciousness whom thisplace persons casually hurl
to annihilations much less serene than Lileplagak's will be: specula-
tions neither profound nor shallow, neither exhilarating nor de-
pressing, upon the final contemplation of which the starman reaches
into the mechanism/organism of himself and deliberately *shuts
down* the variegated forces providing motive power and perhaps
even will to his own hands, heart, and hardware, the penultimate
sound in his inset ears the raucous outraged cry of a kitty cat driven
scrawny-bellied and hackle-fritzed into the nethermost intestines of
the hide-a-bed upon which his unsupported body has just collapsed
with a sprawling impingement of weight that even Lileplagak would
have to describe as "dead"; miaow, miaow, miaow, miaowmiaow-
miaowmiaowmiaowmiaooooow! . . .

XVI

CARRYING a duffel bag, Julian strolled into the lobby of the Regency. Eleven P.M. and still as bright as a generous noon. Colored lights
played upon the pagodas of water rising and falling in the central
fountain. And now I'm going to live here, Julian told himself. What

would Mama Queequeg think? He sauntered past the Kafe Köbenhavn and the fountain to keep his rendezvous with Yetunde, who was waiting in the hotel's insta-caffe shop eating a blueberry pastry and searching the courtyard for him. Tonight she looked like Nefertiti, her hair under a brocaded crown-hat.

"It's all fixed with the LPA," she told him when he sat down on a stool beside hers. "They know you bein' publicly useful now, Mistah Julian—in a private sort of way."

When he twitted her about being up awfully late for a little girl, she said, "Don't you worry; I get my cat-naps," and, after signing her prom-for, took him up to the hotel's twenty-first floor and led him down a corridor which ended at a door belonging more appropriately on a bank vault than a hotel suite. Their reflections rippled in the door's metallic surface as they approached, but saying, "That's Cygnostik Land through there. We ain' goin' in jes' yet," Yetunde turned him aside and introduced him into an immense room off to the left of the corridor. This room was Julian's.

A tray of mint-green boxwoods enlivened the balcony fronting on the Regency's interior court. Other accoutrements were magnolias on the wallpaper, a carpet of golden shag, and a circular bed looking very much like the heaped-up petals of a giant, pared-away artichoke—a bed, Yetunde told him, that would go up and down at the touch of a button, or slowly revolve if you wanted to spiral into sleep.

"You're a gopher," the girl said after Julian had looked around for a moment; "you go for this, you see, and you go for that. Look here."

From the top of a Formica cabinet Yetunde picked up an official-looking certificate bearing the city's official-looking seal. She gave this to Julian, and at its bottom he saw the signatures of Saganella Ruth Lesser and Cyd Cynara, Psychosocial Demographer to the First Councilor. It was Cynara's job, Yetunde explained, to count and analyze populations, not merely of people, but of dogs, cats, and pigeons too. What sorts of pressures did these animals feel? why were they living here rather than there? what contributed to the suppression or the burgeoning of their reproductive instincts? Julian's job would involve winnowing those populations which threatened to get out of control; the cat population, specifically. If he were caught hunting these animals, however, Councilor Lesser, in spite of the authorization now in Julian's hands, would disavow any knowledge of his activities.

"Ortho-Urbanists are big antivivisectionists," Yetunde told Julian confidentially, "and ole Saganella's a Ortho-Urbanist. Even so, Cyd Cynara's done tol' her the re-renewal areas are overrun with cats. That's why you get this small-game license."

Then the girl showed him his equipment; it included a miner's helmet with a lamp mounted above its bill, a pair of jackboots, a pair of elbow-length gloves, a sedative pistol, and several boxes of tranquilizer pellets. She also showed him three collapsible "capture crates," four sacks of dried cat food, two-and-a-half sacks of KitLax litter, an aerosol bomb of flea foam, a box of twenty-five blank tape cassettes, and an offset pamphlet containing information about several different varieties of apples. Julian took in this lot of goods numbly, abashed and bemused, while the girl went to a closet and fetched back to him a knee-length greatcoat with dark brown synthafur at its collar, hem, and sleeves.

"It's cold in Cygnostik Land," she said. "Abu-Bakr used to wear a nose-plug sometimes, too. You want one?"

"I'll try it without. To begin with."

"Okay." She tilted her Nefertiti headgear. "Cousin Fiona wants you to meet 'em all tonight, the Cygnostikoi I mean, but first we got to go see her. C'mon."

Yetunde led Julian across the hall and knocked on the door. A voice, recognizable to him as Fiona Bitler's, bid them enter, and in a moment they were standing in a large suite decorated in black and white leather (or a facsimile), with scarlet draperies, throw cushions, and carpets. Soft islands of light were distributed about the room, and in one of them, in a straightbacked chair, sat Fiona Foe Bitler.

On the wall behind her was a small mosaic, a triptych, depicting three stylized scenes from the ministry of her first husband, Carlo Bitler. Forty-two years dead, that man, and somehow still alive. In the mosaic's central panel he stood like a Manichean messenger, his arms outspread.

While Yetunde made the introductions, Julian embarrassedly lapped his greatcoat over his forearm and juggled the helmet that he found in his hands. How had it got there?

Doughty and humorous, Fiona's eyes played upon him like spotlights. "Do you know, Julian, what you're getting into?"

He admitted that he didn't, not exactly. He said that even though he had been in the Bitler Memorial Chapel on Saturday and had seen a Cygnostik in, well, person, he was nevertheless trembling in his slippers.

"You know," the old woman said thoughtfully, "I have no more idea what last Saturday means than you do, young man."

"It means Lily's got religion," Yetunde interjected.

Fiona laughed. "I don't know. It may simply be a part of the Cygnostikoi's very gradual Coming Out, Yetty. If it is, maybe we can finally persuade our compatriots to do likewise."

"When's Em comin' home?"

Fiona took a letter from the drawer of a tea table next to her. Without opening the letter she said, "Wednesday the twenty-fifth, very, very late. But he wrote this on his second day there, and it arrived only this afternoon. He may have had to change his plans."

Julian shifted the burden of the greatcoat, fumbled with his helmet. "Will he bring more Cygnostikoi?" he asked, conscious of his brashness in asking.

"Just one." Fiona stood. "I'd take your coat, Julian, but Yetty's going to introduce you to our family now and you may want it. Put it on. You're not afraid you'll appear ridiculous before us, are you?"

He put the coat on, clapped the helmet on his head. "Some."

"You look like a polo player on a cold day," Fiona said appraisingly. "Which is no more ridiculous in essence than I must often look. We're all a little ridiculous, it's part of our chromosomal heritage."

"You better give him somepin' to take 'em," Yetunde advised Fiona, "so's they'll like him as much as old Abu."

"A bribe? All right." Fiona exited the room and came back with a bowl containing six apples, which she gave to Julian. "Julian," she said, touching his lapel and letting her hand fall away slowly.

"Yessum?" (Mama Queequeg again; *her* talk, *her* inflection.)

"My only recommendation is to keep an open mind." And she sat down again and began reading the letter from Dr Nettlinger again, too.

In the corridor Yetunde told Julian, "She spent the day on Level 6 with Abu-Bakr's family. Funeral tomorrow. Cousin Fiona knows how it is to lose somebody to meanness."

So do I. They always give you plenty of chances to learn. He couldn't keep any bitterness in his thoughts, however, because the bank-vault door at corridor's end showed him a lanky figure in a tsarist greatcoat and a silver hardhat carrying a bowl of apples and following a little girl whose eyes were fixed upon his reflection rather than her own. Very funny, Yetunde; very, very funny.

At the door the girl held up her thumb to be scanned, then bid Julian listen to the tumble of its lock-wheel. "It's ready for you too, Mistah Julian. We got your print-pattern from the Housing Authority late today."

"Are the Cygnostikoi locked in there? Prisoners?"

"Uh-uh. People are locked *out*, is all. The Cygnostikoi jes' prefer to be where it's sorter like home, I guess."

XVII

THE stoutly hinged door went *chik-chik* and opened for them. Simultaneously a puff of steamy cold and a whiff of strange decayings struck them. Eerie. Was this how that Armstrong fella felt when he stepped out of his LEM onto the moon? Maybe. Maybe not. He'd been pretty certain, after all, that he wasn't venturing into *inhabited* territory. . . .

"Turn your lamp on, Mistah Julian."

He did. Geysering light, his helmet lamp picked out indistinct silhouettes, angular panels, all the tricky architecture of a labyrinth. Walls in Cygnostik Land had been knocked out, moved, and in some cases halved. An alien disarray, with coves, inlets, grottoes, and bays on the periphery of the huge, seemingly empty area directly before Julian. The temperature was just barely above freezing, and the odors assailing them suggested a number of things. Spoiled suet. Cheap cider. Motor oil. Old paper immersed in water and left to shred. And, unmistakably, cat shit.

"They got what useter be twelve rooms," Yetunde whispered. "Decorated it themselves. Refrigeration courtesy of the management."

Julian remembered that very early in the Cygnusians' residency here a single *Jour/Con* reporter had been given a chance to enter their suite. He later described their rooms as smelling of vinegar, a detail Julian had remembered and made use of in the monologue Tybourn had rejected as unsuitable for visicom distribution. Vinegar wasn't the half of it, though. At least there weren't any flies.

"What's that?" Julian pointed out a shape against a truncated wall.

"A orp'," Yetunde said. "Lily plays it. It's a interpreter, sort of. Em says Lily asked for it the first week they moved in here."

Whoops! Something fled past them in the gloom. Tilting his headlamp after it, Julian saw only a hide-a-bed, a section of wall, and an expanse of floor littered with something like either sawdust or sand. The soles of his street slippers were already gritty with the substance.

"Cat," Yetunde said, explaining the apparition. "They like 'em fresh."

"Just where are they, Yetunde?" The apples in the bowl he was carrying were knocking against each other.

"In here somewheres. Don't worry. Maybe it's get-together night for 'em." Then she shouted, "Lily! Hey, Lily, wanna meet Abu's 'placement?!"

The deadness of the suite was intimidating; maybe they didn't want to meet Abu's 'placement.

"C'mon." Yetunde was in butterfly sleeves and ought to have been cold, but she led him through the desolation and terror of Cygnostik Land as if through a patio garden in Summer. Julian's headlamp slashed out swathes in which furniture, rubble, and fleeing cats were briefly visible against the backdrop of the penthouse wasteland. Twelve rooms? More like a hundred. Fulton County wasn't so large an enclave. . . . At last they stumbled into a room (it was a wall and a half short of perfect roomhood, really) in which the six Cygnostikoi had secreted themselves. The apples in Julian's bowl rolled about like overweight roulette balls.

Five Cygnostikoi stood in a ring about one kneeling starman. Oblivious to the beam of light stuttering among them, they tore strips of either the hanging flesh or the tattered mummy-cloth (which was it?) on their whirring forearms and fed these into the rigid mouth of the Cygnostik on his knees. This sight, in combination with the odors colliding and ricocheting about, lowered a thread of nausea into Julian's stomach. He tottered.

"It's okay," Yetunde whispered. "Grows back in a day, those strips. Em says it's sorter like a Eucharist to 'em, is all."

After a few more stomach-turning feedings in glitchy three-quarter time, the party of Cygnostikoi broke up. The kneeler got to his feet, and the six of them, cartilage crests looming like suns, staggered or glided toward Yetunde and him, some almost spastic, some bewitchingly graceful. Julian noticed that their eye patches were glowing faintly, each individual's with a distinguishing color, orange, blue, amber, and so on; while their forward-facing pupils, slitted almost to extinction at first, grew larger and more bulblike as they approached. Finally Julian noticed the fierce parallel nose ridges that ended in a single, hyperventilating nostril. In person, the Cygnostikoi were spooky critters.

"Lily," Yetunde said, "Julian Cawthon, who's taken over for Abu."

"Here," Julian said and he impulsively held out his bowl of apples. Lily was the Cygnostik in front of him, with lemon-yellow eye patches and a lignocelluloid noggin fit to grace the top of any Algonquin totem pole.

With ritual courtesy, their fingers humming, each starman helped himself to an apple, placed it whole into his mouth, and five or ten seconds later brought it out . . . cored.

"Here, Mistah Julian," Yetunde said, "let me innerduce you to 'em more formally." As she said this, one of the starmen hitched away into the gloom. "That un'll be back, don't worry. Look here now."

Julian, teeth chattering, swung his attention back to the five Cygnostikoi still clustered around them.

"I been sayin' Lily," Yetunde said, "but this un's real name is Lileplagak, you know." His eye patches brightening, Lileplagak nodded.

A profound uneasiness stole over Julian as he glanced quickly at the girl. "What did you say?"

"Luh-LEP-luh-gak," Yetunde enunciated. "It's a hard name to say, all right. That's why we say Lily."

Yetunde turned to the next Cygnostik and took his arm. "This is Claxspkr, Julian. CLAX-spur-kur's how you say it. That's his name."

"That's his name," Julian numbly echoed the girl. He wanted to run. The other starmen's names were Podor, Elabelaberi, Snoke, and— "Yyrzstine," Julian said, interrupting Yetunde. "The last one's name is YERZ-stine. That's how you say it." . . . The frightening thing was that none of this could be coincidence. The chances against it being coincidence were . . . astronomical. That was certainly the right word. *Astronomical*.

Yyrstine, the starman who'd stalked off a few moments ago, returned from the wastes beyond carrying a dark-haired Bella Donna Babykins.

""Look, Mistah Julian," Yetunde exclaimed, her eyes upon him in deep and admiring surprise that he should have "guessed" the last alien's name, "it's Olivia. Ole lovely Livvie. She's already ready for tomorrow." She took the doll and hugged it.

Ready for tomorrow, Julian repeated to himself. Ready for tomorrow. If only I were ready for this very moment; for this weird, weird Now. His breath ballooning out before him, he looked at the vaguely synthetic-seeming visages of the Cygnostikoi and winced with each twitchy pulse beat in his temples. . . .

XVIII

"RIDICULOUS," Tonsured Billy muttered angrily. He was wearing a Saganella Ruth Lesser physiognograph, and a thumb print under the First Councilor's nose gave her portrait a silly *mein Führer* look. Even without a smudge under his nose, Billy's look was equally silly.

"Yes, it's ridiculous," Margot agreed, putting a hand on Billy's knee to silence him. "But you can bear it for an hour."

"Ludicrous. Tyrannical."

"Shhh."

They were eight rows up in the A-section grandstands at Grant Field, surrounded by every student, professor, administrative worker, and menial from the King Theological Complex, and by most of the Ortho-Urban clergy. It was Tuesday noon, and Margot felt sorry for Bishop Holman, who was responding with neither cogency nor wit to yesterday's cruel mischance.

Down on the field, on a specially erected platform, Lieutenant Bishop Sara Coryea was saying a funeral mass for Asbury Holman's horse Cherokee. On the platform with her were Holman, the stable boy Eddie, and First Councilor Lesser. The orpianoogla music was "Upward for Aye on Wings."

"Listen to that," Billy whispered. "You'd think we were eulogizing Pegasus."

Margot said nothing. Nobody cared that Billy was ridiculing this ridiculous affair. He could have walked up and down playing a piccolo without offending the students in the A-section. . . . None of them had seen Cherokee's head kicked in nor its eye gouged out. Would *that* have made a difference? No, this was still a travesty of a sacred Ortho-Urban rite. Embarrassing. Saddening.

Fredelle Fowles, who was behind them, leaned over and said, "Can you believe Saggy Nelly put in an appearance for this?"

"Why not?" Billy countered. "Twenty-five years ago they were schoolmates. Sweethearts, maybe. They've declined into senility together."

Margot steeled herself against her classmates' cynicism, which acts like this funeral mass inevitably and necessarily gave rise to, and watched a pigeon circle overhead.

On the other side of the city, on Mosque Block, in a ceremony of which Margot knew nothing, a New Islamite congregation was ushering to sleep the remains of a man named Abu-Bakr. . . .

XIX

A CYCLONE fence circled the I-20 receiving point on the southeastern periphery of the Dome, and inside the fence stood a barricade of plywood and cinder block to conceal the work area to which the fence merely prevented access. It amused Nessim Charles that a receiving point was one of the few places in the city where an unenfranchised Atlantan could go and an enfranchised one (but for supervisors and travelers with portfolio) could not. That the privilege suggested the Nucleus's contempt for the influence of the unenfranchised didn't bother Nessim very much; he knew that only the Negative Elect (all the stevedores at the receiving point) could go with impunity into the series of locks whose final gate revealed the stars or storms of the Open, the nightland outside.

On the twenty-sixth day of Autumn, an hour before shift-change, the receiving yard was full of discolored, gummed-together pickups and freight rigs. Arnold Glom, the point bursar, dispatched stevedores from dock to dock to speed off-loading; and the teamsters, all of them outsiders, were sent back through the locks as quickly as their trucks could be emptied and their palms crossed with barter currency. A few wheeled back out with loads of processed cloth or waste-derived fertilizers as payment for their deliveries. The receiving yard itself lay under the still, astringent glare of magnesium lamps, and winged beetles clicked against the lamps or spun about on the asphalt after being trod on. Puffs of chill steam came out of the refrigeration lockers next to the point bursar's house.

"Why's it so busy?" Menny asked. They were unloading squash, okra, eggplant, and tomatoes, the last crops of the season, from an old Ford carryall.

"Because morning-shift loafed," said Clara Schnozz, a white woman with an abraded-looking nose. "Now Glom's gone hyper."

Across the yard on the pier in front of the point bursar's house, Arnold Glom gesticulated and shouted, jabbed his clipboard at the still air. The arc of dome behind Glom reminded Nessim, in spite of its girdering, of the interior shell of a gigantic egg; Glom's jabs were futile pecks at the shell. Jab, jab; peck, peck.

"I heard him say Emory Nettlinger comin' through tonight," Nessim told Clara and Menny. "Back from Scandipol."

Menny straightened. "Nettlinger?"

"*C'mon, you three!*" Glom shouted, looking across the yard at them. "You've been on that one fifteen minutes. Move, now!"

They cleared the carryall, toting the produce baskets down the ramp and stowing them in either the refrigerator lockers or the waiting delivery carts. Work sped up. Behind them, on the ten-meter scaffold above the locks, Jastertree was releasing each newly cleared vehicle through the three gates of the "egress channel." Pretty soon the yard was empty for the first time since they had come on-shift.

Twenty minutes remaining until shift-change, the stevedores loitered about in the yard listless and expectant. The occasional tailspin of a beetle drew everyone's eyes. Jastertree stayed on the control scaffold, however, and Clara Shnozz said she thought he was holding someone in the "access channel." Finally Glom strode from the bursar's house to the middle of the yard and announced that anyone who wanted to could check out early. A choked sort of hurrah went up from the yard, and several of the stevedores moved off over the yellow docking patterns on the asphalt toward the plywood barricade and the fence beyond it.

"Those lunkers're gonna get marked down on Glom's piss-list as 'short on zeal,' " Clara Schnozz said. "He's checking up."

Menny disagreed; he said that Glom was just trying to get as many stevedores gone as possible before Nettlinger came through. As for him, he was going to stay to see the little physicist. Glom returned to the bursar's house, and they could see his bent head through its boxlike window. Apparently he wasn't going to run off any roustabouts who'd chosen to work through their shift, and among these Nessim counted Jastertree, Lou Griner, Shabazz-Brown, the young FUSKCONite Arjuna, and one or two others.

On the control scaffold Jastertree suddenly made a huge wheeling motion with his arms and shoulders, and like a guillotine hoisting its blade the gate went *chik-chik, chik-chik, chik-chik.* The final lock revealed to them a battered pickup with a canvas tarp jutting up over its truckbed, and this vehicle rolled into the yard with a lurch and halted. An old black man got down from the driver's side.

"Jonah Trap," Menny said. He left Nessim and Clara Schnozz and started across the yard. Nessim hurried to follow. As they approached, the other door swung open and a small blond man stepped down.

The point bursar was there to greet him. "Welcome home, Dr Nettlinger. Hello, Mr Trap. Your granddaughter isn't here yet."

"Yip yip, yip yip yip," Menny said quietly, a trace of falsetto in his voice, and Nessim tried to stop his friend before he made a gibbering ass of himself. What was he doing?

The men at the truck turned toward them. The faces of both Nettlinger and Trap seemed to convey recognition, astonishment; they'd seen Menny before and wondered how to respond to him now. Jonah Trap, the nearer of the two, appeared ready to shake hands, and Nettlinger came around the pickup to confirm his identification of Menny.

"Alexander Guest, isn't it? You were with a resources-reclamation team that came to the Phoenix Plantation five years ago."

"That the one," Trap said. "I ain' gonna forget how he woke up the house when Lily and Clarence come in that night to talk to you. No, sir. How'm I gonna forget this fella, whoopin' like he did. Little Carlo 'most got his pants skeered off." Trap chuckled amiably.

"Menewa," Menny said, ignoring all this. "You can call me Menewa. Maybe I should call you Oglethorpe, bringing your Indians in for a show."

Glom, livid at this odd impertinence, tried to turn Menny aside; he ordered the big man to go home even as Menny began walking about the pickup as if mesmerized by the irregular shape of its tarp.

"Indians?" Menny asked Nettlinger, shaking free of Arnold Glom. "More Indians? Or is it colonists bringing wisdom this time?"

"One Cygnostik," Nettlinger said. "And a statue."

Nessim saw that an old confusion had overtaken his friend, the inability to fix clearly in his mind the terms of the analogy he was obsessed with. Innocents or exploiters? Who was who? Trying to save Menny from himself, Nessim followed him to the rear of the truck.

"Guest!" the point bursar cried. "Guest, what the hell are you doing?'' He waved his arm at Jastertree on the scaffold, at Clara across the way.

Menny yanked the truck's tailgate down, and a bolt-and-washer assembly fell onto the asphalt. Looking into the truck from behind Menny, Nessim saw a Cygnusian regarding them with an expression alien and unreadable. Behind it was the statue Nettlinger had mentioned, an ungainly thing carved out of shadows, pricking up the canvas covering the truckbed. Suddenly the living starman hitched forward out of the dark, causing even Menny to retreat, and obtained the ground as if by extending its legs and then telescoping to its original height; its moist eye patches shimmered in the glare.

Menny began shouting something unintelligible about unwanted wisdom and his need of a screwdriver. The Cygnusian, holding up an arm from which hung strips of a tissuey substance, sidled away to the left. Berserk, Menny rushed the starman, knocked it over. The sound was like a whole *box* of bolt-and-washer assemblies falling off a truck. Now Menny was yipping like a maniac and standing threateningly over the Cygnusian.

Jastertree, Clara Schnozz, Arnold Glom, and Jonah Trap, hurrying to help the helpless Nessim, at last subdued the man and wrestled him away from the alien. The next time Nessim looked, the starman was on its feet again, swiveling its head experimentally. Then it nibbled a bit of tissue from its arms, and Menny fought to get at it again. Five people restrained him. Four, Nessim thought, would have been one too few.

Blip, blip, blip: Three tiny suns went nova in front of them, and Nessim saw a little girl in tightly wound cornrows holding up a camera.

''No photographs!'' Glom shouted. ''No photographs in here!''

Nettlinger took the camera from the girl and hugged her to him. Menny, dazzled by the flashbulbs, ceased struggling, and Nessim could almost hear the big man's heart beating as if it were his own.

''Be good if we could get Kee Wig to someplace cool,'' Trap said, gesturing at the starman. ''At least till you ready to leave, Dr Em. He been out o' the cool twelve, fo'teen hours, you know.''

So Glom had Clara escort ''Kee Wig'' to the refrigeration lockers, while Jastertree and Nessim walked Menny, like a big, tranquilized dog, to the refreshment patio beyond the yard. Then Jastertree left them to help winch Dragsted's statue out of the truck and to operate the locks once old Jonah Trap was ready to leave.

Slapping his clipboard against his thigh, Arnold Glom came to the patio table where Menny and Nessim were sitting and said, ''Guest, don't come in tomorrow. Wait a day or two. Commit hari-kari if you like. I'll ask around for a taxidermist.'' And then, self-importantly, he ambled off.

XX

LIKE Abu-Bakr before him, Julian was a katzenappler. He hunted cats in the re-renewal areas where they had thrived even before the construction of the dome, and he hauled home apples from the Dixie-Apple Market & Delicatessen on the Level 4 Mall. Katzenappler was a term of his own devising which he preferred to "gopher." Maybe he worried too much about what he ought to be called, but his worry grew out of the strangeness of his position and the very real adjustments it required him to make. He had come to terms with the morality of what he was doing, however, and believed himself an agent of good purpose to both the Cygnostikoi and the citizens of the Urban Nucleus. He hoped he wasn't rationalizing his katzenapplership and didn't really believe he was.

On Tuesday, the twenty-fourth day of Autumn, his first morning on the job, Julian carried out the hurriedly devised orders that Yetunde gave him before going to bed. He drove a battery cart to the enclave called "Jacksonville," roamed the vacant streets with his equipment, and returned to the Regency with three mangy specimens of Atlanta's prowling catdom, discovering in the process that he wasn't a very good shot. And no wonder. He couldn't help worrying about the correspondence of the Cygnostikoi's names to those in his first story, "No Other Gods." Had he been fated from the beginning to take this job? Don't think about it, he told himself.

Although the Cygnostikoi themselves didn't exactly *talk* to him, they still made known their wishes and commands. Every day Pal Lily prepared an orpianoogla recording, and every midnight, a minute or so past the hour, Julian went into the icicly barrens of Cygnostik Land, locked himself in a special bath-booth, took the cassette out of the medicine cabinet into which Lily had placed it, seated himself on a chintz-curtained commode, and let the rumbly-bumbly voice of the orpianoogla thunder out of the shower stall where the cassette-player rested. Lileplagak could make the old orp' talk, and every command sounded like "Upward for Aye on Wings." . . . The first time Julian heard such a performance was the Wednesday morning of Dr Nettlinger's anticipated homecoming, and he still recalled how nervous he had been sitting in the bath-booth, his head-lamp ablaze, waiting for the moment when an alien—an *alien*, for crissake!—would communicate directly, sort of, with Mama Queequeg's little boy, Julian. He turned the player on.

All at once the bath-booth reverberated with a full-bodied mag-nificat, the shower stall shook, the player hummed and buzzed almost inaudibly beneath the strains of Pal Lily's overture. And the words, Julian realized, were awesomely arranged doggerel. Dog-gerel having to do with cats, a magnificat menu.

> One that's black for Lileplagak
> *Gopherkatz!*
> A booted trekker for both Snoke and Claxspkr
> *Hal-le-LU-jah!*
> Toms with no odor for Yyrzstine and Podor
> *Hal-le-LU-jah!*
> For Elabelaberi, a Persian janissary
> (Make it very hairy! Make it very hairy!)
> *Gopherkatz! GopherKATZ! GOPHERKAAAAATZ!*

After two more repetitions of this menu, the tape player expelled the cassett into the shower stall, where, emitting a seethe of steam, it dehisced like a well-baked apple and went fizzling over the drain in an alarming fury of sparks. Julian's first thought was that someone had rigged a timed device inside the cartridge, but the fizzling soon stopped and the moment was defused of its terror.

Later Yetunde told him that all the tapes Pal Lily made were programmed for "auto-demolishment." Everything that the Cyg-nostikoi communicated by means of the orpianoogla was confiden-tial for the present; you couldn't be too careful in your safeguarding of any Cygnostik artifact.

"Tapes can sink you, you leave 'em lyin' around. Look at History."

Julian tried his best to fill Lileplagak's orders that night. He betook himself to Bondville, the tenement section where he'd once lived with Gramma Mary. In the aftermath of the "Glissador Revolt," as a concession to the dispirited and angry, the city had pulled down many of the area's sorriest homes and buildings, but nothing had been put back to replace them, and Bondville was now a desert of brick, shingle, Sheetrock, snaky electrical cable, and mysteriously moving dunes of gypsum powder. There seemed to be little hope of bagging a "Persian janissary" or two "toms with no odor" in such a place, and Julian didn't.

He did get a small calico, two yellow toms reeking of musky asteroids, a grey yearling with a star on its nose, and a large rat, which he wasted no time in discarding. That was it. As Weather Control began dialing up dawn, he returned to the Regency feeling glum and inadequate. After he had slept six hours, Yetunde came to see him on her lunch break from the Witness-and-Work program.

"Yetunde," he said, "I'm not going to be able to fill orders as specific as the one Lileplagak gave me last night. It's impossible."

"Course it is. Lily likes to see what he can do with the orp', is all. He likes to play poet, too." She explained that Lily's directions were not intended so much to be followed as to be appreciated. The art of it was important to the starman, the poetry he coaxed out of the orpianoogla.

"He doesn't talk to Nettlinger or your cousin this way, does he?"

"What way?" the girl asked.

"With an orpianoogla."

"Uh-uh, they sholy don't, none of 'em."

"How do they do it, then? Can they talk as we do?"

"I don't know, Mistah Julian. They *don't*, that's for sure."

"How, then?"

"They want you to know, they'll show you. I promise."

"The other way has to be better than squatting on a toilet at half a degree above freezing and listening to a concert."

"Depends. Don't you like the music?"

"The music's astonishing, Yetunde. It's the squatting and the freezing." And the smell of the KitLax, he could have added.

Yetunde's hair was in cornrows today. She drew a finger along one of the rows and smiled at him reassuringly. Then she urged him to buy a few apples that afternoon and take the evening off. All he had to do was listen to Pal Lily's tape and leave.

"Yetunde—"

"Cousin Fiona won't mind. The Cygnostikoi's taken care of and Em's comin' back tonight. Visit your old cubicle if you want."

"Yeah. From the Regency to Malebolge, from Rich's to rags."

"That's right," Yetunde said, grinning, "jes' backwards o' how it oughta be. Come back tomorrow mornin'." The girl was almost out the door when she remembered something and swept back to his bed flourishing a small baton of paper. "Name sheet. Tells what else we call the Cygnostikoi. That's what I come to give you in the first place. 'Bye."

The door closed. He unrolled the baton of paper and read over the

list with the detachment of a ward rep reviewing someone else's
crime statistics.

> Lileplagak
> Claxspkr
> Podor
> Elabelaberi
> Snoke
> Yyrzstine
> Lily, Pal Lily
> Clarence
> Peter, Petya, Dorian
> Beelzebub, Beriberi, Bela
> Snake
> Yogi, Yuchi, Justin

At the bottom Yetunde had written, "Any these nicknames OK.
Easier to say than real names." Their real names . . .

XXI

AFTER an egg'n'orange in the insta-caffe lounge, Julian traveled
down to Level 4, that underground network of corridors, open
courts, grottoes, and hidden bazaars. He passed prayer booths,
tattoo parlors, tress-sculpturing emporia, everything. He even saw
on display a number of acrylic portraits, on nappy black velvet, of
the Regency starmen. Two or three of these paintings were of Pal
Lily's "conversion", rendered from Tybourn's photographs, and
without exception they were terrible.

Later, a five-kilo bag of apples in hand, Julian fought his way
back to the Level 4 lift-station.

Along the way he saw a stall he hadn't noticed going in. Several
male FUSKCONites, pigtails tossing, danced and chanted beside

this stall soliciting contributions for their literature and looking for converts. Above the stall stretched a saffron banner proclaiming in thin red letters, "Federated Urban Society of Krishna Consciousness," and below the banner, thumbing through the literature on display with a bored expression, was little Saba Dearborn.

Julian paused. Hadn't Saba, in a roundabout way at least, brought him to his position as the Cygnostik katzenappler? If she had, he didn't know whether gratitude or resentment was the proper response. She belonged to a piece of his life that had already swirled away in the eddies under the Waterfall of Now, and she had never been, not ever, a member of his *karass*. Julian decided to pass on by.

Back in Cygnostik Land he distributed apples, fed the plangently miaowing cats, cleaned up after them, and returned to his room. Supper was sent up, and he ate alone. Later that evening the telecom unit buzzed.

"Tybourn here. Got your com-code from Yetunde. Congratulations on landing the job. You surviving?"

"So far. Two days. Thanks for recommending me."

"Julian, I've told Idhe you're working for Mz Bitler and Dr Nettlinger. And I showed him the story you wrote about Margot Eastwin."

"Why?"

"Because it didn't seem so badly done. Idhe liked it. He's going to run it with tomorrow morning's tapes."

"I have a job, Mr Tybourn."

"You can have two if you like, one involving writing. . . . And Idhe'd sort of like you to keep notes on what your're doing."

Julian saw a tape cassette auto-demolishing . . . the seethe, the stutter, the rind of fire. Nicholas Tybourn was proposing, or relaying Idhe's proposal, that he preserve for posterity some record of his time among the men from 61 Cygni. A daily record, maybe. He was wanted for a spy. . . .

"Mr Tybourn, I promised Yetunde I wouldn't divulge the nature of my work. I can't do what your're asking."

"Okay." An exhalation of relief, clear as a bell note.

"Why doesn't Idhe get Josie Cixous to ask Yetunde."

"Yetunde wouldn't do it."

"I can't either, then."

"I know, but I had to ask. I work for Idhe, you know. . . . But, Julian, for all our sakes, you ought to take mental notes of what's going on. Don't let anything by. Absorb. Blot up everything. Let you yourself become the record. That could be important."

"Idhe again?"

''No. That's me. Come around when you can, Julian.'' He broke off.

On the verge of funk Julian set his alarm for eleven-fifty, buried himself at the heart of his room's great pile of artichoke leaves, and settled back for a nap. Almost at once he spiraled down into sleep. He dreamed that Parthena Cawthon, his great-grandmother, whom he had never seen was alive, was holding him on her lap and giving him very explicit directions for journeying from Bondville to a small community in the Open named after the Confederate hero Robert Toombs. Parthena, Julian knew, had never in her life left the Urban Nucleus, not after coming into it as an integer in one of the early Evacuation Lotteries. Why did she want him to go to Toombsboro? How did she know all the landmarks along the way?

Julian saw his dream-self nuzzling Parthena's scrawny neck as he sat in her lap, holding on to her as if to the essence of his own life and weeping like a motherless child. Parthena comforted him with long cool hands and her plaintive plantation drawl.

—*Hush, you jes' be quiet now, evvythin' gonna be fine.* And she stroked his head tenderly from nape to brow, for brow to nape, whispering comfort to him all the while. —*Toomsboro, Julie, 's where the ole Phoenix Plantation is, and that bird she do rise up again, she sholy do. You hush now.* And the long cool hands soothed his tears away, soothed him toward a sleep within a sleep. . . .

''NO!'' Julian shouted, sitting up in the dark. His alarm was buzzing faintly. He shut it off with a violent grappling of fingers. A vinegary fragrance hung in the air.

Someone or something moved away from his bed, paused at the door, then let itself out. The silhouette in the door-crack loomed tall and crested. When it was gone Julian realized that its hand or hands had been upon him, touching his hair. Oddly, the presence of a Cygnostik at his bedside, and the intimacy it had assumed with him, disturbed Julian less than did his dream of Parthena Cawthon. He wasn't really frightened of the Cygnostikoi anymore, but his great-grandmother, he felt, was hailing him from a distance much greater than eleven-point-one lightyears. . . .

It was time to listen to Lileplagak's recording. No matter what Pal Lily had requested, Yetunde had given him the rest of the night off. Julian got out of bed and dressed.

In the Cygnostikoi's bath-booth he activated the tape player. The swell of music galvanized him, as it had one midnight yesterday. From the soles of his boots to the tips of his elbows the music set up a tremor in him. He quaked. And then the libretto, the lyrics, the lilt of stipulation and answering hallelujah—but the words were the

same as the night before, exactly the same, and he let his teeth
chatter in disappointment.

No, wait! A little different. Something had been added. Julian
cocked his head and listened to a new stipulation.

> And for Kee Wig, one wee and one bi-i-i-ig
> *Gopherkatz! GopherKATZ! GOPHERKAAAAATZ!*

Kee Wig. The seventh Cygnostik. The final one, according to
Fiona Bitler. If it was midnight (and it was) Nettlinger must have
arrived in the city with this newest starman. What about the name,
though? What did it mean? It hadn't come from "No Other Gods,"
at least; he'd devised only six alien names for that lamentable piece,
and they were already in use, every one of them. . . . On the repetitions of the magnificat, however, Kee Wig underwent a subtle
change. Kee Wig became Kweek Weg, and on the second repetition
Kweek Weg became—

Queequeg!

Julian got up, kicked open the door of the bath-booth, and stalked
out of Cygnostik Land even before the tape player could eject the
cassette. He was being manipulated, taunted. Who do they think
they are, anyway? Just who do they think they are? Maybe he *would*
take notes. Why not? Maybe he would. . . .

XXII

STEINFELS had enjoyed the mass for Cherokee. On Wednesday he
spent the first thirty minutes of his seminar punning at Bishop
Holman's expense. Staring drolly through buttery green contacts,
Old Turtle had Holman looking gift horses in the mouth, changing
horses in mid-stream, examining horses of different colors, offering
his bishopric for a horse, and riding a cock horse to Banbury Cross.

It was too much, more disillusioning in its way than the High Bishop's several shortcomings. . . . The upshot of all Steinfels's banter was that Holman had gone glitchy since Saturday. First he had accepted a Cygnusian into the fellowship of Christ; then he had arranged a public ceremony to translate the soul of a poor, dumb beast to heaven. You could either rant or laugh, Old Turtle's tone implied, and he chose to laugh. Maybe that was healthy, but Margot couldn't help feeling that there were other alternatives. Commiseration. Charity.

Finally Billy spoke: "Dr Steinfels, you're suggesting an analogy between yesterday's mass and Saturday's conversion, aren't you?"

"Am I?"

"Yes, sir. I think so. Just as only human beings deserve or can benefit from a formal mass, only a human being can undergo the sacrament of baptism. Mediations of grace don't count where grace itself isn't possible."

"Is that what I was saying?"

"Not quite so eloquently, but yes. You kept dragging in horses."

"Whereas the real subject," said Steinfels, "is . . .?"

"Human beings. Horses don't qualify. Bishop Holman himself probably realizes he was bestowing an *honor* on Cherokee, not *grace*. But what about the Cygnusians, sir? Couldn't they perhaps qualify as a variety of Man, with a claim on salvation through Christ, particularly if they acknowledge Him—as one of them has done—as their Savior?"

"Christ's death on the Cross," Lewis Potter said, "was an historical as well as a spiritual event. The Cygnusians are outside our history."

"Not anymore," Margot said.

"That's right," Tonsured Billy agreed, "and if physical presence at Calvary is a requisite for salvation, we're all damned."

"But can they co-opt our Savior?" Fredelle Fowles asked. "Christ became Man to take upon Himself the sins of humanity, not of those . . . things in the Regency. It may not be time for *them* to be saved; Christ may not have chosen to show himself to the Cygnusians yet. Out there, I mean."

"Why would He have to?" Billy asked. "Especially if *they* came here, where He's already shown Himself. Their coming here could be part of the plan."

"Are you suggesting, Mr Björkman," Steinfels put in, "that God might be inadequate to the task of redeeming the populations of other planets? That he might not choose to undergo crucifixion, or its equivalent, more than once? Don't sell God short. Don't underestimate omnipotence."

"Far be it from me. It's not selling God short to assume He might arrange for a single Passion to suffice for all Creation. It could well be that of all the sentient creatures He made, only human beings and Cygnusians transgressed against His original law. Maybe only we and they sought to eat of the fruit of the Tree of Knowledge, and one Passion's enough to save both fallen species. Therefore we ought to accept these . . . these starmen, I suppose . . . as fellows in our Lord's all-encompassing sacrifice.''

"Jesus died to save *people*," Mz Fowles insisted. "People made in His image. Look at the Cygnusians, just look at them.''

"And their appearance," said Billy, "suggests medieval carvings of saints. Archangels. Figures in Byzantine mosaics.''

"Also piston assemblies and motorized prosthetic equipment," Old Turtle said, glowering, hands upon his paunch. "You're not trying to resurrect that twentieth-century hokum about 'ancient astronauts,' are you?

"No, sir. Just pointing out that their 'image'—the Cygnusians', that is—isn't so far removed from ours, finally. One model for both species isn't an impossibility.''

"Do you see God in baboons, Mr Björkman? In orangutans?''

"I hope," said Billy warily, "that I see God in everything.''

This response stymied Steinfels. He rubbed his eyes with his knuckles, tugged at his tattersal waistcoat. "The question is," he said at last, "how do we know they're not horses?''

Drawing a series of looping figure eights on her desk Margot said, "We try to find out if they have immortal souls.'' Yes, it sounded obtuse and quixotic, but if you had an immortal soul, a sliver of divine spirit, you qualified for grace, didn't you? Margot's figure eights got larger.

Fredelle Fowles said, "How do we do that?''

"Perhaps we ask them," Old Turtle said. "Is that it, Mz Eastwin?''

"It's a possibility, sir.'' She looked at Tonsured Billy, who seemed, for once, to be on her side. "But it may be they've already answered us. At least one of them has, only four days ago.''

"If it isn't a satanic wile, Mz Eastwin.''

"What if it's the truth, sir?''

"Then it might be possible," Old Turtle said, drumming his stomach, "that their immortal souls don't belong to Christ, and this alleged conversion is still a lie.'' Gone were the horse puns. Steinfels didn't want to admit the Cygnusians to grace, and he was treading on doubtful theological territory to keep from having to do so, even hypothetically.

"Dr Steinfels," Margot said, "if Creation's all one, and if they *do* have immortal souls, Who else but God would their souls belong to?''

Quickly, mocking a bit, tempting Old Turtle to snap, Billy said, "You're not postulating a Manichaean cosmology, are you, Dr Steinfels? Surely you don't regard our God as the Demiurge, or as a co-Creator of some sort? That's heretical, isn't it? Anyway, Mz Eastwin raises a good point: Who else could the Cygnusians' souls belong to?"

"We haven't determined," Old Turtle snapped, "that they *have* souls." To himself he mumbled, "Young people are raving literalists." He got up—something he rarely, if ever, did—and hobbled along the wall to one of the slit-windows in the balloon of Ogrodnik Hall.

"What have we decided?" Fredelle Fowles asked.

"That Cygnusians are horses," Alvar Caballero said.

Slowly, Steinfels came all the way back to his desk and put his fingertips on its surface, like a spiritualist awaiting a "voice." "I've decided," he finally responded, "to dismiss you early. Assignment: Research the matter and write me a one-thousand-word paper on the eligibility of our interstellar visitors for salvation through the mediation of Christ. You may go."

"Sir—" someone began.

"That's all. You may go." Old Turtle tucked his notebook under his arm and like a doctor leaving a sickroom let himself into the hall.

Tonsured Billy was the first to stand. " 'No' is the safest, I do darkly perceive," he announced to the class; "but 'Yes,' 'Yes' is—"

" 'Yes' is more exciting," Margot concluded for him.

XXIII

THEY spent the afternoon together in the Complex's library, a large hemispherical balloon whose orangelike segments were decorated with vivid scarlet and yellow likenesses of pre-Federation "writer divines." Going in, you passed beneath the twin colossi of Cotton

Mather and Edward Taylor. The library's interior was five floors of visicom carrels around a central computer well, information depot, and display shaft perpetually flooded with soft light. You could browse through the holdings of the entire library by sitting in a carrel, punching up preselected call numbers, and then perusing the computer-summoned material in privacy. There were no books or cassettes anywhere in the balloon, and the first-floor information depot housed only a holdings catalogue and a sunken work area for the five or six lost-looking phantoms on duty there.

On the third floor Margot and Billy took adjacent carrels, sitting together without the privacy guard that could be drawn out from the wall between their consoles. Where did you begin, though? If Christ had indeed come (as He had) to take upon Himself the sins of humanity, who qualified as human? What, Margot asked herself, is a human being, after all? You could go crazy seeking a cogent definition: *Man is a political animal. Man is determined yet free, free yet enslaved. Man is . . .*

"Billy, who said that a human being is a hairless biped without feathers?"

"A contemporary of either Aristotle or Plato, to which the Great Man himself replied, 'If that's the case, then a plucked chicken is a man.' Something like that. The anecdote's hazy in my memory."

Man is a political animal, Margot thought again, and she looked at her classmate's pale forehead, its paraffin translucency, and wondered why she had so deep a suspicion of the ones who governed the city. She recalled that a week ago Billy had been frightened of what was happening in Atlanta, whereas this morning he had seemed almost buoyant in his defense of the creatures that Steinfels, if given his head, would summarily excommunicate from any hope of fellowship in Christ. In the interval, of course, The Event had occurred. Something political would be manufactured from it, for the city's politicos, pretending to knowledge, would twist it to their own ends. Real knowledge, however, lay with the Cygnusans, and only with them. At least that was what Billy seemed to feel now. As she herself had put it, "Yes" was more exciting. . . .

They studied, calling up microfilmed tomes of mythology, theology, and philosophy, ancient and modern: Origen, Augustine, Aquinas; Barth, Teilhard de Chardin, Ogrodnik. They didn't find very much they hadn't already known or couldn't have deduced for themselves, and it appeared their papers for Steinfels would have to spring full-blown from their own tortured brows, Athenas of subtle artifice. . . . But in the course of their "research" Billy called up an illustrated copy of the Egyptian *Book of the Dead* and fixed on his visicom console a color photograph of a mortuary painting.

"Look, Margot. Ra in his solar barque." The sun god bore an ankh, symbol of authority, and he resembled a falcon with an oblate disc on his head. Ra-Harakhete entering the Cave of Night, there to struggle with the serpent Apep, there to defeat the powers of darkness.

"See the ankh. What does it look like to you?"

Margot pondered. "A cross with a circle on top."

"A cross with a handle, in other words. An ankh is an ansate cross, Margot, and 'ansate' means 'having a handle.' "

"All right. And what does that mean?"

"Margot, I *stumbled* across this illustration, but I've stumbled serendipitously, I think." He tapped the screen. "What about Ra? What can you say about him?"

"A falcon with a lopsided O on his head. Like a safari bundle. Maybe he has his laundry wrapped up in there."

"Doesn't the O suggest something to you, mean something?"

"Well, it could be the sun. Or a halo."

"And the idea of the sun and the idea of the halo, Margot, are to some extent tautological notions, at least symbolically. Would you accept that, Margot, along with man's natural tendency to associate divinity with the sun?"

"All right. Since you seem to want me to."

"Good. . . . Then I can't help feeling that this old mortuary painting supports my belief that the starmen qualify for grace. It illustrates that you needn't be made in a *strictly* human cast in order to grip the handle—the invisible handle—on the Ortho-Urban cross. Without being an 'ancient astronaut,' you see, Ra is a Cygnusian."

Inter. Connected. Ness.

"To carry this further, do you remember the poem by that English Jesuit, the sonnet called 'The Windhover: To Christ Our Lord'?"

" '*Daylight's dauphin, dapple-dawn-drawn Falcon*,'" Margot quoted. "Is that the one? Gerard Hopkins?"

"Hopkins," Billy agreed. "There's an odd analogical pattern in the poem: Falcon equals Christ. Or, at least, the falcon represents Christ's order on earth, as a manifestation and a glorification of that order. By extending the analogy we can conclude that Ra equals Christ, too. If we *can* conclude that, it isn't impossible to see Christ in essences—*quiddities*, if you like—other than the human. You almost have to, in fact, for if He was sent to save humankind, he nevertheless suffuses the whole of Creation, Margot; His spirit is shot through the fabric of the farthest galaxy as well as that of our little local backwater." Billy's hand caught hers, and his usually pale face darkened with excitement.

"But why equate Ra with Christ, Billy? You're jumping about on the basis of awfully tenuous associations, aren't you?"

"Like Tagomi?"

"I could follow Tagomi. I'm not following you." And she became aware of Billy's hand around her own; the heat of his palm reminded her, by contrast, of Jenny-O's frigid clasp in the weeks before she died. And Billy's hand, together with her memory of Jenny-O, made her think of that old woman's frivolous carnality. Tenuous associations, all of these. A woman already in her seventies when Margot had first gone to her, Jenny-O had among her bric-a-brac a finely carved medieval monk, arms outspread, whose tonsured head you could push down with your thumb in order to expose pink and perpendicular out of the front of his cassock a gargantuan prick. . . . Jenny-O had thought that one of the funniest things under the Dome.

Now, holding Billy's hand, Margot found herself retrospectively embarrassed by the premeditated impiety of a toy monk pointing an accusatory hard-on. Why? The boy's touch didn't enflame her; she didn't even view Billy, once they were ordained, as a potential partner in Ortho-Urban service. Their differences had temporarily united them (the Forthright Lummox, the Secretive Snob), but there was nothing romantic, in either a courtly or a sexual sense, in their union. . . . Why the ambiguous heat of this touch, then? It was a weird series of associations rather than arousal that had made her think of that randy monk. . . .

"See if you can follow this, then. Ra is a falcon. The falcon is Christ. Christ is a Cygnusian. Stop.

"Now consider: The poetry of Hopkins was influenced by the theology of Scotus, who emphasized the concept of *haecceitas,* or thisness, the specialness of each individual attribute of God's Creation as a means of understanding the whole. It follows, then—if you're still with me—that we must accept the thisness of the Cygnusians in order to understand the universal that both they and we *partially* embody. Know thyself, the Greeks said. But self-knowledge is solipsistic, it's incomplete knowledge. Our contact with the Cygnusians is giving us a chance to encompass a knowledge of that which encompasses us. Their thisness plus our thisness may reveal the What behind Creation, Margot."

"You baited Old Turtle about falling into heresy. Aren't you on the brink yourself?" She squeezed his hand, released it.

"Only if anticipating revelation is heretical. What a time to be alive, Margot." He stared at the sumptuously colored painting for a long time, then aligned the automatic copier over the frame and punched for two plastisheet reproductions. The console produced these at once.

Carrying one of these filmy sheets, Margot parted from Billy and caught the *Tillich Carrier* back to the rectormitory.

In her sleeper-cove she smoothed the plastisheet film onto the wall above her bed, where it adhered. On the opposite wall was a small wooden crucifix. Margot could almost feel the tension of the contradictory, or at least antipathetic, resurrections these gods stood for. . . . And yet Billy had perceived a blood relationship between them. Could it be that the Paraclete was a falcon rather than a dove? . . .

In her paper Margot argued that the Cygnusians were eligible for grace. She attempted a definition of *homo sapiens* based not on biological criteria but on metaphysical ones. She decided that a human being was that distinct and unique creature who tried to define himself, at least in some small measure, through his acceptance or rejection of the concept of divinity-in-creation. . . . Will that hold up? Or have I qualified my definition to the point of meaninglessness? If it does work, then the Cygnusians are human beings and Christ is their Savior as He is ours. One's *concept* of self, the question of solipsism aside, is a measure of what one actually is. . . .

Margot imagined Steinfels cross-examining her: "How do you know that whales don't have a notion of divinity? Porpoises? Pigeons?" . . . "I don't, sir." . . . "What if they did? What if they did?" . . . "If my definition's correct I suppose we'd have to say they were eligible for grace, too." . . . "*Whales?*" . . . "Yes, sir; unless they haven't fallen and don't require it." . . . "Fallen? *Drowned*, you mean!" . . . It did sound ludicrous, didn't it?

At midnight, her paper finished, Margot went to bed.

XXIV

"ANYBODY home?" Julian pounded on the door of his parents' old shop; he felt cold and exposed.

A small black man whose eyes pointed in opposite directions cracked the door and poked his head out. "Yah?" he said. He looked like a gnome or a troll. "Who're you?"

Julian told the gnome his name and asked for Menny.

"That's my landlord, Nessim," Menny called from inside. "Let him in."

Nessim ducked apologetically out of the way, and Julian passed into the customer area that had once rioted with ferns, hanging baskets, terra-cotta pots and vases. Now Menny's battery lantern gave back to him other images: a scarred linoleum floor, a trellis guyed with spiderwebbing, and an empty fountain.

"Come on," Menny said good-humoredly. "We're sitting out here." And toting the lantern, he led the way to the greenhouse. Julian remembered orchids, roses, fuchsia, lilies, some in polyethylene blisters, some in boxes of treated sphagnum moss, some simply in pots containing soil that could still be dug at various places inside the Dome. . . . Now the lamps in the greenhouse had all either burnt out or fallen to pilferers. Why did the desolation surprise him so? Menny, after all, had moved in long after vandalism and neglect had transmogrified the shop. . . .

"Odd hour for a visit," Menny observed, not at all unpleased, and Julian explained that he hadn't been to the Kudzu Shop in a long time and had only hoped Menny would still be awake when he arrived.

"He awake awright," Nessim Charles said. "Lucky he ain' dead, though." The little Muslim told the story of Menny's assault on a starman. "Second time in five days I had to walk him home."

"Yep," Menny acknowledged. "I went crazy. I knocked the Cygnusian down, and if somebody'd given me a screwdriver I'd've taken it apart."

"Why?" said the incredulous Julian.

"I don't like 'em. And they keep bringing them in. Pretty soon anybody who ain't enfranchised's gonna get kicked right out the door."

"Tonight's was the last one, Menny."

"I don't believe it," Menny responded quietly, fatalistically.

Nessim, seeing that his friend had company now, decided to go home, and Menny and Julian stood on the sidewalk in front of the Kudzu Shop to make sure he got out of Coweta Town without being set upon by huggermuggers. Back in the greenhouse, Menny began to undress for bed. He folded his clothes and stacked them in the outer office. "Want to sleep here, Julie?" Completely naked, a brown, heavy-gutted, heavy-scrotumed giant, Menny waited in grainy lantern light for Julian to reply; his breathing suggested infinite patience.

"Sure," Julian said finally. "I'd like to sleep here."

In a utility closet they found a piece of canvas, and with this and a moth-eaten dressing gown Menny lined a flower tray that the two of them had struggled to mount on cinder blocks. Still wearing his underclothes, Julian lay down at full length on the tray. He closed his eyes, then quickly opened them again. "What if they make it rain tonight?"

"We'll get wet. Just like I did Sunday morning."

A few yards of heavy-duty plastisheet and some carpet staples, Julian suggested, would be all they needed to repair the greenhouse's broken panes, at least provisionally. Menny mumbled something. It was clear he wasn't listening. Julian raised his head and saw Menny sitting in an adjacent tray, feet on the floor, his gnarled knees jutting upward. Seeing Julian, Menny pointed at a patch of skin beneath his sagging breastplate and squeezed the area between thumb and forefinger.

"See this?"

"Uh-huh," Julian replied dubiously.

"Doctor who does the medicaid physicals for the receiving point told me it's an adventitious nipple. An extra one, you know."

Julian could see nothing but Menny's encircling fingers. "An adventitious nipple?"

"That's what he said. Which seems funny, having an extra one. I've never had to use the two real ones."

Julian admitted that having an extra one did seem funny.

"I never married, Julie. I never had children. And I'm a man. But I've still got a . . . an *ad-ven-tish-us* nipple. Why is that?"

"I don't know, Menny."

"When you're a human being," Menny said thoughtfully, "there just isn't that much difference between you and another one, man or woman, Saggy Nelly or Nessim Charles. We've all got nipples, even if they don't work."

"I guess we do." Had the incident at the receiving point befogged Menny's brains? Were the two of them *really* discussing . . . nipples?

"Some of us even have three. And the doctor told me the third one almost never works, the adventitious one, even if you're a woman."

"Well, being, uh, adventitious, it wouldn't."

"Of course not. But do you know who it is, Julie, that lacks even the genuine articles?"

"The Cygnusians?" Julian guessed.

"That's right. The Cygnuisances. . . . And we still let them come into the city, more every year." He released the unfunctioning gland and struck the side of his flower tray. "This is worse than when Oglethorpe landed at Savannah, Julie. At least Oglethorpe had nipples. . . ."

Lord, what would Menny think if he knew I was working for the

Cygnostikoi, living with them, catering to their appetites? . . .

"It's on my 'milk line,' " Menny began again, tapping his flank. "The doctor said everybody has a milk line, from your armpits down to your groin. You can have extra nipples almost anywhere along the milk line."

"I didn't know that, Menny."

"Gospel truth. People are animals. We evolved from animals. Have you ever looked at a cat's belly, or a dog's?"

Without volunteering that he had done so quite recently, Julian said that he had.

"Well, the female ones have adventitious nipples that aren't adventitious at all. They work, those extra nipples. They're all on the milk line, and they work; the milk just flows, Julian, an amazing thing." His eyes intercepted Julian's and held them. "Cats, dogs, pigeons, and people. We've all got to stick together. We all have milk lines."

"Pigeons don't have milk lines, Menny. They're birds."

"But they were born here. It's possible to identify with them. They're human, at least."

"A little, maybe. . . . Menny, have you lost your job?"

"I don't know. Glom wants me to twist a bit. . . ."

Julian abruptly changed the subject: "Hey, Menny, can I see the trees? The bonsai?"

Readily agreeing, Menny walked with him to the open patio at the rear of the greenhouse. Julian saw the trees, and in this alien and familiar place, eight years after their deaths, equated the two bonsai with his parents. Surely, even if no God existed, the spirits of Papa Ty and Mama Queequeg inhabited these two trees, maybe as airy projections of Julian's memory of and belief in them; if nothing else, maybe that.

"Goodnight, Aoyagi," Menny said. "Goodnight, Zakura." And the two men returned to the greenhouse.

XXV

DEACON-CANDIDATE FINDS CALLING / AFTER FINDING ABANDONED INFANT, the headline read. Her sleeper-cove was illuminated solely by the glow of the visicom screen; outside the city grew grey, then pearly, as dawn slowly clocked the darkness aside.

The story was about her, of course; a moving story, despite its familiarity. She read it twice, noting the way Julian had contrived to suggest a parallel between her discovery of "little Moses" and the starman's apparent discovery of Christ. . . . But she had trouble equating herself with the Margot Eastwin in Julian's story; oddly, this distance from herself as a "character" gave the account of Moses's rescue more reality than it sometimes had in her memory. What an intimate gift for a stranger to give her. . . .

Margot read the newstape story a third time, then shook her head and turned the console off.

I'm here because of that child, she thought. I service-assisted this past Saturday because over five years ago I heard an infant crying in a parcel locker and rushed to take it in my arms. . . . I told the story, the story's been retold to me, and now the story has an existence apart from that of either teller. . . .

"Margot!" Tonsured Billy's voice called her from beyond her door. "Hey, have you seen it?"

She drew on a white dressing gown cut to resemble an alb and let Billy in. "I've seen it; I've just now dialed it out."

"We ought to have it copied and show it to Steinfels."

"I don't want to do that, Billy. If he's seen it, that's all right—but I don't want us to be the ones to bring it up, I really don't."

She was conscious of a loss in the gift that Julian had given her; she was conscious of the incongruity of her selfishness. She wondered if young Cawthon had any idea of what he had done by making the discovery of "little Moses" more real in print than it was in her memory. Subtly, she was changed. Her faith was narcis-sistically renewed, as if through the witness of someone whose values she respected. But I *know* what I believe, Margot told herself, and shamefully I don't desire to carry my witness into the world; I can't help that, I really can't. . . .

XXVI

ON the way to UrNu House with Fiona he thought of what he had seen and heard since returning from Scandipol. The Event. Abu-Bakr dead. A funeral mass for the High Bishop's horse. The assault on Kee Wig at the I-20 receiving point by a man who had gone crazy at Trap's plantation five years ago. . . . It was difficult to believe that so many things could happen in ten days' time.

Although not in bloom, the azalea hedges on the interior promenade of UrNu House gave the Cherokee-marble walk a cosmopolitan elegance reminiscent of New Free Europe. Along the walk, behind the azaleas, fluted columns made a circle around the building's central court. Inside that chamber over there, where Carlo Bitler had been shot to death, the Council/Conclave was meeting in closed session, Saganella Ruth Lesser presiding.

"Is that it?" Fiona asked him, pointing into the court.

"That's most definitely it," Emory said. "I can tell even though it's covered." Somehow the morning-shift stevedores from the point had wrestled Dragsted's statue onto the lawn, where it reared up in front of a mirror pool protected by an empedestaled marble phoenix. Under its stiff sheeting the statue dwarfed the phoenix, laid its reflection on the pool like a shroud, and put Emory in mind of a flour-and-water Matterhorn. He led Fiona to a bench beside the pool.

She took off her street slippers and dangled her feet in the water. Fortunately, the statue hid Fiona from the pair of columns through which the First Councilor must come to greet them. In the clear water Fiona's feet were whey-colored lampreys making love.

"Why are you doing that?"

"My second childhood, Em; we're all in the childhood of the soul." She wasn't challenging him, but he took his own slippers off and aligned them side by side on the bench.

Then he extended his feet toward the water. Because his legs were too short to do this comfortably, he had to stand so that he could alternate the dipping of his feet. Dipping them, he saw Councilor Lesser appear from behind one of the sheeted slopes of the statue. She approached and shook hands with each of them, her hand as limp and warm as melting cheese, her smile faint and vacuous; and Emory noticed on the concrete walk beside the pool the several dark footprints he and Fiona had made—footprints that told him Fiona's arches were higher than his.

"Isn't the statue *large*?" the First Councilor said. "I've decided that on the thirty-fifth, the Saturday after this coming one, we'll have a formal unveiling. At the same time, you see, as our new promenade is dedicated." She looked down. "Your feet are wet."

"We were bathing them," Fiona replied. "Em wanted to dissuade me, I think, but didn't know how."

"Can you draw a fish?" asked Saganella Ruth.

"I beg your pardon," Emory said, and the First Councilor immediately gave him her arm so that he could support her while she removed her slipper and dunked her right foot in the pool. With her wet foot—or rather its wrinkled big toe—the woman drew this figure on the walk: The fish at once began to fade.

"An ancient sign of greeting among the first Christians," Saganella Ruth explained. "The fish stands for Christ. Has to do with the Greek letter *chi*, if I'm not mistaken, a principal sound in both *Khristos*, Christ, and *ikhthus*, fish. *Chi* is sometimes written *X*, as in X-mas, and you will notice that the tail of my fish forms just that alphabetical symbol where it joins the fish's body.

"Of course," she continued, drawing a new fish, "the early Christians drew this sign in the dirt with their bare or sandaled feet, usually when they were talking with a stranger and wanted to establish a bond. If the stranger didn't remark the sign, they realized they had encountered one outside the Faith and nonchalantly wiped out their fish with a smudging of dirt. This was in the days of the Roman persecutions, you see, when one could lose an ear or a hand for professing belief in Jesus. . . . Oh, that one's gone, too. Please join me in drawing them."

Following the First Councilor's lead, Emory and Fiona spent three or four minutes dunking their feet in the pool and drawing little fishes on its concrete verge. At last they put on their slippers and sat down.

"You attended Abu-Bakr's funeral on Tuesday, didn't you?" Saganella Ruth asked Fiona. "Well, other business called me away—but I want you to assure his widow and children that I haven't forgotten Abu's service to the Nucleus. Before you leave, remind me that I have a gift for them."

"We will." Fiona clasped her long hands. "We came to you on two matters today—"

"First, the statue," said Emory, "a matter you seem to have disposed of already with your plans for an unveiling ceremony."

"I have indeed. And the second matter, Mz Bitler?"

"A message from the Cygnostikoi. Soon after the newest star-man's arrival they asked me to make a request of you. . . . All but Pal Lily, who's already been, want to attend an Ortho-Urban service."

"That's fine, I should think. But I wonder why you ask me; the ecclesiastics are the ones who'll have to make the preparations."

"We ask you," Fiona said, "because of what happened last time. Abu-Bakr died, we believe, because a perfervid few thought they'd been given a license to kill 'infidels.' The Muslims and the FUSKCONites look upon The Event as an attempt to undermine the faiths of their devotees, as a pretense to harass them. If six more Cygnostikoi convert, what might happen?"

"Do they intend to convert?"

"We don't know," Emory said.

"But," Fiona put in, "it seems likely. They often move in concert. . . . With the new one's arrival, Councilor Lesser, they appear ready to embark on a program of active involvement in the city's life. We originally brought them hoping their visibility might awaken the Nucleus's citizenry to other vistas—" (Emory saw Saganella Ruth purse her mouth at this borderline treason.) "—but now we're unsure whether harm or good will ensue from their activities. Therefore it's your responsibility to make the decision, Councilor Lesser. Em's a physicist, I'm a freelance 'educator.' "

"You're both Church, aren't you?"

"I have a membership," Emory said. "Or a lapsed one."

"I'm Church," Fiona confirmed, "if you accept skeptical be-lievers of a somewhat Eastern persuasion. Carlo was privately a Monophysite because of his study of the Copts and the Syrian Christians—but he never preached Monophysitism as an essential part of his gospel. He sought social reform as much as allegiance to Christ, I'm afraid."

"He got both. Eventually."

"Or their appearance," Fiona countered. "The razing of por-tions of our tenements and the institutionalization of faith."

Emory cleared his throat and stood up. Why was Fiona being so recklessly honest with the First Councilor, who, her religious fanaticism completely aside, was still probably a madwoman? Gazing into the pool, Emory saw his own small face undulant with worry.

"You're trying to suggest I ought not to permit the Cygnostikoi to attend service. You lack sympathy for Ortho-Urbanism and don't wish your wards to spur its growth."

"No, ma'am," Fiona answered. "The *consequences* of six more conversions—conversions even Em and I don't understand—ought to be your foremost concern. We just want to focus your attention on the problem."

"*Why* don't you understand them, Dr Nettlinger. You've observed them several years, haven't you?"

Emory turned. "Yes, ma'am. We don't understand them because they're not human beings; they look, they act, they function differently. What they know is different from what we know, and *that* makes mutual comprehension—the discovery of common denominators—a dicey affair."

"What of Lily's acceptance of Christ as a common denominator?"

"Councilor Lesser, we don't know what that acceptance *means*."

With her cadaverous cheek bones and spaced-out eyes Saganella Ruth looked as if she tilted with windmills in her dreams. "My decision is that the six remaining Cygnostikoi *may* attend a special service."

"Very well," Fiona said, unperturbed.

"But Lily ought to go, too. Having converted, he ought to try for perfect attendance." Saganella Ruth bent to the hem of her gown and wrung it between blanched fists. Then she wiped her hands on her thighs and summoned one of the guards on the promenade. "Go to my office and fetch back my gift for Abu-Bakr's family; it arrived this morning from Beatty's." The man departed, and the First Councilor sighed.

"I *can* treat those outside the Faith with fairness," she said finally. "And I seek private contact with FUSKCONites and Muslims in order to learn what they're thinking and how they feel."

Emory tried to imagine Saganella Ruth going incognito into the streets to eavesdrop on the *vox populi*. He couldn't.

"Abu-Bakr is a case in point. Soon after I gave Abu his small-game license, you see, I asked him to drop by the Hill every few weeks to talk to me about whatever *most* occupied his thoughts. . . . Did either of you know that Abu was a man with an obsession? You didn't, did you? Well, it's true. . . ."

And the First Councilor proceeded to tell them a complicated and unlikely story about Abu-Bakr's "obsession," the capture of an animal that he called either Macavity or The Great White Tom. His obsession had begun when this huge white cat, unexpectedly reviving after being tranked, took a bite out of Abu's lower lip and shot away into the dark. This experience developed in Abu-Bakr an irrational hatred of the dumb beast and a desire to bring it back to the Regency as a prize. But Macavity always eluded both Abu's pharmaceutical weaponry and his clumsy traps, and the poor Muslim grew more and more desperate, more and more obsessed.

One night Abu chased Macavity three flights up a condemned building into an apartment illegally occupied by a renegade guru nearly a hundred years old. This man was seated cross-legged amid a ring of cinerary urns containing the remains of several of his deceased followers. The Great White Tom darted into the guru's lap and crouched smugly there, gnawing on the web of skin between the old man's thumb and forefinger. Abu burst into the room in pursuit of the cat.

"You've got Macavity!" he shouted at the old man. "Grab him!"

"I don't have any cavities," the guru responded, cupping his ear and showing his gums. "I don't have any teeth."

The Great White Tom bounded into a further room, and in pursuing the cat Abu-Bakr stumbled through the old man's urns, toppling and breaking two or three of them. "Sacrilege!" the old man cried. "Sacrilege!" When Abu did reach the bedroom, Macavity darted from it, spinning Abu about, and leapt over the guru's head toward the open front door. Abu hurriedly fired his sedative pistol and to his chagrin and regret stung the old man in the neck; he tried to help his victim into a more comfortable posture before drowsiness overtook him, but the old man irritably shooed Abu away and began sweeping up the ashes of his departed friends. Remorse-stricken, Abu-Bakr clambered after Macavity. . . .

"The object of Abu's obsession had escaped him again," Saganella Ruth concluded. "The Great White Tom had fled. And this is just one episode in the saga of your persistent gopher's frustration. It was all Abu-Bakr could speak of when he came to our open conferences. My heart went out to him, New Islamite though he happened to be. . . . That is perhaps the moral of my story. In fact, I several times resolved to aid Abu with confederates or more weaponry in his quest for The Great White Tom, but before I could really do so he was killed."

The guard whom Saganella Ruth had sent off to her office returned carrying something frowzy and white, and Emory recalled that Beatty's was a taxidermist's.

"Oh my behest," the First Councilor explained, "a unit of special-assignments police officers went out on Monday morning and finally turned Macavity at bay. The beast was then delivered to Beatty's for urgent attention, and here, Dr Nettlinger, here it is."

Emory accepted the stuffed cat from her hands; it was much smaller than Saganella Ruth's story had led him to picture it. . . . On the way back to the Regency Fiona asked him if he thought Abu-Bakr, whom they had both known quite well, the sort to be overcome with an irrational desire for vengeance against a cat.

"No," he responded. "Not at all. It may be that Saganella Ruth is herself The Great White Tom she so considerately had stuffed."

XXVII

THE Littlest Angel care center unrolled beneath the sanctuary and the chapel of the church off Hunter Street like an underground Great Plains. Only a few lights were on, and the lambency-blowers that generated its air walls during the day would not be turned on for three or four hours. Nothing impeded the eye in its long sweep over the hall except an occasional vitrofoam "clamber tree" or a pegboard divider.

After Saganella Ruth's telecom on Thursday afternoon, Bishop Holman had decided the Littlest Angel would be a perfect place to hold a brief special service for the six starmen who wished to follow in their born-again compatriot's footsteps. Therefore, at four A.M. on the twenty-ninth day of Autumn, Asbury Holman led a procession of six Cygnusians and four human beings onto the floor of the Littlest Angel and marched them to a pegboard divider halfway across. A Church musician pedaled along behind playing "Upward for Aye on Wings" on her orpacycle—softly, so as not to awaken the overnighters in the nursery.

Father Roland Flinders, the director of the Littlest Angel, showed the others how the collapsible desk chairs folded out from the floor like mushrooms popping up. Because the chairs had been scaled to five-year-olds, the adult human beings and the ungainly Cygnusians sitting in them gave Holman pause. He overcame this and preached a sermonette based on the Biblical account of Creation.

Afterwards the orpacyclist played "Come to the Church in the Wild Wood," and all six Cygnusians hoisted themselves from their chairs and hitched forward to accept the Bishop's Invitation to the Altar. He had hoped this would happen, and he blessed each one in turn. Once he had been a licensed executioner in the city's employ, but now it had been given to him to redeem not only men but soulful beings from beyond. Mysteriously, everything evened out in the end. . . .

At the conclusion of the service Father Flinders escorted Mz Bitler, Dr Nettlinger, and the six converted starmen to the transit-station adjoining the Littlest Angel; and Holman drew aside the young man who had become the Cygnusian's new gopher. What was a gopher? Holman didn't know, but Saganella Ruth had said that he would be the one to approach.

"Mr, uh, Cawthon . . . we'd like you to write up what you've seen here this morning and send it to your friend Tybourn of the city newstapes."

"Sir?"

"The First Councilor assures me your employers want this news released; they didn't, however, want any photographers on hand this time. . . . You've already published a piece on Mz Eastwin, haven't you?"

"Yes, Your Holiness. But without a byline."

"That takes nothing away from the reporting. The First Councilor asked Idhe for the name of the writer. She was surprised to learn it was you and decided—along with your employers—that you might as well do this write-up, too. Will you?"

The boy agreed, and Holman strolled about the care center for thirty minutes after the others left. I'm too greatly blessed. Too greatly blessed. He was tempted to climb into a clamber tree and crow for sheer joy.

XXVIII

IN Steinfels's class that week they spent much of their time arguing about the newest turn in the strange drama of the Cygnusian presence in Atlanta. One convert had been an exhilarating challenge; six more were an exasperating, somehow divisive one. Margot had the impression that her classmates felt their territorial rights had been encroached upon, a sentiment theologically akin to "Ah ha, there goes the neighborhood. . . ."

Outside the Complex, in the city at large, rumors circulated to the effect that the conversations had not taken place at all; that the Cygnusians were latter-day prophets; that already four or five groups worshipping the starmen as The Great Sepipartite God had mimeographed treasonable, heretical leaflets proclaiming a new millennium (no one had seen such a leaflet); that Malcolm Muhammed and the Right Enlightened Lamar Coomaraswami of the FUSKCONites had met to consider united action against the religious/political "provocation" of these spurious conversions; that the world was finally, after all this time, *truly* coming to an end. . . .

On Wednesday Margot received an invitation from the High Bishop, who was going to deliver the closing benediction, to attend the unveiling of a statue at UrNu House. Bring a friend, Holman suggested. So she asked Tonsured Billy—William Erasmus Björkman—to go with her, and they arrived at three in the afternoon, well ahead of the other invited guests.

Between the columns on the circular walk were pristinely laid tables: starched tablecloths, unopened bottles of red and white wine, virgin cheeses, tissue-veiled meats and crackers; and out on the enclosed lawn, in surprising contrast to this spotlessness, Dragsted's statue under a mottled sheet of canvas. Billy and Margot stared at it over one of the tables on the promenade as the other guests arrived, and at last an amplified voice bid everyone enter the courtyard for the unveiling.

"Hey," said someone beside them in the semicircular crush of people in front of the mirror pool.

"Julian!" Margot was genuinely pleased and surprised to see him, and she introduced him to Tonsured Billy, who scrutinized Julian closely. She explained that the High Bishop had asked them to attend, and he said that his invitation was from Mz Bitler. "I didn't know you knew her, Julian. I thought you might be here to cover the unveiling. . . . Billy, Julian wrote the article about me in last Thursday's newstapes." Billy shook hands with him again, warmly this time.

"No, my connection with the *Jour/Con* people is on again, off again. But I know Mz Bitler and her husband through that little girl over there, Yetunde Trap." He pointed to a little black girl with a camera. She and Julian's friend, Tybourn, were prowling the grounds for good shooting sites.

"I liked your story—" Margot began.

To the strains of a twentieth-century movie theme the First Councilor, the High Bishop, Emory, and Fiona ascended the speakers' platform to the left of the statue. Saganella Ruth smiled and drew a sign in the air that looked to Margot like an incomplete infinity symbol, for its lefthand loop was unclosed.

"You've been invited here this afternoon," the woman said a moment later, "to witness the dedication of our new promenade and the unveiling of a gift from the Scandinavian Polity." For twenty-five minutes she spoke about good will, the sanctity of the Urban Nucleus, the Christian implications of Atlanta's motto *Resurgens*, and the need for C/C members to make better use of their official cafeteria. Then she introduced Fiona Bitler to polite but doubting applause.

"Thank you," Mz Bitler said. "In this building we have a walkway called the Promenade of Universal Amity. Calling it so doesn't make it so. I'm going to point out that this is an *interior* courtyard, in an *isolate* political building, in an *insular* city, in an *introverted* network of domed 'nuclei.' Four I's, you see. And despite the introduction into the Petri dish we live in of an altogether unique strain of intelligence, we're still as provincial and island-bound as we were two centuries ago. For today at least, this is a 'Promenade of Universal Amity' in hope more than fact. . . . But maybe, just maybe, we've come to unveil that hope as we unveil this statue from Scandipol. And maybe one day we'll rise spoorlike out of the old cultures and institutions nurturing us to a new and better union in diversity. Because our cultures nourish us at a price, I think. We're all nomogenized and we're all stunted. But a 'Promenade of Universal Amity' is a good idea, anyway. And all of us on the platform hope you like the statue we're going to unveil."

She sat down in discomfiting silence. Margot looked around. Maybe the councilors and ward reps, accustomed to Saganella Ruth, were stunned by the speech's brevity. Tentatively Margot touched the heels of her hands together and then very lightly began to applaud. Like a novice concertgoer, Julian began clapping too. Tonsured Billy joined in. The sound of six hands clapping was maybe more embarrassing than silence.

At last the First Councilor, bowing to Fiona, began soundlessly patting her hands together in front of her chin. The dignitaries on the lawn hurried to follow suit. Only Emory Nettlinger, who seemed quietly contemptuous of this display, and Fiona herself, did not applaud. A wave of the First Councilor's hand restored the lawn to silence and summoned an attendant from the walk. This man denuded the canvas Matterhorn by hoisting its sheet aloft and holding it in the air like a levitating avalanche.

The crowd's response was a grim, lengthening silence.

Julian whispered, "Why don't you start things off again?"

"I can't," Margot said truthfully.

The Cygnusian was perfect, and so tall and alien as to be frightening. But the Fiona Bitler was an abomination. Margot looked back and forth between the living woman and the statue of her.

Later, during the enforced sociability of the reception, Margot found herself walking along one of the tables in Julian's company. She was struggling with a suspicion nobody else had come to, or maybe one nobody wished to talk about.

"Julian," she said, halting him. "Look at the statue."

Obediently he gazed over a tablecloth stained with wine and dropped hors d'oeuvres.

"I think the Cygnusian's really a Cygnusian. A starman who's been, I don't know, *turned off* somehow and given a burnishing. See?"

"Do you mean you think it's dead? A corpse they've loaned us for the formal dedication of the promenade?"

"I don't know. Maybe dormant rather than dead. But the discrepancy between the two figures is enormous, a Praxiteles beside a casting in plaster. Dead or dormant, there's still this question: Why would the Cygnusians *want* one of their own to impersonate a statue?"

"Probably not because of the hours." Julian laughed and took up a glass of scuppernong wine. "If your suspicion's correct, Margot, one answer to that is that it doesn't matter to them what their dead or their dormant do. After all, a human being is claiming credit for the statue, and the statue apparently came about through *human* initiation and labor."

"Yes, but with Cygnusian cooperation. Otherwise, no statue."

"Okay. How do you answer your own question, then?"

"If I were Saganella Ruth, I'd be afraid the Cygnusians were plotting an invasion. Each one of them, entering the city as a statue, could be his own Trojan horse, and soon the parks and p-courts would be cluttered with 'computer-twinned' statues waiting for the right moment to jump out and destroy us."

"Yeah," said Julian, smiling in admiration of her ingenuity. "But you aren't, thank Saggy Nelly, Saggy Nelly."

"No. And *I* wonder if the starmen haven't allowed a dead, or a dormant, Cygnusian to impersonate a statue to, well, to *promote* universal amity. That's a possibility many would overlook."

"If so, Margot, it may be a wasted gesture."

"In the event of the crucifixion resides the symbol of the crucifix. One way to regard the Cross, Julian, is as the mnemonic artifact of Christ's suffering. It's possible that that Cygnusian out there—" She gestured across the lawn. "—suffered a voluntary death, or shutting down, in order to become a *symbol* of the concept of amity. A sacrifice. Amity's a variety of salvation, after all. And over a period of time, conspicuous in the courtyard of UrNu House, the gesture may not be wasted."

"Julian," a voice at Margot's back said, "this is a girl I'm going to have to be introduced to."

Startled, Margot turned to see Fiona Bitler on the arm of her husband. Both of them, this close, had a suprareality deriving in part, Margot knew, from her knowledge of who they were: jewel-bright eyes, flesh like satin. Julian, unaffected, introduced her to them.

"I liked the way you started the applause," Fiona said. "You dictated the behavior of a yard full of politicos."

"They were following the First Councilor's lead, not mine."

"Maybe. But *she* was responding to you."

"Mz Eastwin thinks the Cygnusian in Dragsted's statue is a real Cygnusian," Julian interjected after a time. "Dead or dormant."

Both Emory and Fiona glanced involuntarily into the court. Margot could tell that this possibility had never crossed their minds. Emory's face betrayed chagrin, as if ashamed that he hadn't considered this hypothesis before anyone else. He started to speak.

And was interrupted by First Councilor Lesser, who came up to them glassy-eyed and tottery, the High Bishop in tow. Behind Holman Margot saw Billy with a coffee cup in one hand and a dish of dissolving purple sherbet in the other.

"Mz Bitler," Councilor Lesser said, "your address has confounded some of my colleagues."

"Why? I tried to be direct."

" 'Isolate.' 'Insular.' Those words—you may not have known this—are proscribed adjectives." Saganella Ruth drew Fiona and her husband away. "And Petri dish. What in the world is a Petri dish? . . ."

Holman was conventionally attired in business clothes. When the others had gone he took Margot's hand in his. "You came, didn't you? And this is your friend. Nice to see you again, Mr Cawthon."

"The friend I brought is behind you, Your Holiness."

Tonsured Billy managed to set his sherbet dish on the table and wipe his palm dry. He shook hands with Holman. "What happens now, sir? Now that we've accepted all the Cygnusians into the Church?" Billy's interest was real, but Margot could tell that he was still smarting from his mandatory presence at a horse's funeral. His chin jutted belligerently.

"Well," said Holman, "I've just about reached a decision that will startle many. My heck, it's going to *anger* some people."

They waited for him to go on. The reception was concluding. Most of the dignitaries originally present had gone home.

Absently the High Bishop bit at the right-hand droop of his Marshal Earp moustache. "I'm an impulsive man. I'll trust to your discretion, even though I've told no one else yet. It's this: I'm thinking seriously of ordaining the Cygnusians."

"*Ordaining* them?" Billy said shrilly. "As what? When?"

"As priests in the Church, Mr Björkman. Perhaps at Christmas."

Margot felt a coldness come over her. Intellectually she believed it appropriate, maybe even imperative, to cast the starmen in humanity's pageant of salvation—but that they should willy-nilly be made priests. . . .

"Why?" she asked. "Why would you ordain them, Your Holiness?"

"And why as *priests*?" Billy added. "Students at the Complex study five years just to be ordained as deacons. I don't begrudge the Cygnusians *membership* in the Church, but elevating them to the priesthood is a miscarriage of rationality, it's probably even a breach of canonical law, it's certainly—"

"Slow down, Mr Björkman. You don't know my reasons."

Billy quieted, and Julian asked the High Bishop what the Cygnusians themselves might think about his plan.

"I don't know. And I don't think Fiona and Em are very excited about asking them for me, Mr Cawthon. There's time, however."

"Sir, you've told us your decision," Margot said. "Can't you tell us your reasons too?"

"All right. The Cygnusians are more than converts, Mz Eastwin;
you see, they're also messengers. That's *part* of my justification,
although there's more. . . . Maybe I invited you today just to tell
you. But you've got to pardon me now. Tomorrow's another leath-
er-cracking day." And the High Bishop excused himself and
strolled off down the row of tables lining the curved promenade.

XXIX

MARGOT persuaded the others to walk home with her. She needed
time to think about all that had happened at the dedication, particularly the High Bishop's outrageous plans. Julian said that he would
go with them as far as the Regency, and they walked together
without talking.

Outside the Regency a uniformed doorman was trying to hustle a
pair of young people out of the lobby. Billy pointed out that those
getting the hustle were yearlings at the seminary. The three of them
watched as the doorman shoved a male student through the hotel's
front door; a young woman in a yellow vinyl cassock, however,
broke free of him and headed back inside. Turning to catch the
woman, the doorman saw the man he'd just evicted go back in
through an adjacent door.

"What's going on?" Julian asked.

"Christ if I know," the doorman said, flapping his arms. "Go on
in. The big crowd's inside."

They filed through the lobby. Beside the fountain, dwarfed by its
spiraling jets of water, seven first-year seminarians stood in ranks of
two, one student at their head, and chanted an odd litany at the
hotel's topmost floor. The two students who had just escaped
eviction stood side by side in the final rank. Each yearling wore a
vinyl cassock.

"*By the seven gold candlesticks,*" Margot could hear them

saying, "*and by one like unto the Son of Man. . . .*" The litany went on for a while and then concluded, almost brutally, "*Depart, depart, depart!*" Then another student came to the front of the group and they began the chant again.

"An exorcism ceremony," Billy said. "They believe the starmen emissaries of Satan, if not actually his fragmented hypostases."

Margot remembered that during the past two weeks Steinfels had several times suggested that the starmen's "immortal souls"—if they had any—didn't belong to Christ. To whom, then? These earnest yearlings had decided for themselves. If the Adversary had wooleyed their superiors (as they believed He had), then they would do what they could to atone for their superiors' blindness.

"*Depart, depart, depart!*" they chanted. And then began again.

"They're using one of the books from Newman's Extrapolative Theology seminary as a model for the ceremony," Billy said; "the course they instituted year before last, remember?"

"*A Case of Conscience,*" Margot said.

"That's right. The Jesuit Ruiz Sanchez pronounces an adjuration against the serpents of Lithia and their entire planet goes *poof!*"

"That book's proscribed," Julian said. "I've tried to find it."

"We had it on a study cassette," Margot said, "along with *A Canticle for Leibowitz* and two or three others. Newman warned us that none of them had been granted an imprimatur under the Urban Charter. For seminar use only." The Extrapolative Theology class had been inaugurated because of the presence in Atlanta of the "Bitlinger" starmen; otherwise those books—"quasi-philosophical fantasies," Newman had called them—would have remained buried in the silt and debris of the barbarically giddy past.

Finally the seven cassocked figures separated and began filing out of the lobby, ignoring a hundred hostile stares. Those who might have approved, Margot realized, probably didn't understand what had been happening.

"Quadrini! Hey, Geneva!" Tonsured Billy hailed a woman who lived in their rectormitory section. "What're you people up to?"

Quadrini halted, surprised to see Billy and Margot; she approached them, then, brushing back a rope of pale hair. "This was supposed to be a counter-ceremony to the one at UrNu House, but we got started late. The doorman kept chivvying us, you know."

"The top floor hasn't gone *poof!*" Billy said.

"We didn't want it to. But we hope they're lying dead up there, seven burnt loaves in the infernal kitchen."

"It's *cold* up there," Julian said.

"Well, if they're dead, you know, their essences are in Hell. I gotta go.'' And Quadrini, her juniper-green cassock flicking in and out about her feet, whirled away from them.

"We'd better go too, Billy."

Julian grabbed Margot's wrist. *"Wait."* Flustered by his own action, he immediately let her go. "I think I'm going to stay, I mean. Nobody from the newstapes was here to cover this. I ought to do it.'' His mouth slightly parted, Julian seemed ready to whisper a confidence or peck Margot gently on the forehead. Instead he smiled, pivoted, and strolled off toward the insta-caffe lounge beyond the fountain, leaving Margot unaccountably perplexed.

"He swaggers like he owns stock in the hotel," Billy said.

"He lives in the Basement. All the way down, I think." And she turned and led Billy off after the brightly clad exorcists. On the way back to the rectormitory Billy asked her if she knew which service program she'd be assigned to at the end of the current session and, recalling that appointments were only ten days off, Margot told him that she had requested the Littlest Angel care center.

"You'll get it," Tonsured Billy assured her, taking her hand. "Nobody wants to mess with kids these days."

XXX

NESSIM was glad Glom hadn't fired Menny, only laid him off for a week to think about his bad behavior. The week away from the receiving point did nothing to humble Menny, though; the big man had spent the last six days on the job in a glowering, tight-lipped mood that had somehow—on the Monday following the special service in the Littlest Angel—turned even sourer and more difficult to deal with. At the same time, Menny's stevedoring was above reproach, energetic and efficient.

On Wednesday night, however, he began mumbling to himself as he worked; along with crates and pasteboard barrels he tossed down phrases filled with funny names and obsessive repetitions: *Okanas-*

tota, Azazel, Oglethorpe, Andrew Jackson, Hothlepoya, Armstrong, Horseshoe Bend, milk line, and *nipples.* Nessim remembered most of them because Menny said them so often.

Inside the refrigerator warehouse one night Menny put his hand on Nessim's arm and said, "You know how the white man received book learning before the Indian, Nessim? Do you?"

And using their presence in the chill storage area as a cover for his narrative, Menny related how God came down to both white men and Indians after He'd made the world and put a piece of beautiful paper in the hand of Kanati the Cherokee. The white man snatched the paper from Kanati and ran away, thereby depriving the Indian people of a written heritage; the theft of the paper also explained why Long King, the Creek micco, had gone to old General Oglethorpe looking for knowledge when the first Englishmen landed on the Georgia coast. Later on, Sequoyah made up a syllabary that restored to the Cherokee their stolen piece of paper, and Elias Boudinot began a newspaper at New Echota printed in both English and Cherokee. That paper was called the *Cherokee Phoenix,* long before Atlanta was burned by Sherman's troops and its citizens had a good excuse to call their town the "Phoenix City."

"Paper didn't last long," Menny said. "Everybody got shipped off to Oklahoma."

Nessim glanced nervously at the door, slitted now on the brilliant white light of the receiving yard.

"I've been trying to accommodate for thirty years, Nessim, just like Boudinot and John Ross and the others who tried to fit in. Just like old Menewa, Crazy War Hunter himself, after the Creek War—"

"Menny—"

But Menny went on talking about the Great Removal, Andrew Jackson, the Battle of Horseshoe Bend, Hothlepoya and his Red Sticks, and his own irrational desire for enfranchisement—all the things he had been mumbling about. None of it made much sense to Nessim, and he was relieved when his friend allowed himself to be led back into the yard.

Above the innermost lock gate Arjuna, Lou, and Clara Schnozz were using a mechanized lift, supported inside a gantry next to the control scaffold, to stevedore produce and handicraft items aboard a girder-car poised tail down on one of the continuous tracks of the dome. Light blazed in its long windows, and the girder-car's running boards were slathered with shifting gold nimbi. Shuffling in electromagnetized boots, Arjuna winched containers up the running board and handed them through an open door to the girder-car pilot. On the gantry below him Lou and Clara wrestled with the boxes sent up to them from the yard.

"Nessim," Menny said, watching the activity, "I want you to help me get everybody on our shift over to Steve & Dory's after the Friday pull."

"Get you who I can. You know that."

Menny said nothing else in explanation, and on Thursday he bucked and toted as well as before but with better grace. Nessim, whenever the occasion arose, drew aside the other stevedores and talked briefly with them. Curiosity worked in his favor, and he got more yesses than noes.

At two o'clock on Friday afternoon, right outside the receiving point, Nessim saw Menny coming in with a canvas bag slung over his shoulder. This bag, whose contents he revealed briefly to a puzzled Arnold Glom, Menny put in his locker; then he came sauntering back into the yard and began offloading produce from the afternoon's first vehicle before Nessim could get his coveralls on. What was in that bag?

The shift dragged by, Nessim never daring to ask, and at midnight everyone straggled out of the yard half dead, like poleaxed steers, eyes fixed on the point's phosphorescent docking patterns.

Seven people straggled away to Steve & Dory's, a tavern and beer garden three blocks from the point. To get there they had to leave the asphalt outside the cyclone fence and angle through a city block canopied by pecan trees; no houses here, only foundation stones and half-buried water spigots. Music drifted through the trees from Steve & Dory's, UrNu-sanctioned "city-and-suburban funk-phalt," proletarian laments and lovesongs. Nessim found himself compulsively mouthing the lyrics of one of these songs as he and the others approached. And he hated the songs too.

> I only beat you up
> Because I love you.
> I only tie you down
> Because I care. . . .

The beer gardens consisted of a well-trampled lawn enclosed by four Atlantic Coastal Line freight cars and the ancient tavern building itself. Japanese lanterns were strung between the boxcars, and pecans lay underfoot like huge worry beads popped from a score of necklaces.

Sebastian, the head waiter, pointed the seven stevedores across the empty garden to the freight car called *Lady O'Connor*. Arjuna and the Jastertree remained in the tavern to fill everyone's order while the others clambered into the boxcar, sprawled out on cushions, and waited for Menny to begin. He paced, and whatever he was carrying in his shoulder bag rattled and clacked as he did. Arjuna and Jastertree returned from the tavern.

> I'm inside the city,
> The city's inside o' me.
> What a pretty way
> For 'most anyone to be. . . .

Arjuna slid the door to with a bang, and the funkphalt lyrics lapped against freight car *Lady O'Connor* as if from a great distance. It was dark. The flambeaux inside the car were flashlights that had to be taken down from their wall mounts, turned on by hand, and replaced. The car's ceiling, Nessim saw, was mildewed.

Menny told the others everything he had told Nessim in the refrigerator locker at the receiving point. He explained that the Great Removal had taken place without regard to services rendered, allegiances declared, or past property signed over. He told them that, lacking enfranchisement, they could all expect similar treatment when the flood of Cygnusians into the city forced the Public Housing Authority to reconsider its placement policies. Pogroms might well be in the offing.

That said, Menny opened his canvas bag and distributed to everyone in the car a perfectly smooth baton painted a garish red. The batons were each as long as Menny's forearm.

No, not batons. Red sticks . . .

"What we s'posed to do with these?" Jastertree asked, his bent knees and elbows making him look like a huge cricket.

"If you agree the Cygnusians are dangerous, keep them."

"What if we don't agree?" Arjuna asked. He was the only FUSKCONite in the boxcar, the youngest of them all, and his politics were dictated by the Right Enlightened Lamar Coomaraswami or by his own independent enthusiasms.

"Keep it for a while, Arjuna. If you give it back to me in the next three days, I'll assume you're not interested."

"Monday's Halloween," Nessim said. "We got the shift off. Autumn the forty-fourth, you know."

"Okay. Keep your Red Sticks *four* days, then. If you've still got them on Tuesday, you'll *be* a Red Stick along with Nessim and me. Just like Hothlepoya's warriors at Horseshoe Bend."

Holding their symbolic batons like candles, Menny's fellow stevedores greeted this declaration with silence. Nessim felt chills dancing in arpeggio runs on his spine.

Clara Schnozz laid her baton at her feet. "Nessim told us you were going to prom for a round. That's why we all come."

"I'll go get it," Menny said. He yanked open *Lady O'Connor*'s door and jumped down into the pecan-littered court. Rita Radney was singing.

> I told the barman
> Jes' what you are—
> You're not a starman,
> But still you're my star. . . .

XXXI

HALLOWEEN was an odd institution in the Urban Nucleus. So many people dressed bizarrely as a matter of course that discerning the *intent* of a costume had its chancy side. If you played, the game could be vicious. Anyone opening his door realized that the act invited mayhem; anyone knocking understood that his prospective trickee could himself well be a trickster lying in wait with all manner of surprises, from pails of water to bazookas; only sometimes were there placatingly preferred "treats." Nevertheless, the Council/Conclave had made Halloween and the Day of All Saints following it official Ortho-Urban holidays.

Julian didn't want to go out on Halloween; he wanted no part of the crazies who would be plying their madness in the Basement and the Towers, no part of a madness capable of corrupting reclusive milquetoasts into Torquemadas of inquisitorial invention. Uh-uh. He wanted to stay home.

But on Monday morning at one A.M. Julian stationed himself on the commode in the Cygnostikoi's bath-booth and listened to Pal Lily's latest orpianoogla chorale; he heard the same thing he had heard on his first night in the booth. Only once in the nearly twenty days that Julian had been working at the Regency had Lileplagak failed to compose something new and startling for his gopher's midnight concertgoing: the second night's tape had been a repetition of the first's, with the unsettling addition of a request for "Kee Wig." Since that line was now about to come up again, Julian almost shut the machine off.

He was convinced that the Cygnostikoi had picked his mind for their names, but he could discover no malice or even rationale behind their having done so; and in Cygnostik Land he had even learned to greet the newcomer Queequeg with a friendly nod of the head. But the name still bothered him, and he had to will himself not to shut the tape player off when it came time to hear the offending lyric again. He desisted, however, and immediately afterward he heard

> On All Hallows' Eve I do believe
> *Hal-le-LU-jah!.*
> That to help you track Luh-LEP-luh-gak
> *Hal-le-LUUUUU-*
> Will go with yoooOOOOO!
> *jah! Rum-tiddly-tiddly-tiddly-TUM!*

Pal Lily wanted to go with him at the height of All Hallows' Eve itself?! No. His patience was at an end. Lunging angrily up, Julian slipped, fell sideways, and saw his right foot coming down in the tray of KitLax. Balancing himself with both arms outstretched, he looked at his enmired foot, pulled it free, and held it shedding sand over the knocked-askew tray. His boot resembled an overripe banana rolled in crushed nuts. Finally the player ejected the cassette, the tape seethed to destruction, and Julian stomped out, leaving behind him a spoor like driblets from a broken hourglass.

In the wasteland outside he lurched into Lileplagak. "Lily, you're not really going to try to go with me, are you?"

Lileplagak, his eye patches glowing, lifted his arms as if to embrace Julian, but instead dipped his crest in response, a humble yes.

"Lily, you haven't thought this through."

In an outdraft of litter stench (Julian wondered why his mouth was running with spittle when it ought to have been dry) the starman's head dipped a second time, confirming his intention to go.

"Let's go see Yetunde. Maybe she's still up."

Julian trudged away, and the starman, lowering his arms, hitched along behind him. At the vault door Julian allowed his thumb to be scanned, stumbled through into warmth and brightness, and heard Lileplagak come clicking out in his wake. When he knocked at Fiona's suite, Yetunde opened the door and held up a hand before he

could say a word. "I know," she said. "That's why I stayed up."
She let Julian and the starman in, and Julian's eyes went involuntarily to the stone-worked triptych of Carlo Bitler, the central panel of
which so fascinated him. By a force of will he returned his eyes to
the girl and blurted, "It's unreasonable! Whose idea is this,
anyway?"

"Lily's, I 'magine."

"But it's a joke, something out of a bad dream. And the
danger—"

"Em and Fiona say he can go and you s'posed to take him. Lily
wants to trick 'r treat like a reg'lar citizen. It's the first thing he's
asked for since convertin'."

"He asks for apples every day! And cats, lord, the cats—!" But
that wasn't what Yetunde meant, Julian realized that; Lily wanted to
forward his mysterious program of contact with the natives, something like that, who could say? . . . "Yetty, my job's supposed to be
carried out in secrecy, and here you are asking me to go out in public
with Lileplagak!"

"Nobody gonna notice. Everybody out's gonna look funny,
anyhow, costumes 'n' all. You'll jes' be two more hobgoblins
hobblin' around."

"But what if we *are* discovered?"

"It doesn't matter, Mistah Julian. Things are openin' up some.
Em and Fiona don't understand it, but the Cygnostikoi want it and
maybe folks are used enough to 'em being here to 'cept it. . . .
'Sides, you been helpin' with the Comin' Out too, ain' you?
Publishin' stories and keepin' notes."

Lileplagak, like an overgrown and fantastic cocker spaniel, was
observing this exchange with his head lolled to one side. As Julian
felt a tremor of apprehension pass through him, Lily's head rolled to
the other side. Uh-oh, Julian thought, how does Yetty know that?

"I peeped," she said. "I talk to Garamuni when he's changin'
sheets some times. A notebook fell out o' your mattress. You got a
passel o' stuff about the Cygnostikoi wrote down in it. What for?"

"A kind of historical record, I guess. Idhe wanted stories for the
newstapes from my notes, but I've never written him any."

"You've written him three, ain' you?"

"Yes, yes I have. But none from my private notes, Yetty." He
checked them off in his mind: the one on Margot, the one on the
special service in the Littlest Angel, the one on the exorcism
ceremony.

"Okay, Mistah Julian, it's okay, don't worry none. That
notebook's lovely shit. Even Fiona says so. Lily *wants* us to know
about his folk now, don't you, Lily?"

Whirr, said Pal Lily agreeably.

"But you still gotta take him tonight, Mistah Julian. No ifs, buts, or uh-uhs. You hear?"

"I hear," he said disconsolately. "But don't make me take him before ten o'clock, okay?"

"Deal," Yetunde said. She struck Julian on the chest to seal the bargain and ushered the two of them out.

XXXII

THE next evening, Halloween, Julian rode with Lileplagak down the service elevator. Outside the Regency he tried to devise a route to Bondville that would make use of alleys, back streets, and little-traveled p-courts. A block or so from the hotel Pal Lily stopped in his tracks and refused to go any further.

"Lily," Julian said wearily, "what's the matter?"

The starman, who was carrying a Consolidated Rich's shopping bag, popped it open and pointed back the other way; the bag mouth gaped like a hungry animal.

"You don't really intend to trick 'r treat, do you?"

The bag popped its affirmation.

"Where?"

Lily turned and led Julian, pulling his capture crates on a dolly, back toward Peachtree. On a gingko-lined expanse of concrete they ambled unmolested, maybe even unregarded, among the groggy Halloween pedestrians. A sense of their sore-thumb salience nagged Julian. This can't last, it just can't last. But the people in the courts brushed by them without so much as winking. "Cheap attire, cheap effects," the looks of some seemed to say, and Lily busily took in everything, his front-facing and peripheral pupils contracting and dilating in concert.

In ten minutes they had arrived in the quadrangle of the theological school's rectormitory. Windows blazed all around them, but the walks in the courtyard were empty.

"Lily, these kids won't have much to give you."

Lileplagak contradicted this assessment with a flap of his shopping bag, and a new uneasiness assailed Julian. Why the rectormitory? Pal Lily had maneuvered him here for obscure reasons of his own.

"Lily, the security systems in the foyer won't pass us."

And, in fact, a scroll-emblazoned grating blocked the corridor of the rectormitory building. Television monitors mounted overhead showed them that they were being mechanically observed. No way in presented itself.

A vinegary fragrance welled up in the foyer. With his long fingers Pal Lily tore a strip of flesh (or forearm binding) from his arm, crumpled this into a chamois, and wiped each of his arms as if rubbing down a rifle barrel. Then his legs extended. Using the same makeshift rag, he wiped the face of the monitor on the left, then the one on the right, laying down a film on the sensitized surface of each screen. Then Julian's and Lileplagak's images were absorbed into this film, or concealed by it, and the sheen of the monitor-cameras turned into a glossy grey blankness.

"Lily—" Julian began, scandalized in spite of himself.

The starman dwindled to his original height and ate the rag with which he had eradicated their images; then tore another strip from his arm, swabbed his upper limbs, and proceeded to wipe down the bars of the grating, which began to hum as if in transferric sympathy with Lileplagak's ratcheting arms.

"Lily—"

The grating popped open, and Julian instinctively hung back as Pal Lily went gaily from door to door, knocking. At the fourth door a brown-skinned young woman put her head out and looked Lileplagak up and down. Pretending to be a doorjamb, Julian pressed himself against the corridor's wall.

"Hey, that's a splendiffy garb-up," the woman said, and when Lileplagak snapped his shopping bag, she grinned indulgently, disappeared for a moment, and returned with some goodies. She looked down the corridor at Julian. "You want some too?"

"No, ma'am. He's asking for both."

"Okay, then. *Vayan con Dios.*" And she shut the door.

Lileplagak knocked at seven or eight doors on the first floor and received goodies from three of those who opened to him; all but one of the others apologized for not having anything on hand. After two more floors of trick or treating, Lily's bag was heavy with booty and Julian tried to persuade him to leave. "You can't get anything else in there, Lily, and half of it's probably booby-trapped, anyway."

The starman looked around as if to say, *"Booby-trapped? In a rectormitory building?"* and stalked off down the hall. A male student in a dressing gown passed them, and Julian sheepishly said hello.

On the fourth floor Pal Lily didn't knock on a single door; he hitched and glided right down the corridor until he came to a door outwardly no different from any of the others. Julian nevertheless had a premonition, and when the starman knocked he slunk guiltily aside, with no idea why he should feel guilty, and heard Margot draw in her breath at her first unexpected sight of a two-meter-tall Halloweener. She recovered quickly, though, and asked Pal Lily if he would accept two or three packets of instant mint tea in lieu of candy or fruit.

Lileplagak could no longer pop the mouth of his shopping bag, so laden with goodies was it, and in response he grabbed Julian by the arm and pulled him into the doorway for moral support. Or maybe for unfathomable Cygnostik reasons of his own.

"Hey, Margot."

Without even realizing it Julian made a mental catalogue of the points at which his and Margot's lives had coincided, like graph lines on a grid of appalling size. For the most part these lines seemed to have been plotted for incompatible quadratics, but occasionally they touched, ran together, and in cataloguing the touchings Julian became aware of a strange glimmering inside him. He smiled and lifted his hands.

"Hey, Julian," Margot said, returning his smile, and inevitably she asked him what he was doing there.

"Taking my friend around for goodies. Lileplagak, Margot. Margot, Lileplagak. I hope that's how that's done."

"It'll do." Margot asked them in. Although she pointed them to a sofa and a hammock-bottomed chair, only Lily sat. His legs and arms bent at a hundred impossible joints, and his head lolled gratefully against the wall.

"That's our first convert!" Margot said, startled.

"Yeah. I'm supposed to be taking *him* trick 'r treating, but he brought *me* here. On purpose, I think. A Cygnostik's a cagey critter."

"Cagey about what, Julian?"

That was the question, all right. Julian didn't know how to behave toward Margot or what he could say to justify their intrusion. Still, his presence in Margot's rectormitory cubicle *felt* right, and even Margot, caught off-guard in an abbreviated kimono, seemed aware of the weird and radiant rightness of his being there.

Matchmaker and chaperon, Lileplagak rummaged a Winesap out of his shopping bag and five seconds later dropped the threadless core on the carpet.

Julian took a step forward and lifted Margot's hand to his chest. "I wanted to ask you to marry me," he said, amazed and not amazed by his words.

"Why, Julian?" She studied him keenly.

"I don't know."

Margot withdrew her hand from his and walked to the kitchenboard. From beneath it she took three packets of instant tea. Then she crossed the room and dropped the packets in Lily's bag.

"Because I love you, I should have said. I do, Margot. I want you to marry me." It was altogether true: he had experienced no emotion so intensely since his overmastering grief at the deaths of his parents.

"If you hadn't asked me," Margot said, "I would have asked you. That's the truth, Julian."

"What about Tonsured Billy?"

"My closest friend. A brother. He doesn't love me like you do."

"Marry me tomorrow."

Lileplagak cored another apple, probably a Delicious; it was hard to tell the variety just from the core.

"My service assignment came through today, Julian. I'll be at the Littlest Angel until the end of the year, six weeks in all. Let's wait until after Christmas and the graduation ceremony."

"Okay. We'll marry on Year Day."

"In the Church?"

"What?"

"Will we marry in the Church, Julian?"

"I'm an agno—"

"That doesn't matter now. I'm asking you if you'll allow the ceremony to take place in an Ortho-Urban Worship Center."

"All right. If I don't have to pretend to something I'm not."

"I wouldn't ask that."

Lileplagak ate one of the packets of instant mint tea, wrapping and all. He didn't spit the wrapping back out, either.

"Margot—" Julian wanted to kiss this woman. He wanted to slide his hands inside the midnight blue silk of her kimono and caress the long curve of her back. He wanted to pull her to him and discover if the beating of his heart had a partner in the beating of hers. Deep inside his chest someone was tenderly, poignantly skinning a baby rabbit; the pain was sweeter than the preludes to even his most recent guilty dreams. A deacon-candidate in his arms. How much of his passion could he expect her to return?

Margot looked across the room at Lileplagak, a huge figure

crushing the cushion of her rectormitory-issue sofa.

"Lily—" Julian said, understanding her hesitation.

The starman's head revolved toward them. His eye patches glowed with an understanding of his own, and, laying both forearms along his thighs and making a sound like *chik-chik*, he grew weightily rigid in his place.

"Julian—" Margot began.

"It's the 'little death,' " he explained. "It's like sleep, or being shut down, or even having died with the possibility of a willed resur—"

"Kiss me now."

He kissed her then. His hands slid inside the midnight blue silk of her kimono and caressed the long curve of her back; the beating of his heart had a partner in hers. Over her shoulder he could see her sleeper-cove and the end of her bed. He drew his hands forward so that their heels were cupping her breasts and clumsily began walking her backward toward the cove. Briefly she acquiesced in this, then gripped his leg between her own and put a hand on his stomach.

"I want to wait for the sacrament. Help me do that."

"Bodyburning's a sacrament now, Margot, if entered into with love and commitment." *Heaven is in your arms*, he heard funkphalt chanteuse Rita Radney warbling in his mind just as a crescendo of "Upward for Aye on Wings" drowned the cheap ballad utterly and his temples began pulsing like orpianoogla pipes. Elsewhere, one of his physical members was nosing a zipper facing. I can't help it, I look like the letter Y. Why?

"Bodyburning's a sacrament only for laymen," Margot said, kissing his throat. "We're supposed to adhere to a more rigid standard."

Then adhere to mine, Julian wanted to say. I've raised it in lust, longing, and love. That's Y. . . . He caught his breath, moved his hands down the carnal smoothness of her ribs to her hips, spoke into her hair, fragrant with Lime Mime. "The missionary position, Margot. Surely it can't be a sin, the missionary position. . . ." Was this really him, beseeching favor so piteously? No, it was the Y he had become; it was the dying, yearning animal he was tied to. . . .

"Julian," she said, and the belt at her waist fell away, her kimono opened from throat to knees, and her chaste, delicately paneled body was revealed to him in a frame of silk.

He wanted to remove the panels, touch them with kisses, discover the mortal engines of love and love's contentious familiars operating in concert to create the *person* of Margot Eastwin. Margot, surrenderingly, was whispering his name. . . .

Chik-chik said Lileplagak, rising from the dead. He lifted his laden shopping bag and strode whirring and fizzling to the door.

"Lily—" Julian began.

Margot, with a look teetering between relief and frustration, cinched her kimono together. "From the day after tomorrow to the eighty-third you can find me at the Littlest Angel, Julian. And you . . . ?"

"I'm working for the Nettlingers. Ask for me at the main desk of the Regency." He kissed Margot and backed away without taking his eyes off her. "Farewell. Farewell, Margot."

"Godspeed," she said, responding with an archaism of her own.

Lileplagak grabbed Julian by the elbow and pulled him into the fourth-floor corridor. The closed door seemed a cruel joke to Julian.

"It's a Cygnusian!" cried a man's voice. *"Just look!"*

Looking, Julian and Pal Lily saw four seminarians standing at the west end of the hall. The woman was Quadrini. The three men were unfamiliar to Julian, although the one who had just spoken was the student he had said hello to on the third floor before coming up to Margot's.

"Depart, depart, depart!" this young man said, pointing at Lileplagak. The others, also pointing, joined him in repeating the chant.

"Come on," Julian said. He started off at a trot.

Registering that the seminarians were going to follow, Lily dropped his bag, scooped up Julian in his arms, and reached the opposite stairwell in four strides. The seminarians armed themselves with apples spilled from Lileplagak's goody bag and began heaving them at the glass door at the end of the hall. Behind this door, momentarily fascinated by the pursuit, Lily watched the apples splatter or rebound away with heavy thuds.

"Put me down," Julian demanded. "The Christians are after us."

Instead Lileplagak held one leg out over the empty stairwell and calmly extended it. When it was resting firmly on the landing below, he did the same with the other leg. Then, like a capsule in an elevator shaft, he descended smoothly to his original height. A moment later a hail of apples was pulping and ricocheting around them.

"Avaunt, Satan!" one of their pursuers cried.

"We're trying to avaunt!" Julian shouted, and Pal Lily, extending his legs and collapsing upon the extensions, took them down from landing to landing until they were in the first-floor foyer. The starman passed through the open grating there, closed it, and set

Julian down. Julian saw that an apple had lodged behind Lily's halo-crest like a big angry tumor, and so reached up and pulled the apple free. The starman took the apple from him and promptly cored it.

Then the two of them hurried out into the sweet, concealing dark of the quadrangle and the p-courts beyond.

It was the witching hour.

XXXIII

AFTER only three meetings, and without having previously exchanged anything more loverlike than a smile, she and Julian had just declared their love for each other. Very nearly they had gone to bed. What did it all mean? Margot tried to think. . . .

Into her mind came a recollection of Jenny-O's startling wooden monk. She thought, too, of the old woman's secret tattoos, a butterfly under her heavy left breast, a faded blue hummingbird on each of her emaciated thighs. And if bodyburning was a sacrament, by her own testimony Jenny-O had celebrated it many times in her pre-Dome youth. And afterwards, too.

What had Paul written? That woman was the deceived, woman the transgressor. That one should put aside "the earthly in you: immorality, impurity, passion, evil desire," etcetera, etcetera. All of which Margot understood and accepted, but parted with that holy sexist, as did Ortho-Urbanism, on the stipulation of woman's role in the Church and the definition of those acts giving evidence of "the earthly" in one.

If the product of regard, commitment, and passion, bodyburning was a mediator of grace. A sacrament. Out of the ashes of such passion here could rise the yoked firebirds of two self-canonized lovers. That was something almost everyone admitted. . . .

Without knocking, Tonsured Billy burst in. "Hey, did you hear all the commotion in the halls?"

Margot, sitting where Lileplagak had sat, raised her eyes to Billy.
She had heard nothing.

"There's a funny smell in here," Billy said. He looked at the
floor. "Boy, you must have been hungry, Margot."

"We're going to be married on Year Day, Billy."

Tonsured Billy blanched; the pink island of his pate, however,
somehow managed to flush a delicate crimson.

"Not you and me, Billy. Julian and me."

The boy's face and crown traded colorings as he relaxed in the
welcomeness of this clarification. Her closest friend. A brother.
"Hey, I'm happy for you, Margot, if you're happy for yourself. Do
you really know him well enough to consider marrying him?"

Margot pressed Billy's hand as he sat down beside her. Everything was decided. She didn't want to talk about the rightness or the
wrongness of her decision with someone who had no conception of
what had triggered it. Somehow Julian's friend, Lileplagak, had
seen through to the passion in a relationship seemingly platonic and
had hurried that passion into the light. How could you explain that to
someone who hadn't experienced the strange warmth of Pal Lily's
mediation? It was almost a question of grace, like the one she'd
been mulling when Billy burst in.

"Did your service assignment come through, Billy?"

"Just what I requested. The Barrio Mission Patrol."

"Good," Margot said, suppressing her joy with a minor happiness. "I'm really pleased for you."

XXXIV

OVER the two weeks since the remaining six Cygnusians had converted, the First Councilor had taken to visiting his private cham-
bers every other night or so. Holman tried to be understanding.
Saganella Ruth was lonely; she had given up everything to govern
the Urban Nucleus, and even today beneath the spaced-out mask of

her autocratic idealism, Holman could see the contours of the fresh, spaced-out face she had owned in her youth. Therefore, when she chatted away at him, he listened. When she simply sat staring at the icons on the mantle, he also stared, wearing a look of profound sympathy. At times during these silences he realized that she wanted him to reveal something of his own feelings about recent events, but he worked hard not to talk about himself and so avoided divulging his plan to ordain the Cygnusians.

More and more Holman was convinced that their ordination as priests was what God had willed him to accomplish, but Saganella Ruth's frequent visits made it hard for him to put his final signature on this conviction. He knew that she would agree out of hand with his decision and congratulate him on its originality and power. And could anything that Saganella Ruth herself desired coincide with the will of God? Holman was afraid that, beyond solace for her loneliness, the First Councilor wanted aid in the formulation of city policy, the imprimatur of his office, and that fear made Holman unhappy.

It was witching hour, the interface between the eve of revelry and the day of saintly celebration.

Holman stood across the room from Saganella Ruth stroking Cherokee, who at the First Councilor's recommendation had been stuffed at the taxidermist Beatty's. Tonight the woman's face had an impetuous pale glow; tonight she would not be put off. Holman's unhappiness grew, and he brushed horsehair from his palms to hide his gloom.

"Don't be evasive, Asbury. You've had something on your mind ever since I started these visits. What do you intend to do with the Cygnostikoi now that they've all accepted the Faith? What do they mean to you?"

Cygnostikoi was her word; she had gotten it from the Nettlingers. But no matter what you called them, his plans were set and he reluctantly told Saganella Ruth what they were.

"Oh, Asbury, God's will is revealed in this. Seven Cygnostik priests will lead directly to an increase in membership! Think of the infidels, agnoes, atheists, and dissenters who'll discover the True Path." Her long teeth gleamed with yellow enamel highlights.

Holman could not help thinking about the new horse Eddie was training for him now, an Arabian stallion he had already mentally christened Crusader. Listening to Saganella Ruth, he thought of this wonderful animal and touched his own lips, heart, and shoulders.

"Why do you cross yourself, Asbury?"

"Uh? Oh. My decision. I'm praying it won't provoke violence."

"Nonsense. Two weeks ago the Nettlingers cautioned me that six new conversions might have that effect. But so far, not a ripple—

even with a newstape story about the second special service."

"Ripples? There've been ripples. The New Islamites won't venture out except in each other's company, and the FUSKCONites have almost stopped street and p-court solicitations altogether. They're fearful. I have to ask myself if I'm going to frighten them further."

"What does your conscience tell you, then?"

"That the Cygnusians are messengers sent to us directly from God to confirm us in the Church's traditional values."

"Good, good. Then you'll go ahead with this?"

"I've been having a strange dream, Councilor Lesser." He stopped. Why was he telling her this? "The dream makes me doubt my reading of God's will, makes me wonder if I should even attempt such a reading."

"What sort of dream?" Her eyes coruscated in the lamplight, and the glitter in them reminded him of the wide, liquid eyes of that last hostage-holder he had lined up in the crosshairs of his Sniper's Pride police rifle, eyes that had glittered in his scope right up to the moment that the right one exploded and filled with blood. . . .

In self-defense Holman began to pace. "All right," he said. "One of the disturbing things is that the person in my dream isn't me at all. I become the young man who filed the story for us, Julian Cawthon, you know. Except that his *consciousness* is really mine. Do you understand?"

"Surely. You're dreaming Cawthon's dream and see young Cawthon as an actor in it, but the actor's mind really belongs to you. Fascinating, Asbury. You're yourself and somebody else at the same time."

Holman halted and sucked at the corner of his moustache. The First Councilor was not a dull-witted human being, as some had said. At least a few of her wits she had kept admirably honed. . . .

Pacing again, he began to tell his dream, which always occurred in two parts. In the first part he was down on the Level 4 Mall, not as himself but as Julian Cawthon, trying to buy kitty cats at the Dixie-Apple. At the Fresh-Meat Retreat he showed his Feasters Sodality chit, placed his order, and received seven beautifully denuded, cellophane-wrapped cats from the butcher on duty. Whereupon he was immediately shunted into the checkout lane and incomprehensibly translated to a surfaceside re-renewal area. Here, late of a spring evening, he would find himself empty-handed and alone.

"Marvelously arcane, Asbury," said Saganella Ruth, that disturbing, glinty gaze still playing in her eyes.

Somewhat daunted by this look, Holman told her the dream's second part, in which he always trudged through the half-lit streets looking for and calling to . . . well, apples. "Here, Jonathan," he

would call. "Here, Winesap, Wenatchee, Delicious, and Crab."
Then he would go into a suitable-looking building, where the smell
of rich dirt and apple blossoms instead of plaster and boiling
cabbage assails him. The tangled roots of apple trees hang down
around him from the first-floor ceiling. He climbs from landing to
landing until on the fourth floor he discovers the branches of the
trees. He's disappointed because he has come too early in the season
for fruit and must go back down the clotted stairs with empty hands.

"The significance is all very clear to me," Saganella Ruth said.
"But I have access to information that, heretofore, you've been
ignorant of, Asbury. . . . The young man you become in your dream
is the Cygnostikoi's gopher and it's his duty to keep them supplied
with enough cats and apples to insure their good health. It's what
they subsist on here, you know."

"I didn't know," said Holman, stroking Cherokee.

"Well, it is. And your dream, Asbury, is a message to you from
God. He's telling you to go ahead and ordain the Cygnostikoi, that
your role vis-à-vis the starmen is comparable to but different from
that of young Cawthon. It's all very, very clear to me."

Holman said nothing. It wasn't clear to *him*.

"All right, Asbury," Saganella Ruth said indulgently. "What
sort of needs does Julian Cawthon help the Cygnostikoi fulfill?"

"Physical needs, I suppose."

"Certainly he does. And in real life how would he go about
securing cats and apples for his charges, Asbury?"

"Cats from the re-renewal areas, apples from the Dixie-Apple."
The woman's Socratic method offended Holman, made him feel
like a schoolboy.

"Which is what, Asbury?"

"Exactly the reverse of what I do in my dream."

"Which suggests—?"

"That my relationship to the Cygnostikoi is akin to young Cawthon's but different somehow." And I can say my catechism,
too. . . ."

"Amen. The reverse of the physical is the spiritual. Your
dream's telling you that you're the Cygnostikoi's spiritual gopher."

Maybe she was right. He *knew* he was a spiritual gopher. His
whole life, after his sniper duty, had been directed toward saving
souls rather than dispatching them. "But what about my empty
hands?" he asked, resisting her interpretation out of pride. "And
the trees have no apples."

"You're too early in your dream," Saganella Ruth said. "That
suggests you've been correct in withholding your plans to ordain the
Cygnostikoi as priests. But since you've chosen tonight to inform
me of your decision to ordain, the time must now be ripe to

announce to the city what you intend to do. The ordinations at Christmas will be part of a splendid revival of Ortho-Urban enthusiasm, and the announcement you make tomorrow—on All Saints' Day—will be the first trump sounding this revival, Asbury!''

Revival. He didn't like that word. Had the Church been dead? It had not. It hadn't even been sleeping.

Holman could not understand how the First Councilor could so shamelessly mix politics and religion, but neither did he know how to refute her interpretation of his dream (in spite of her illogical contention that the *absence* of apples suggested their ripeness), and so remained silent. When, smug and animated, she at last said goodnight, he repeated his evening prayers and went to bed.

The fragrance of apple blossoms filled his dreams, and when he climbed to the fourth floor of his indoor orchard he found the branches of the trees crippled with tumorous fruit. A family of howler monkeys moved back and forth through the branches dropping down to him all the apples he could ever wish for. . . .

XXXV

LATE in the afternoon of all Saints' Day Nicholas Tybourn came to the Regency and had the main desk summon Julian downstairs. Julian—his heart thudding the syllables of his fiance's name, *Mar*-got, *Mar*-got, *Mar*-got—noticed at once the generous mood his friend was in. Tybourn's glum expression was today merely a facade to hide the exuberance welling in his soul. Julian had never seen Tybourn so happy. ·

"Idhe's run my ass off today. This is the first chance I've had to sit down to a meal. Come over to the Kafe Köbenhavn with me.''

Tybourn politely told the table steward, who was happy to be contradicted, that his choice of a table was unsuitable, they wanted one in the cafe's dark, inner corner. When the waiter arrived, Tybourn rebuked him in a mock-scurrilous way for being late. The waiter did an excellent imitation of a man who has taken offense, and patrons at other tables averted their eyes playfully just as if the argument were real.

What a fine day it was, a perfect day to praise all the saints numbered by the Church. Julian's heart thudded *Mar*-got, *Mar*-got, *Mar*-got, and it was fine how everyone in the cafe, looking at him and the newsman sidelong, congratulated him in his joy and approved of his choice of a table companion.

When his *smorrebrod* and lager came Tybourn gave the waiter the pleasure of returning his sandwich meat to the kitchen to be reheated. The waiter stayed a long time to see that this was done right, and Tybourn remarked loudly that the Kafe København certainly did everything it could to treat its customers like princes.

"They treat you like a goddamn prince here, don't they?" His good humor was contagious, and most of the other patrons turned to their plates to show how much they appreciated their meals.

Then Tybourn told Julian that Fiona Bitler had called the Newstapes Building that morning to say that Bishop Holman's plans to ordain the Cygnusians at Christmas could now be reported to the city. Fiona had called at Councilor Lesser's request. Julian replied that ten days ago Bishop Holman had hinted at this intention and sworn his listeners to secrecy.

"Well, there's no longer any need for secrecy, Julian. Mz Bitler told us we could use any available source for information about the starmen, including you."

"She's a generous and sympathetic woman," Julian said.

"This wasn't her doing, only. The First Councilor seems prepared to lift most censorship requirements in our coverage of the Cygnusians."

"Councilor Lesser's a—" Julian stopped. He had been about to say a "magnanimous and compassionate woman," but the words wouldn't come and he saw that Tybourn's exuberance had fled. What had altered his mood?

"She's a charlatan and opportunist," the newsman concluded bitterly. "But we're going to make use of her self-serving stratagem to find out all we can about the Cygnusians. That's why I've come to you, Julian. I want you to write a piece on your job. Even *I* don't really know what you do."

The waiter returned with Tybourn's *smorrebrod*. He was in a churlish mood in direct contrast to his earlier suppressed gaiety. The world's abruptly contracted indifference to his happiness settled upon Julian like a chill, and his heart stopped saying Margot's name.

"Okay, Mr Tybourn, but why don't you just come with me one

night.''

"All right. When?'' Tybourn looked up at the waiter. "Now you've burnt the bread. . . . Never mind. Maybe I'll eat the god-damn thing.''

When the waiter had stalked off, Julian said, "What about Thursday evening? Friday morning, to be accurate.''

"Good. I'll meet you in your room at midnight.'' Tybourn drank off his lager, nodded, and left the cafe via an angry swagger and a nearby gate.

On Wednesday Julian rode over to Capitol Hill and arrived during the Littlest Angel's afternoon recess. A jumble of four- and five-year-olds was swarming the equipment in the playground, and one of the adults meandering among them was Margot. Seeing her surrounded, Julian was embarrassed to present himself and his heart began going *Mar*-got, *Mar*-got, *Mar*-got. The children climbing on the monkey bars where Margot and he had introduced them-selves twenty-five days ago seemed awfully well-mannered and agile. Their taunts were witty, and the children who fell on the asphalt only cried because it was expected of them. A familiar-looking little priest showed Margot how to calm a little boy feigning hysterics for her benefit, and Julian's thudding heart overflowed with the astounding *goodness* of people.

So as not to disturb Margot on her first day, Julian turned around and floated back to the Regency.

Two or three winos slept in the gutters between Hunter Street and Peachtree, bothering no one and dreaming noble dreams.

A battery-van driver at Five Points shook a friendly fist at Julian when he stepped in front of the van. In order to spare Julian injury and warn him against the perils of city traffic, the driver shouted, "Watch where you're going, fuckhead!''

God's in his heaven, Julian thought. All's right with the world. . . .

BOOK THREE

REVELATIONS

XXXVI

Margot arrived for duty at the Littlest Angel at six o'clock on Wednesday morning. Father Roland Flinders, a man not much larger than a child himself, greeted her and tried to set her at ease. The children would begin arriving about seven, he said, and in the meantime they ought to look around.

"During the six weeks you'll be with us, Mz Eastwin, you'll assist in each of our four divisions; infants and runabouts up to two, the three-year-olds, the four-year-olds, and the 'seniors.'" The "seniors," he explained, were mostly five, with a few sixers in amongst them.

The Littlest Angel was Church-financed and Church-run, which meant that the salaries of the directors and teachers came out of tithe monies and city taxes; the staff consisted of graduates of the King Theological Complex. The Center's motto was "Suffer Little Children to Come Unto Us." The nursery itself occupied at least two levels of the hive's subsurface strata, for the floor of the Worship Center Sanctuary and chapel was a good fifteen meters overhead and the "clamber trees" coiling up from the floor looked quite tall when you began thinking about climbing them. There were no rooms per se in the Center, only discrete areas preserving their separateness by means of noiselessly blowing air walls of different colors. You could see these walls, and walk through them, and admire their shimmering pastel beauty—but sounds were muffled by them, and as a result the Center's acoustics were amazingly good. Tables and chairs folded up from the floor and collapsed back into it when they weren't in use.

"Do you know why we selected you for this assignment?" Father Flinders asked Margot as they walked.

"My performance at the Complex? My interest in this sort of work?" But she privately feared that Bishop Holman had intervened for her. . . . No, he probably hadn't done that. She had impressive enough credentials without the High Bishop's assistance. Good marks. An extension course in child development. A background of voluntary involvement in the work of children's agencies and care centers. The fact that she herself had been an orphan. Surely she had come by this assignment on merit; Father Flinders assured her as much by both his attitude and his words.

As they walked toward an area separated from the main floor by glass dividers (a sign on the door said *The Incubator*), Margot recalled a day school where things had been far less tidy. A deaconry assignment had taken her and some others to a center in which the children ran free, in spite of the whistle-blowing and arm-waving of their supervisor; the sanctuary was a shambles, pews had been overturned, and from the chancel railing the children hurled clothes and feces. Naked was the rule, fingerpainted like players in a Royal Nonesuch was the fashion. The kids' behavior, Margot's professor said afterwards, was confirmation of the Golding Thesis; proof of the anthropological, as well as the theological, accuracy of the concept of Original Sin. . . .

"Let's go in," Father Flinders was saying. "I'll introduce you to Deacon Russick."

The Incubator was really just a nursery for the infants, with a carpeted runway for the charliechaplin toddlers. The only person on duty when Flinders and Margot entered was Deacon Jack Russick, a thirtyish young man with blue jowls and a nose as flat as a putty-knife blade. He had a raw puncture wound in his bottom lip.

"Kid kissed me two days ago," he explained, shaking hands. "Put his only tooth right through there."

Because she was going to be working in The Incubator her first week or so at the Littlest Angel, Flinders left her with Russick. She saw the director at a recess for the older children that afternoon, but she spent most of her first day, and most of her first *nine* days, working with Russick or Emma Goslin or one of the other Incubator staffers. She had lunch with Julian on Thursday, and he and the Cygnusians occupied her thoughts even as she acquainted herself with her new duties. Babies and Cygnusians seemed equally inscrutable to her, as if they had secrets an adult human being could never hope to learn. . . .

"This is MAMA, Mz Eastwin," Russick told her that first morning. "I invented, designed, and built her."

"MAMA?"

"Right. Stands for Maternal Automaton, Ministerial Anthropoid. A boon to our work in The Incubator. Ask Deacon Goslin."

MAMA was a furry, mammary-equipped servitor resembling a gorilla with flashlight lenses for eyes. It had no legs, only a massive lap grading into a circular base mounted on a magnetized plate. When Russick first introduced Margot to his invention, MAMA's dead eyes studied her with chimpish dignity.

"What does it do?" Margot asked.

"What does *she* do," Russick corrected her. "Just about everything except change a kid's diapers, unfortunately. MAMA's very versatile."

She was indeed. Margot eventually saw MAMA give suck, roll and rock, hum lullabies, and tell prerecorded Beatrix Potter, Dr Seuss, and Level Stalker tales in a strangely genderless voice. One of her stories had to do with a whale in the Miami Oceanarium giving birth to a brand new baby beluga. . . . As for the nourishment MAMA gave, Russick explained that it came in the form of a lacteal solution providing the same immunities as genuine mother's milk.

"Immunities," Russick counted on his fingers, "lactoprotein, and love. What else could you ask for?"

Well, answered Margot silently, what about a mien a bit less monstrous? Because one of MAMA's talents was frightening the bejesus out of runabouts who'd never seen her before. Navigating by sonar, MAMA never once ran over anyone; even so, newcomers watched warily as she backed up, whirred forward, turned in circles, and "blinked" her flashlight eyes.

The day after news of Bishop Holman's latest decision had appeared in the newstapes Russick said, "MAMA ought to be ordained, don't you think? She's just as deserving as those Cygnusians."

"*You're* just as deserving," Margot said. "And you're only a deacon." That was what worried her about Holman's decision: the slight it occasioned to people who had striven long and hard in service to their God. In this, Tonsured Billy's complaint was her own. . . .

Diaperings and feedings went on as relentlessly as the days of the week fled by; Margot, Russick, and Goslin monitored toilet training, and on Monday, Autumn the fifty-first, Russick entered The Incubator with two pairs of wired underpants.

"These are emission-sensitive drawers," he told Margot and Emma Goslin. They buzzed, he said, at the first suspicion of an accident, whether the tiniest droplet of urine or the faintest easing of wind. The buzz alerted the runabout wearing the drawers of nature's call and sent him scurrying to a potty chair. That was the theory. In practice Russick's invention sometimes proved its own worse enemy. *Buzzzzz!* the underpants would go, and the charliechaplin would usually be so badly startled that he'd finish whatever he'd begun. Still, Russick had faith in this invention, and on two or three occasions the emission-sensitive drawers did their duty before the runabouts did theirs and the potty-chairs came into day-saving play. These times were the exceptions, though, and Margot more than once found herself arguing with Russick about his wired underwear.

"Give it a chance," he'd say, gesticulating. "It's the application of technology to an age-old human problem. The first real advance in this business since the invention of the breechclout. You're too impatient."

"Jack," Margot would respond; "Jack, it's your impatience with people that's making you patient with this, don't you see?"

Uh-uh, he didn't see, and off on one of The Incubator's runways they'd hear the angrily saccharine *buzzzzz!* of some kid's sagging drawers. . . .

One day while changing a spindly five-month-old, through The Incubator's glass facing Margot watched a group of seniors perform a kind of snake-dance in and out of their tables and chairs. They seemed to be lifted out of innocence by their dance, out of innocence and into a darkness where they all became demigods or devas beyond her touch or understanding. Of what use was theological training here? Did a knowledge of Church history qualify you to see into the heart of a dancing child? Or to wipe off the slick, begrimed buttocks of a five-month-old? . . .

The baby she was changing shifted under Margot's hands, and she was conscious of the saliva running in her mouth. It struck her that she *always* salivated while diapering, and this thought disturbed her. You salivated, after all, when you smelled something appetizing, not because you were wiping away someone else's processed waste. What was the matter with her?

Margot lifted the baby to her, hugged it, and set it on one of the runways among the charliechaplins.

Stimulus/response, that's all it is, Margot told herself. Involuntary. The odor provokes it, the odor and simple proximity. No way to halt it, even if you're stupidly ashamed of the process. . . . Stop it, Margot. Everyone's beyond innocence, finally, and to be ashamed of that is to be ashamed of what we can't help being. Excrement—shit—is a symbol of our humanity, and the tender cleansing of a slimy bum is only an act of necessity, an act of love.

And love is a necessity, after all. Through it we're redeemed.

Aloud she said, " *'But Love has pitched his mansion in/The place of excrement.'* " And with no one there to hear what she had said but a room full of two-and-unders, Margot could feel herself reddening. Her embarrassments were embarrassing. . . . Finally, gripping the sides of a bassinet, she said, "I renounce my guilt. At least in this, I renounce it."

Buzzzzz! said the drawers of one of Russick's wired runabouts. . . .

XXXVII

A HALF hour after midnight on the forty-seventh, Julian and Tybourn set off for Coweta Town. Although Menny still lived there Julian felt sure he could avoid the immediate environs of the Kudzu Shop. You had to go where the game was, and Coweta Town was a likely place to show Tybourn what his katzenapplership involved.

Five captures in two hours, without getting clawed or drawn into a fatiguing chase. A good start. And Tybourn seemed to be enjoying himself. He kept up with a minimum of huffing and puffing and now and again complimented Julian on his shooting.

"Hey, Julian, you've got a sniper's eye, you do."

"Practice, sir; I've had a lot of practice since coming on with the Cygnostikoi." And he downed his sixth cat in a row, this one a three-legged calico which fell atop a manhole cover. "Ah, a female."

"How do you know that?"

"All calicos are female. Something to do with genetics." He'd learned that, of course, since coming to work at the Regency. He took a new clip of sedative darts from his belt and started to slide it into his pistol. When he tilted his head, the lamp on his helmet went out and he and Tybourn made their way to the calico in heavy darkness.

A voice said, "Killing unarmed pussy cats, tsk, tsk."

"And a three-legged one at that," another voice responded.

The voices had seemed to originate from a concrete bunker off one of the crumbling sidewalks. Julian saw two shapes rising from behind a brick wall fronting a set of stairs where there had once been a basement apartment. Both shapes grew more grotesque and top-heavy as they climbed into view. One was a man wearing a nylon stocking, a length of it falling off to one side like a scalp lock. The other man's head was unsteady beneath a store-bought hood. Once on the sidewalk the two figures separated and approached Julian and Tybourn predatorily.

"Halloween was three nights back," Julian said.

"Put that ammo clip away," the stocking-head warned him. He and the other had waited for Julian to spend a clip before revealing themselves, and now both huggermuggers were jiggling knives in their hands.

"Back to back," Julian told Tybourn. "Take off your overtunic and wrap it around your right arm." He nudged the calico aside with his foot, and he and the newsman shuffled together hastily, back to back, rump to rump. The beating of his heart seemed to echo up and down the street.

The hooded thugster leapt forward and slashed at Tybourn's arm with his knife. Julian could hear cloth tearing.

"Siggy, damn you, the old man's mine."

Then their two assailants stalked them without speaking. Julian could feel Tybourn's butt turning on his own as they tried to keep the thugsters in front of them. He knew that unless he and his friend hit upon a novel stratagem or a bit of blind luck they would be murdered in the street, cut down like human weeds.

Suddenly prideless, Julian shouted, "MENNEEEEY!" He shouted it several times. He heard Tybourn land a walloping blow on the hooded thugster's ill-chosen headgear, a sound followed by the *ticka-ticka-tick* of a knife stuttering over asphalt. The other man began cursing violently when he saw that his companion had been disarmed.

Julian broke and ran, hoping to draw one of the men after him. No one followed, and he looked back to see Tybourn confronting both thugsters. The hooded one was trying to right his latex mask, and the stocking-head was drawing back his curved blade in a slow, deliberately mesmerizing sweep, as if to hypnotize and then behead the newsman. Having none of this, Tybourn butted his attacker to the street.

Then, coming on halt-footed, he caught up with Julian and grabbed him by the shouders. "Benedict Arnold! Quisling!"

"Come on, Mr Tybourn. We don't have time for this kind of pleasantry." He shouted Menny's name again, loud and long.

Up the street "Siggy" gave up on his latex hood and helped his companion get off the pavement. Then the two men took up the chase again. When Julian whirled to face them, his helmet lamp jolted back on and revealed the huggermuggers' distorted faces and hurtling limbs. He and Tybourn ran, Tybourn snorting like an asthmatic dog, winded already. In a crossroads Julian dug in his heels and caught Tybourn by the arm. In another thirty seconds the clash would be joined. Feeling that he was trapped in a nightmare, Julian shouted, "MENNEEEEY!"

"Here," Menny said, miraculously appearing alongside a project house across the intersection. One elbow was cocked in a stiff V behind him, and in his hand was something resembling a billy stick. Behind him, clustering forward out of the darkness, came five or six more people brandishing billies of their own. Their appearance was so threatening that the thugsters in pursuit of Julian and Tybourn halted several meters up the street. Julian turned away from Menny and looked at their assailants.

Although both men seemed to understand the changed nature of the situation, they didn't begin to back away.

Siggy, without his hood, was quite an ordinary-looking man approaching thirty. Julian heard him call his companion "Kit." Kit held his face in profile and squinted through the mesh of his stocking at the group advancing across the intersection.

"Hey," he said questioningly. "Which side you goin' with?" He asked this of Menny, who was now abreast of Julian and lumbering forward without pause or greeting.

Julian could tell that Menny had deduced everything; now he was committed to slaking a bloodlust of his own. Tybourn fell into step behind the big man, and the other Red Sticks drew up in a phalanx. Julian felt nauseated, more queasy than when he and Tybourn had been the pursued. He had no doubt at all as to what would happen now, and the film frames previewing in his imagination horrified him.

Why? He had no sympathy for creatures twisted out of their humanity into symbols of evil they were too small and too banal to justly represent. But who or what had done the twisting? Did they do it to themselves? Maybe. Maybe sometimes they did. Julian didn't know. . . . As he fell in behind the others, wondering how he would acquit himself in the massacre almost at hand, he felt sick and prematurely remorse-stricken.

"Just a second," the thugster named Kit said, holding up a hand. "Just a second. Aren't you starfolk, too? . . . Hey, c'mon now."

Finally, seeing that it was no use, the two men backed away, retreating crablike with their blades before them. Then they broke and ran, as earlier Julian and Tybourn had done from them.

Menny braced himself and hurled his billy stick. It struck the unhooded thugster behind the ear and toppled him to the street with a painful explosion of breath. Almost at once Menny, a big white woman, and one of the blacks had dropped to their knees beside the fallen man.

Julian, continuing with the others, didn't stop to see what else Menny did to the thugster, but he thought he could hear a concert of blows behind him, the pummeling of wood upon bone. Maybe not. The victim didn't cry out, after all, and maybe the pummeling was the sound of running feet over broken asphalt. It was impossible to know anything but metastasizing pain and the sick fury of the chase. . . .

The second thugster, Kit, threw his scimitar against a building and ran like someone hyped on A-juice or spedicol. Ahead of Julian, crazily pursuing the man, were Nessim Charles, a young FUSKCONite with a scalp lock bobbing like the tail of Kit's nylon stocking, two muscular black men, and Nicholas Tybourn. . . . Where had Tybourn found the reserves of energy to keep up? And why am I trying to compete with him? Julian asked himself. Why am I chasing a man who's going to be mercilessly run to ground without my help?

His sides heaving painfully, Julian caught himself up and stopped.

Tybourn and the others dragged down the thugster named Kit. In five minutes they had methodically bludgeoned him to death, allowing him only a scream or two in protest. Then the street was quiet, and directed by the beam of his helmet lamp, Julian walked toward the group. His footfalls echoed among the project houses like hammer blows. What he saw when he arrived was unsettling.

Tybourn, straddling the dead man's body, had pulled the stocking from his head and was now tenderly wiping blood away from his battered features. "Kit," he was mumbling. "Kit, Kit, Kit. Short for Christopher, I guess. . . . It wasn't a name I ever called him by."

The FUSKCONite and the black called Jastertree helped Tybourn to his feet; no one said anything. The FUSKCONite, in fact, took a pocket knife from his loose-fitting work jacket and cut his scalp lock off; then he threw it into the darkness, as Kit had cast away his scimitar.

"He wanted to behead me," Tybourn was saying to everyone and no one. "Why? . . ."

Menny approached them with a glazed look, saw something further up the street, and walked past with only an incurious nod at the dead man.

A choked laugh came out of Tybourn's mouth. He shook his head, rubbed his eyes. "Fitting," he said, almost inaudibly. "Very fitting." He let his eyes rove over the faces of the assembled Red Sticks.

Menny came back carrying the stunned calico limply over his forearm. He turned the cat over and peered into its fetid mouth. He felt gingerly about its belly. "Pregnant," he said. "See how the nipples're swollen." He handed the cat to Julian, then ruffled its fur and discovered the wound Julian's sedative pistol had made. "You really do this?"

"It's tranquilized, Menny, that's all. . . . I'm supposed to keep the city's wildlife at a viable population level. That's all I can tell you."

"Viable population level?" Menny turned to Nessim Charles. "Does that fetch? Viable population level?"

The walleyed black man shrugged, asking everyone's forgiveness for having been asked. Tybourn inhaled noisily, pushed Jastertree's hand away, and went over to sit on the stoop of a project house. Julian followed and sat down two steps below the newsman; he put his hand around Tybourn's ankle and stared back into the street.

Moving like sleepwalkers, the Red Sticks picked up both their victims and carried them to the opposite sidewalk for the semiweekly Sanitation Patrol death carts. Then they regrouped and ambled off toward the intersection in which they had first materialized. Menny, absentmindedly stroking a three-legged calico, stood in the canyon of the project houses and muttered curses against yahoos and starmen and psychosocial demographers—so that Julian realized his former cubicle-mate no longer blamed *him* for what had happened to the cat. Instead, Menny had projected responsibility for its stunning on an abstract hierarchy of power that no doubt had a real analogue in the city's government. Julian felt vaguely uncomfortable that Menny had shifted the blame from him to a nameless power structure. To comfort himself as much as Tybourn, he squeezed the newsman's instep. Values here were gloriously bollixed. . . .

"Julian," Menny said at last, "I've got to get back to the others. You come and see me, hear?"

After Menny had gone, taking the cat with him, Julian and Tybourn sat on the stoop watching a pair of girder-cars pass in the night on the wide inner shell of the Dome.

XXXVIII

HE called for her on Sunday afternoon, between services, and back in the Regency, in a bed like a huge, cool green pile of artichoke leaves, they mediated grace. It was as if her body was remembering an old and esteemed ritual rather than trying to learn a new and maybe unproven one, and everything was all right. Utterly all right.

"Just one thing you have to worry about," Julian told her. "It's a quasi-Victorian amendment to Ortho-Urban doctrine called the Lesser Limitation. After Saggy Nelly, of course."

"Yes?" she said, taking the heel of Julian's hand into her mouth. "What's that?"

"No kissing below the belt."

Margot bit him for this egregious witticism and worried about the time they had left together that afternoon. Flinders had let her go with the stipulation that she be back by five o'clock, when there would be an influx of children because of the evening services at which their parents would be presiding or assisting. Five was an hour and a half away.

She and Julian talked. She told him about Jenny-O and that woman's Falstaffian spirit so counter (she had long thought) to her own. Julian told her about Papa Ty and Mama Queequeg and how they had been locked into the Level 9 Coenotorium during a meeting of the Glissador Corps and fed an insidious gas through the ventilating system. Orphans, they were both orphans—but everyone was an orphan, finally. You made your own way. The only parent you could rely on in all things was God, and there were moments, Margot was sure, when even Christ had believed Himself an orphan. . . .

She told Julian how working at the Littlest Angel was dangerous. It was dangerous because some people thought the principal function of a care center was to lay the foundation of a new society, with care-center children—grown to adults—as its immediate architects.

"Who thinks that?" he asked her.

"I do, a little bit." She told him about Deacon Russick and MAMA, who was supposed to be not only a labor-saving device but also an aid in the raising of contented, mentally healthy human beings. This intention qualified it as a weapon in the arsenal of the Utopians—for contented, mentally healthy human beings would do much to set the world straight.

"Unless they're too contented. Then they wouldn't see the need."

"That's right. And that's the other extreme a care center ought to avoid—the Utopians on one hand, the Traditionalists on the other. The Traditionalists want the care center to inculcate orthodox survival patterns in their children, you see, so that the status quo won't be upset. If they thought you were going to use early education as a means of programming kids with new or radical formulas of survival, uh-oh, look out. They'd close down shop, Julian, because it's the Traditionalists who're always in control, the Utopians who're always waiting in the wings."

Lying there beside him, his body looking darkly tropical against the light green sheets, Margot wondered why Julian wasn't more bitter than he was against the Traditionalists in the political establishment. It hurt her to realize—for the nth time—that her Church was supported in part by a tyranny, one that had snuffed out Julian's parents on the pretext that the Glissadors, corridor-running messengers, were plotting revolution against the principles of the Urban Charter. . . . Was Julian's want of bitterness a result of his want of hope that things could be changed? Or did he believe a change at hand? . . .

"If you're not Utopian or Traditionalist," Julian asked, "what *are* you? What are you trying to do at the center?"

"Give a bit of shape to the kids' lives without hindering the way they grow, I guess. A dangerous thing to try." She thought of Karl Tagomi and his words about Eastern and Western religions. Relationship versus identification. The suppression of ego rather than its development. . . . You had to strike a balance. Man wasn't the measure of all things, but neither was he a cipher. You had to get that across. . . .

A few minutes later Julian was telling her about his own "dangerous" job and the assault and counter-assault that had taken place in Coweta Town two nights ago. He told her of the involvement of his cubicle-mate, Menny Guest, in his and Tybourn's rescue and in the death of Tybourn's son. Julian even admitted that he had taken a hand in keeping the story out of the *Jour/Con* newstapes.

"How is the father—Mr Tybourn—taking this?" Even parents, it seemed, could be orphans. . . .

"Numb. We're working on an ethnography of the Cygnostikoi together, and he's thrown himself into it heart and soul."

"An ethnography?"

"Well, a partial one. I'm doing the 'field work' and taking notes, Tybourn's trying to make sense of the material. We'll publish—in the newstapes—in another week, I think. We've got the Nettlinger's permission."

Julian pushed her back and covered her mouth with his own. They mediated grace. Afterwards she returned to the Littlest Angel and tried to discover at least a hint of guilt in herself. She couldn't. Not until she was changing a soiled diaper three days later did she feel the twinge she'd been waiting for, but this had nothing to do with her afternoon with Julian and was soon overmastered.

Sometimes puzzled, often weary, Margot came to realize that she was discontented with the world but quietly happy with her own life.

XXXIX

On the fifty-seventh the ethnography on which Julian and Tybourn had collaborated appeared in the *Jour/Con* newstapes:

THE SECRET LIVES OF THE CYGNOSTIKOI

INTRODUCTION: Although the creatures from 61 Cygni A have been with us for some time now, the average Atlantan knows very little about them. These are the facts he does have: 1) In appearance the Cygnostikoi are humanoid, but far from recognizable *facsimiles* of human beings. 2) Fiona Bitler and Emory Nettlinger brought the first two representatives of this species into the old Georgia countryside five years ago. 3)

Since arriving the Cygnostikoi have lived in virtually kingly seclusion in the Regency Hyatt House. And 4) after the apparent conversion of the seven Cygnostikoi now among us, they have shown an inclination to involve themselves more actively in the life of the city.

Now, because of the researches of a person who has worked closely with the Cygnostikoi, it may be possible to illuminate some elements of their social organization, their physiology, and their mental processes. These phenomena are all uniquely, perhaps even bizarrely, interrelated.

This "ethnography" does not pretend to have any final application to how the Cygnostikoi live on their home world; its observations are limited to their behavior "in captivity," and its conclusions are tentative. In one or two instances the authors have indulged in speculation, but have tried to do so only on the basis of the facts at hand.

THE PENTHOUSE SOCIETY OF THE CYGNOSTIKOI: In their artificial Regency environment, the Cygnostikoi live in a suite of several first-class rooms in temperatures seldom exceeding 0° C, in a deep and perpetual twilight. The odors in the suite are often unplaceable, but the smell of something akin to vinegar usually predominates.

Seven Cygnostikoi live in this sealed-off, unearthly environment. The association of these creatures puts one in mind of the geriatric septigamoklans sponsored by Dr Leland Tanner in the Human Development Towers three decades ago. The intimacies, the antagonisms, and the final group harmony achieved by both aliens and septigamoklanners make this analogy a tempting one. Moreover, it may actually contain a clue to the societal organization of the Cygnostikoi. We make the comparison for two reasons: First (and most obviously), the simple fact that the septigamoklans consisted of seven "marriage partners." Second, the fact that the Cygnostikoi in the Regency are probably not a family in any *consanguineous* sense but are clearly a family by their observation of a *conjugal* bond. They are spouses, our researcher feels, not siblings.

It is also possible that this same "marriage grouping" may have existed on the Cygnostikoi's home world before the probeships of the Scandinavian Polity aided in reuniting its several partners in our own Urban Nucleus. The fact that Dr Nettlinger has no plans to introduce any more starmen into the city, unless something untoward occurs, strengthens this assertion and suggests that seven is the optimum number for a Cygnostik "family."

We cannot discuss the concept of lineage in regard to the

Cygnostikoi, however, because of our ignorance of their sexual nature and because their "family," insofar as we can tell, is a unit of spouses rather than of parents and children. One of their principal behavior patterns, in fact, has nothing to do with the anthropological concept of lineage; it seems instead to be of a religious nature.

The Cygnostikoi, in a prescribed rotational order, *take turns worshipping one another*. This they do in spite of their recent public confessions of faith in Ortho-Urbanism, with no apparent awareness of any contradiction in their doing so.

Julian had learned that after each worship service the Cygnostik god for a day would go off and collapse into a catalepsy so complete that he appeared to have died. Not until the following morning would he revive. The others could do the same thing if they wanted to, but immediately after a service the worshipped one *always* shut down. It was, appropriately enough, his day of rest. . . .

These rotational offerings of praise, prayer, and payment, so much like a Eucharist in reverse, probably do not mean that the Cygnostikoi actually regard the venerated one as a god. Instead he may symbolize for them that concept or quality which they *do* think of as God. This may have something to do with the idea of respect for the individual; hence, each Cygnostik has a turn as the object of worship and is at the same time a stand-in for the ones worshipping him. On a symbolic level, then, no matter who is the focus of veneration, the Cygnostikoi are really worshipping themselves. Such a worship, in their unreadable minds, may not at all contradict a public confession of faith in Our Earthly Savior, Jesus Christ.

The Second Person of the Trinity is an incarnation of God in the flesh of a human being. The Cygnostikoi, viewing themselves as their own "saviors," feeling the power of godhood in their own mortal selves, may therefore look upon Christ as one more suitable proxy in their worship. Like any other Cygnostik, Christ becomes a stand-in for their ritually distanced worship of themselves. They accept Him because, in His incarnation as a human being, He is very nearly an equivalency of themselves.

He contains them, they contain Him.

If this is true, one can no longer look upon the Cygnostikoi's conversions as divine testimonials to the absolute validity of Ortho-Urbanism. By the same token, this interpretation casts a shadow on the advisability of ordaining the Cygnostikoi as

~ priests in the city's official Church; it also undercuts the justifications so far given for taking such a step.

Both Julian and Tybourn understood that this last paragraph was a slap in the High Bishop's face, maybe even a gauntlet flung at the First Councilor herself. But they argued with Idhe, and Idhe finally let the paragraph stand. . . .

CYGNOSTIK PSYCHOLOGY AS IT REFLECTS CYGNOSTIK PSYCHOLOGY: The physiology of our visitors may be a literal embodiment of a synthesis of what, for human beings, are the two commonest ways of viewing the universe, the mechanistic and the animistic. In most human societies these theories are mutually exclusive; you must choose one and discard the other.

The very *person* of a Cygnostik, however, brings these two theories together in one "cybergamic" unit and reconciles them. The deepest level of Cygnostik consciousness, then, is a fusion of the "rationality" of empiricism and the "mystery of magic" of animism, for our visitors are in fact machines and biological entities at the same time. Their hands and arms have much in common with sophisticated prosthetic devices, while their torsos and heads appear to be entirely organic in nature. So well integrated are these organ/components that the "mechanical" parts have the ability to *grow* flesh, cartilage, and various proteinaceous structures, while the ostensibly "biological" parts grade into the mechanical ones so subtly that one can find no clear demarcation between the two.

Despite the likelihood of a chemical incompatibility between our biosphere and their own system, the Cygnostikoi "fuel" themselves by eating simple, Earth-grown fruits and meats [Julian and Tybourn had agreed to be no more specific than this about their diet], but their utilization of these foodstuffs is so efficient that a Cygnostik produces almost no waste material, and none at all by way of either micturition or defecation. What little they do produce is excreted through microlasered "pores" in their prosthesislike limbs as a clear, vinegary-smelling lubricant. An organic process, then, not only powers the Cygnostikoi but also redounds to the benefit of their conspicuously mechanical components. And the mutuality of these purely *physical* processes seems to us a metaphor for the balance between the mechanistic and animistic in the Cygnostik psyche.

Another metaphor for the same thing (although also a

biologically evolved tool for *effecting* this state) is the config-
uration of our visitors' eyes, with their horizontal-hourglass
pupils. In actual fact each eye has two pupils, one frontfacing
and one peripherally located on the curved outward edge of the
Cygnostik eye patch. The two "bulbs" of each pupil are
connected by the thin neck of the "hourglass" which the
pupils help form.

The only example of an analogous morphology that Federation scientists have discovered occurs in the case of the tropical
fish *Anableps*. This creature swims along the surface of the
water with the bottom halves of its gogglelike eyes submerged
and the upper halves in the open air. Each half of each eye
contains its own pupil, and each pupil is evolutionarily suited
to the medium, air or water, in which it principally operates.
Something distantly similar to the adaptation of *Anableps* may
be at work in the structure of the Cygnostikoi's eyes.

One conjecture is that the two front-facing pupils, or A-
bulbs, work together in the same stereoscopic fashion as do
human eyes and have a selective sensitivity to the spectrum
patterns of their planet's primary, 61 Cygni A. The two
peripheral pupils, or B-bulbs, on the other hand, work inde-
pendently of each other, but have their retinal attunement to the
radiation distribution of the smaller sun in the binary, 61 Cygni
B. In this way a Cygnostik is optically equipped to make a wide
range of the discriminations under a variety of lighting condi-
tions; the side-set pupils, in addition, may have survival
specificity against indigenous predators who would use the
murkiness of 61 Cygni B's ascendency as a veil for attack. If
these hypotheses are valid, the two sets of pupils—like those of
the curious *Anableps*—do indeed operate in different
mediums. Water and air for the fish, two distinct light spectra
for the beings from the Cygni system.

We find, however, that during their daily religious observ-
ances both the worshippers and the designated deity narrow
their A-bulbs to such infinitesimal pinpoints that these pupils
almost disappear. The side-set bulbs, on the contrary, expand
and glow with walleyed ferocity. These facts suggest that the
Cygnostikoi use one pair of pupils for coping with the empirical causations of day-to-day reality and another when "seeing" into that supernatural pleroma where such causations
may not apply.

In other words, the Cygnostikoi's B-bulbs permit them to
apprehend physically a spiritual realm which we have access
to, if at all, through our emotions rather than our senses. The
operation of the two sets of pupils is not mutually exclusive,

however; the Cygnostikoi can look at once into *both* worlds, if
they desire, and in fact habitually do so.

This last speculation was Julian's. He had seen the Cygnostikoi in
their prayer groups, and, his agnosticism notwithstanding, had
somehow convinced himself that when the Cygnostik septigamoklan prayed it actually got through to the party on the other end.
Julian's bent wasn't at all Teilhardesque; he rejected the notion of
the Omega Point as so much philosophical/poetic claptrap, the idea
of the noosphere as the clumsily defined never-never land of a Jesuit
mystic. But the Cygnostikoi still made him wonder about The
Realms Beyond that most certainly did exist, those places and times
about which no one, no human being at least, would ever acquire a
sure and unimpeachable knowledge. And he was made hungry
trying to understand the difficulty in understanding even his own
position among things. . . .

CONCLUSION: The Cygnostikoi—the term itself derives
from a combination of the stellar designation *Cygni* and the
Greek plural of *gnostic*, itself deriving from *gnosis*, "knowledge"—is a specis of humanity, if you will, both physically
and spiritually more advanced on the evolutionary ladder than
homo sapiens. In comparison, in fact, it may be that we have
channeled ourselves in o a phylogenetic cul-de-sac from which
only our extinction will remove us.

The fact that it was human beings who discovered the
Cygnostikoi and transported them from their own world to
ours, rather than the other way around, doesn't at all contradict
this assessment. Our technology has been put solely to material
uses (we know of no other way to employ it), whereas they
have integrated their own technological achievements into a
comprehensive synthesis of the physical and the spiritual. We
don't even have the prerogative of berating ourselves for
failing to do likewise; the nature of the beast that we are makes
it *impossible* to emulate the Cygnostikoi.

Finally, it may be that our visitors "converted" for a reason
other than the one we cited earlier, or in addition to it. Having
recognized human limitations, they may have determined that
we require psychological confirmation of the worth of our
religious systems. Their apparent conversions are hence conscious acts of charity and compassion toward us, whatever else
they may be. Further, in accepting Ortho-Urbanism our
visitors more than likely intended to bestow a similar chari-
table approval, by extension, on all human religious systems
acknowledging our limitations and giving us hope of tran-

scending or overcoming these. This is a splendid generosity—but one surely touched for the Cygnostikoi with the knowledge that their gifts will never truly alter the basic circumstances of our poverty.

The end. That was it. The piece's gloomily metaphysical conclusion forced Idhe to run it without any byline at all, but neither Julian nor Tybourn cared. Just getting "The Secret Lives of the Cygnostikoi" on paper had been a catharsis for both of them.

What would happen now? . . .

XL

AT noon on the fifty-eighth, her third day among the three-year-olds, Margot met Julian on the playground. He was swinging from the highest strut of the monkey bars, his arms folded across his chest, and his eyes shut. Margot stepped into the cage and kissed him on the lips.

"Bong," he said, making himself swing like a clapper. "Bong. Bong." His eyes, she saw, were red-rimmed and bloodshot.

"I read your ethnography. Father Flinders called it a . . . let me see, 'a craftily worded exhortation to heresy.' Russick thought it 'interesting.' "

"How did MAMA react?"

"All the blood's going to rush to your head, Julian."

"Good for the brain cells. . . . Margot?"

"Yes?"

"I love you." Studying him, Margot felt certain he was near tears. In the two weeks since he had proposed he had said "I love you" no more than three or four times, always as a kind of guilty concession to what he seemed to believe he *ought* to say. Now he spoke spontaneously. Margot put both hands on his face and massaged the lines of his jaw.

"Early this morning," he said, "Saggy Nelly had the *Jour/Con* building forcibly closed. Idhe's been jailed, and no one knows where Tybourn is."

"Do you think he's been arrested, too?"

"Yetunde seems to think he's just lying low, but nobody really knows."

"Should you? Lie low, I mean."

"According to the law, Idhe's principally at fault, not the authors of the article. But if he revealed our names we'd be subject to dismissal and fines. . . . Yetty and the Nettlingers are under suspicion as the inside researchers for the ethnography."

They were quiet. Then Margot asked, "Are you hungry?"

"Not for food. Kiss me again. Then I'll hie me back to the Regency, deacon-lady, to see my 'family.' "

She kissed him again, and when she turned to go back into the Center, he was swinging in the cage of the monkey bars going, "Bong. Bong. Bong."

The following Sunday the newstapes resumed printing under a hireling editor named Chavers and an official censorship board. Although Idhe remained among the missing, Julian reported that Tybourn had turned up one day at the Regency stoned on liquid THC. Julian got the man home to bed. Other good news was that no one had harassed Yetunde Trap, the Nettlingers, or Julian about selling out to the combine as "undercover ethnographers." Margot prayed that the controversy surrounding the Cygnostikoi would not end in witch-hunting, kangaroo courts, and executions at the stake. Maybe it wouldn't. . . .

Still, the insularity of the Littlest Angel protected one against the forces warring in the streets and p-courts, and Margot wondered if it was right to shield the Center's children from *everything* that was going on in the world. She recalled Fiona Bitler's speech at UrNu House and began to understand why she had instigated a Witness-and-Work program for many of the city's older children.

"Father Flinders," Margot said one day, surprising the man in his confessional-sized office, "isn't it possible to take the kids aboveground sometimes, away from the Center?"

"I'd like to say yes, young woman, but the tension in our city now makes that impossible. . . . You saw, of course, the first new issue of the newstapes containing the High Bishop's evangelical blueprint for ordaining the Cygnostikoi? Well, that makes going out of doors risky."

Her face must have fallen. Father Flinders sprang up from his chair, took her hand, petted it consolingly.

"But that doesn't prevent us from bringing the 'real world,' as you would no doubt call it, down here to the children. I've arranged for Mz Bitler, her young cousin from Toombsboro, and a couple of starmen to visit the Littlest Angel. . . . If Muhammed can't go to the mountain, then the mountain—Uh, that's not entirely appropriate, but you take my meaning?''

"Yes, sir.''

"Good. Mz Bitler taught in an old Van-Ed program for gifted children, you know; Nettlinger was one of them. She ought to do something to, uh, broaden the kids' outlooks, don't you think?''

So. Something to anticipate. The real world was coming to them! Margot suffered doubts. Wasn't the advent of two Cygnostikoi suspiciously like an invasion? How would their preschoolers react to these whirring and ratcheting starmen? . . .

On the occasions when they met, Julian kept Margot abreast of events in the city. Idhe, after spending two weeks in an interrogation center, was released and returned to work in a role subordinate to that of Chavers. Tybourn still had his job, Julian hadn't been arrested by gestapo, and the Nettlingers appeared safe from reprisal too. The physicist's reputation in New Free Europe assured him a degree of immunity from persecution in the Atlanta Nucleus, and this shadowy umbrella covered Fiona and Yetunde as well. . . . As the year wound down toward Christmas, though, agitation among Muslims, FUSKCONites, and other dissidents grew. Militant Ortho-Urbanists responded with parades and rallies of their own. A bomb went off on the mezzanine level at Consolidated Rich's, several Ortho-Urban services were canceled because of threats, police raids were conducted against four or five unauthorized sects quartered in the Basement, and on the seventy-sixth Saggy Nelly imposed a strict curfew while urging everyone to be of good cheer and do their holiday shopping as joyously as in years past. The curfew was to last a week.

"All this because of Holman's plans?" Margot asked.

"The Muslims and the FUSKCONites might have accepted the conversions alone, but the ordinations are too much. Everybody's testy, Margot.''

"How do Lily and the starmen feel about all this?''

"Uh-uh, can't say. But they're coming to see you next week. Maybe you'll find out. . . .''

XLI

MARGOT'S last days at the Littlest Angel were spent among the "seniors," with second-year deacon Vanessa Samaras. They had a group of fifteen children and worked with them in a "room" defined by shimmering, pale blue air walls. In this group was a little boy—Jeremy R. Downson—who took an almost embarrassing liking to Margot and did everything assigned him as if for her alone. Margot was at first afraid that Samaras would be annoyed with her for permitting the boy to monopolize her time and attention, but Samaras only shrugged and smiled when Jeremy R. Downson cornered Margot.

Still, Margot tried to deflect him as often as she could in order to give a little of her time to the others. Often, gazing at her, the boy looked absolutely lovesick, and she found herself reddening under his gaze just as if he were an adult and a stranger.

Jeremy was bright to the point of precocity. He always asked for Margot's help, but he really didn't need it. He wanted her eyes, not her advice, and he drew octopi and whales, lift-stations and churches, pneumato-trains and rocketships, even human portraits, with an eerie skill, almost always with either a black or purple crayon. Flakes of wax adhered to his thin fingers like the scales of dark insects only he could summon.

On the seventy-ninth, just as Father Flinders had promised, Fiona Bitler came down to the Center with her young cousin and two Cygnostikoi. Because the lambency blowers had been turned off so that Mz Bitler's party could navigate the huge floor without hindrance, Margot saw them coming a long time before they arrived at Samaras's group. Containing the kids' curiosity as the starmen approached was a formidable task now, and Samaras tried to occupy their attention by telling them the story of the prophet Elisha's run-in with a group of small boys who taunted him with the epithet "baldhead! baldhead!"

171

Samaras explained how Elisha had then angrily called forth a pair of she-bears to mutilate and rend forty-two of the boys. What was the point? Margot wondered. Respect for one's elders? Maybe Samaras wanted to insure that her seniors received Fiona's party with the utmost politeness. Maybe the deacon did not appreciate the results of yesterday's art lesson during which the children, already aware of the identity of their expected visitors, had painted big, goggle-eyed portraits of the Cygnostikoi and hung them up on a pair of highly conspicuous pegboards. Or maybe Samaras, a gentle and sometimes indecisive woman a year or two younger than Margot, just appreciated the firmness with which Elisha had met an unpleasant situation.

While Fiona's party was still among the three-year-olds, Samaras engineered a discussion. Hands shot up all around, and it was quickly decided that Elisha had over-reacted. Striking his forehead and rolling his eyes upward, Jeremy R. Downson summarized group opinion: "He certainly taught those boys their lesson, didn't he?"

Then a sudden silence descended on the children, and a fidgety boy with both thumbs tucked under his chin reminded Samaras it was time for a bath-booth break. Off everyone went, except for Jeremy; he stayed at his table doodling on its surface with a waxy fingernail.

The visitors arrived at Samaras's section while the children were gone, and Fiona recognized Margot from the dedication at UrNu House. Margot clumsily made introductions. One of the Cygnostikoi was Lileplagak, whom Margot recognized instantly. The other Fiona presented to her as Kee Wig, after which the starmen and Yetunde promptly sat down in three of the chairs vacated by the children. Father Flinders, Samaras, and Jeremy blinked at one another, and Fiona told a brief story about her meeting with Margot at the unveiling of Dragsted's statue. Telling it, the old woman's eyes fixed on the art work displayed on the pegboards behind Samaras.

"Your children, Deacon Samaras, do as well as Dragsted," Fiona said; "they really do." She walked over to the pegboard and fingered one of the drawings as if it had touched a sensitive spot in her. "But this one's an adult's work, isn't it?"

"I did that," Jeremy R. Downson announced, a bit more cautiously than Margot would have expected.

"Without a model?" Fiona asked. Involuntarily everyone looked at Lileplagak and Kee Wig.

"No, ma'am. I did it by heart."

"Well, it surpasses in concept and execution anything that Scandian knave Just Dragsted's ever done. It reminds me of the work

Emory did when he was in my Van-Ed class nearly forty years ago.''

"But Dragsted's Cygnostik is excellent," Margot interjected. "A perfect likeness. I don't think you can fault it."

"It's too good," Fiona said, turning toward her. "And Dragsted had a live model from the Amity Moon Base."

Was that model still holding its pose? The last thing Julian had said to Fiona at the unveiling was "Margot thinks the Cygnusian in the statue is a real Cygnusian." Did Fiona remember that?

"I'll be frank," the woman continued. "Most of the drawings— if you put this one aside—aren't very accomplished, but every one of them is truer than Dragsted's statue, despite its sterile verisimilitude. The magical desire to *make* isn't in Dragsted, not in the way most children feel it. He's a culture hack. Which is why my unveiling address stressed the event over the symbol of the event."

"The Iconoclast's Four I's," Margot said.

"Yes," said Fiona Bitler, laughing. "The Petri Dish Address. You know, Em and I brought the starmen here in the hope that their presence would suggest a vivid alternative to the Dome. Now the city is trying to enlist them in a cause that we can't help but decry."

"Do you mean Ortho-Urbanism?" Father Flinders asked defensively.

"I wouldn't've come if I felt that, Father. My main heresy's a political rather than a religious one, I think."

Yetunde shook her head, and wooden earrings shaped like marabou storks dangled alongside her neck. "Maybe the father thinks you think ole *Asbury* tried to enlist the Cygnostikoi as converts."

"No," Fiona said. "Whatever the Cygnostikoi do now, they do because they want to. . . . Carlo, my first husband, Carlo and I didn't have any children, you know. The children I taught in the Van-Ed programs became my children. After Gerard Nettlinger took Carlo's life, Emory became my only child, and when he was nine we left the city together."

Margot glanced at Samaras and Flinders, who were growing uneasy in the face of these unexpected personal revelations. Children began to drift back into the area. Although Fiona acknowledged them with a smile as they took up places away from the starmen, she did not stop talking. . . . It's to me she's talking, Margot at once understood; it's to me she's saying these things. . . .

"Because of our age differences there's always been something a little Oedipal in Emory's relationship with me. My child grew up to be my husband. Married again, I was again childless, you see. And I suppose you could say we didn't come back to the Nucleus until we had become parents.

"The Cygnostikoi were our children, of course. They came back from New Free Europe with us as pliantly as any of these children would go to the playground with you. But now they've started to demonstrate their independence, as with their pledging themselves to your Church. It happens in every parent/child relationship, I guess. The lesson is—and at seventy you can dispense lessons, you know; people *expect* you to be garrulous—the lesson is that you have to *un*learn being a parent in the same way you first had to learn to be one. That's hard sometimes."

Margot looked down to find Jeremy leaning against her hip, his thin right arm around her waist. When had he approached her? She hadn't even seen him move? . . . Fiona suddenly looked at her and the boy, and Margot interpreted her look to say, "Forty years ago Em and I were as you and that boy are now." This made Margot unaccountably nervous, and she put her hands on Jeremy's shoulders and walked him back to the table.

Emory and Fiona = Jeremy and Margot. What was she to make of that equation? Her last day in the Center was Friday, the eighty-third, and she would probably never see the boy again. She certainly didn't intend to run off with him, and Jeremy himself wasn't very likely to press for an elopement. Ridiculous, her case of nerves . . .

"My children's latest wish," Fiona was saying, "is to visit the Littlest Angel every day this week. To work with the children and try to get to know them. Yetunde will come with them. Is that all right, Father?"

Flinders agreed. How could he refuse two candidates for the priesthood who wanted to work in his Center? A little girl sitting on the floor said, *"Yea!"* and beat two rhythm sticks together.

When Lily and Kee Wig arrived at the Center the next day, Yetunde made it clear that they wouldn't be able to work there unless the lambency blowers were shut down; they didn't care for walls very much. The noise level went up, but the distinctions between age groupings and study sections were almost completely broken down.

The visitors worked like this: Lileplagak covered one vast territory on the northern side of the hall, Yetunde a vague area through the middle of the floor, and Kee Wig the remaining third. At intervals of an hour or so they switched territories. And so it went all day. Margot could look across the hall and see Kee Wig lifting two or three kids effortlessly into the branches of a clamber tree. A moment later, from another direction, she might well hear Pal Lily at the orpacycle playing anything from a Negro spiritual to a lurid funkphalt ditty.

As for Yetunde, she busied herself teaching the preschoolers anatomy with the aid of a Consolidated Rich's Bella Donna Babykins. The doll's nakedness didn't put Margot off, but she felt personally violated every time one of the children probed at its eyesockets or popped its abdomen panels. Relief came when everyone began making decorations for the synthetic Japanese spruce outside Father Flinders's office on the edge of the main floor.

What impressed Margot most during all this activity was Jeremy's behavior. He was animated and bright again, but he ignored her with a will. He attached himself to whichever visitor came into their area and tried to monopolize their time as he had formerly tried to monopolize hers. Kee Wig played "elevator" with him for fifteen solid minutes, and Yetunde let the boy take snapshots of everyone in Samaras's section with an experimental news-service camera.

At one o'clock Samaras and Abercrombie and the Center's other deacon attendants settled the kids down for a nap. With the help of the three visitors this didn't take as long as usual. Yetunde strolled about on her own while Lileplagak and Kee Wig sat back to back in the middle of the floor with their huge arms spread and their halo-crests bowed forward to suggest that it was time for quiet.

A moment later every child in the hall *had fallen fast asleep*!

The starmen kept their heads down and their arms extended for the entire fifty-minute nap period, coming to only when Yetunde told them it was time for activities to resume. The children awoke at the precise moment that Lily and Kee Wig dropped their arms and grew erect.

"I don't think I care for that," Samaras told Margot as the children rose from their chairs. "It's mass hypnosis, sedation almost. I *know* I don't like it."

Flinders didn't either; he had someone tell Yetunde to tell the starmen not to intervene in the nap periods henceforth.

Margot tried to question Jeremy about the strange nap. "Did you dream this afternoon?" she asked him.

"I dreamed a little, I think." He wasn't interested in the conversation; he wanted to show Lileplagak the ornament he was making. "I was at the dentist's, sitting back in his chair. He looked into my mouth with a mirror and told me about how he had a little boy like me, only younger. And that's all."

That's all, Margot echoed silently. Dr Nettlinger's father had been a medicaid dentist; he had also been an assassin. That was a long time ago, though; a very long time ago.

Later Margot learned that Flinders had selected several children at random and interviewed them about their naps. Very inconclusive results. "I just sleeped," Abercrombie reported, was a common response. Some recalled conversing with an unfamiliar adult; others saw a sky full of stars or lights of different colors. Probably the Cygnostikoi *had* used a variety of hypnosis to calm the children and put them to sleep, but this was hardly An Insidious Weapon Against All Humanity. . . .

During nap periods on the following two days, however, the starmen excused themselves, carried brown-bag lunches up the ramp to the playground, and, sitting on the monkey bars, devoured these without even opening the bags. But for their heads and forearm cerements the bodies of Pal Lily and Kee Wig were almost indistinguishable from the bars among which they sat.

On the eighty-third, the last day of Margot's service assignment, two days before Christmas, Father Flinders threw a party for the staff members and all the children of the Littlest Angel.

Bishop Holman, in his Buffalo Bill togs, gave a brief invocation and grace, and then the refreshments were served. Jeremy R. Downson, Margot noticed, refrained from eating or drinking any of these.

Russick impersonated Saint Nick, and MAMA, her lap overflowing with plastic trolls, braided fingercuffs, rubber reptiles, and dollar whistles, followed along behind him beeping and blinking, as a sort of surrogate sleigh. Holman and Russick distributed toys, and Pal Lily played Christmas carols on the orpacycle.

Margot looked at Holman amid the confusion and noise. What revelation did he expect from his "messengers"? Whatever it was, he wanted to put it off for a while. Dispensing goodies, he moved among the children stiffly and his smile came from a long way away. When MAMA's bounty was exhausted, he shouted, "God bless you, everyone!" in a mock-hearty voice and trotted off waving one fringed sleeve over his head.

There were slick, sticky places on the floor where drinks had been spilled, and in one section an argument about the ownership of a stack of ornaments led to a shoving match. When two rival factions began duckwalking under the Christmas tree, it was almost knocked out of its moorings, and one of the girls in Abercrombie's group fell off a stepladder and gashed her chin.

"Somebody put something in the Coke," Abercrombie said to Margot after the girl had been carried off. "We've been spiked on the sly."

"They're just wrought up," Margot replied. "Christmas."

When the nap period began, as if on cue Liliplagak and Kee Wig carried their brown bags outside. But sitting the children down and cutting off their protests required the mobilization of every deacon in the Center. MAMA and Russick played a brief return engagement, and Jolly Saint Nick threatened to disinherit everyone but the still and the meek.

Samaras's group had trouble quieting itself. Jeremy spent several minutes explaining how poorly Russick was costumed and what a sacripornal trick the Jolly Saint Nick legend was. Margot tried to calm him. Five minutes later his head came up again; he snatched a sheet of paper from the tray beneath his table and began compulsively drawing. This movement soon had the other kids wide-eyed and fidgety. Again Margot went to Jeremy, and this time he gave her an incoherent lecture on tooth care. He tried to pass around a poster he had drawn of a decay-ridden molar in cross-section.

"Christmas is a pagan festival," he said when Margot retrieved the drawing and folded it up. "A winter feast. Just like the Roman Saturnalia or the Julmond of the Celts . . . at least when we do it like this." He gestured at the litter strewn about. "You're trying to turn me into one, too. And I'm not, I'm not."

"Not what?"

"A pagan," the boy said. "I'm trying not to be."

A six-year-old Calvinist. Margot touched the boy, but found it hard to sympathize with so silly a worry. What was the matter with him? Jeremy shook Margot's hand off, and it was clear now that his agitation was being communicated to his section-mates. As he babbled on about winter feasts and dental plaque, the other children stood up, pushed, tried to move around.

"Go get the Cygnostikoi," Samaras directed Margot. "If we can just get Jeremy to sleep we'll be all right."

Margot didn't like the idea, but she went. Lileplagak returned with her, and Yetunde was there with Samaras when they got back. Jeremy tried to latch onto the starman, but the other children clamored for attention, too, and the uproar began to disturb other sections nearby.

"Father Flinders ought to be told," Margot said.

"He'll be out here in two minutes if we don't get them quieted down," Samaras responded. "Let's just do it." She nodded at Yetunde, who nodded at Lileplagak.

As on Tuesday Pal Lily sat down, bowed his head, and spread his arms; today, though, he intimately embraced only the kids in Samaras's section. In two minutes' time all the children were asleep, and the Cygnostik seemed to hold them all in a circle of mysterious dreaming.

"Good," Samaras whispered; "just the way things ought to be done."

Margot kept her peace, and at nap's end, when Lileplagak revived himself and his fifteen sleepers, Jeremy was the last to awake. When the boy's eyes fastened on Pal Lily, it was as if for the first time. Rage and disgust twisted his face, and, turning the table over, he suddenly stood up. The boy's face became the mask of an adult, and his section-mates, seeing what he had done and the way he looked, were half panicked.

"You're going to undo everything!" Jeremy shouted at Lileplagak. "You're going to make the mess we're in worse!" He leaped over the capsized table and charged the Cygnostik with embarrassing fury. His right fist pounded on Pal Lily's upper torso, lifted and fell as if it clutched a knife. The starman merely hugged Jeremy to him until the boy's fury was spent and he was weeping uncontrollably in the alien's embrace.

A crowd gathered, and Margot could see Father Flinders picking his way toward them from his office. She scooped Jeremy out of Lileplagak's arms and carried him off toward The Incubator. She didn't know what she was going to do with him there; just get him out of the way, she supposed, just lay him down and somehow try to soothe him. He was hardly to blame for assaulting Lileplagak. . . .

Carrying the boy, Margot gazed at his face with a slowly dawning astonishment. Although he had changed a good deal in the nearly four years since she had last seen him at the placement agency, she understood that Jeremy R. Downson was the same little Moses she had rescued from a parcel locker. She had found him again, only to lose him. Could nothing stay? Did everything fall victim to the world? . . . No, some things remained. This boy had once led her to god's immutable mercy, hadn't he? . . .

Through The Incubator's glass facing Margot saw Russick in his Jolly Saint Nick costume recharging MAMA's power cells.

XLII

LATE Saturday morning Julian met Margot outside her rectormitory building and in the already busy quadrangle kissed her. In eight days they would be married. Margot Eastwin-Cawthon. Or Cawthon-Eastwin. Whichever she preferred. It didn't matter. Julian was in

love with hyphens. Hyphens were the loveliest punctuation mark
ever invented by the hand of man. And didn't Margot look happy,
too? Happy and harried.

"I resigned this morning," Julian told her.

"Why?"

They began striding freely among the morning crowds. On every
street corner, in every p-court, gingko leaves jittered and flashed.
Out of the corner of his eye Julian glanced slyly at Margot.

"For a while," he said, "I was the world's only katzenappler—
unless there's another one in Scandipol. But there's no future in that
line of work. Tybourn thinks the newstapes'll take me on full time,
if I want."

"Good. Do you want?"

Julian stopped walking and caught Margot by the shoulders.
"Listen to this." And he recited for her:

Serene in my agony
I am carved in mahogany.

Once flesh in Gethsemane
And bones on Golgotha,

I'm serene in my agony:
A mahogany man.

Margot made him repeat it. Then she said, " *'Serene in my
agony,/I am carved in mahogany.'* That's Christ, the effigy in the
Memorial Chapel."

"Or Lileplagak, or maybe even Menny."

"Your old cubicle-mate? The one you're taking me to see?"

"The very one."

"Then why the references to Gethsemane and Golgotha?"

"Mythopoeic universals. The garden and the hill of skulls. Out of
the dead, life. . . . Hey, don't wrinkle up your nose."

. "You sound like Steinfels. But I like the poem. Is Idhe—or, uh,
Chavers—going to let you write poetry?"

"No. I'll be a police and biomonitor reporter, murders and
obituaries."

" 'Out of the dead,' " Margot quoted, " 'life.' "

This delighted Julian, but he could only smile to show that it did.
It was easy to see Margot was still thinking about her rediscovery of
little Moses yesterday. And I can't convince her that it was a random
encounter, and she can't decide what it's supposed to mean if it

wasn't. Meaningful? Meaningless? Neither of us knows. . . .

They hurried. Street-corner Saint Nicks asked for donations, and the speakers on a Consolidated Rich's battery van blared out Rita Radney's "I Am Your Fool, You Are My Yule." Through the courts and malls of Greater Peachtree Julian and Margot made their way to Coweta Town and the Kudzu Shop. Julian knocked nervously on its weathered front door.

Remarkably neat in a synthasuede overtunic, Menny admitted them and studied Margot appraisingly. Julian had spent two or three nights with Menny since the outing with Tybourn, and the big man now took a proprietary interest in not only the Kudzu Shop but Julian's private life. He gave advice. He asked questions. In a clumsy, roundabout way he tried to play papa to the prodigal son he liked to imagine Julian to be. . . . But about himself Menny preferred to remain mute; he told his young landlord that the stevedores who had rescued Tybourn and him were simply members of a receiving-point association of which he, Menny, was the director. The billy sticks were symbols of membership, nothing more. . . .

Now he pointed a hefty finger at Margot and shook it at her familiarly. "She reminds me of someone, Julian; she reminds me of someone."

"Who?" Margot asked, not at all taken aback.

"A girl I worked with once. Your hair's a different color and you don't have any freckles, but you favor her anyway. Her name was Cleo Noble."

"A stevedore?" Julian asked.

"Uh-uh. She worked with me and a man named Newlyn Yates on a resources-reclamation team. This was, oh, five years ago."

"What happened to the girl?" Margot asked.

"I don't know. When we got back, the authorities debriefed us and I quit. Soon after that Julian let me move into this place and I never worked for old r.r. again."

On a hibachi in the hothouse Menny fixed them toasted cheese sandwiches, carefully turning the triticale bread and swearing at each touch of the sizzling soy extract with which he'd basted them. They ate sitting on overturned flower trays.

After they had eaten a while in silence Julian said, "Menny, Margot and I are getting married on Year Day. We want you to come."

At first Menny seemed not to have heard. Then he stood up and gripped Julian's hands firmly in his own. "Good, good!" he said loudly, as if trying to disguise his emotion. Then he turned to Margot and gripped her hands in the same way. "I'm as pleased as I can be," Menny told her. "I really am." He seemed to have no idea what else to say.

If news of somebody else's wedding had such power to move him, what did Menny ordinarily live for? Julian was touched. A shambling, paunchy, bursitic Indian, for all his infirmities Menny didn't belong in the Urban Nucleus; he belonged where he could see sunlight wheeling off the back of a falcon or a pharaoh quail. Once he had worked where he could see such things, in the kudzu-filigreed Open. . . .

"It'll be in the Bitler Memorial Chapel," Margot said. "In the afternoon when it's available for private ceremonies."

Menny said that he would probably be working Year Day afternoon, as much as he wanted to come, and Julian suggested that in lieu of the wedding he attend Margot's graduation the following morning, Christmas day.

"Would you like me to get you a ticket?" Margot asked Menny. "Every deacon-candidate receives two for his parents, and my parents aren't alive anymore. . . . Julian can bring it back to you later this afternoon, or you can meet him outside Grant Field tomorrow morning."

It was agreed, and after putting a piece of wood over the smoking hibachi, Menny squeezed Margot's hand, said goodbye, and shambled off to work. When he was gone, Julian took Margot to the patio out back.

A pair of miniature trees sat on the top shelf of a bookcase against the patio's far wall, and curled up on the bottom shelf, five or six shapeless balls of fur surrounding her, was a three-legged calico cat. Menny had given her a ragged blanket to lie on, and the smell coming off the calico and her kittens was a basic one, strong, and fecal.

"One of my victims," Julian explained. "Menny calls her Trippi, short for Tripod. Besides, she likes to get under your feet."

"How old are the kittens?"

"Week or two. Menny midwifed them."

Surprisingly the kittens didn't occupy Margot's attention for long; she stood up from examining them and touched the bonsai on the top shelf.

"Aoyagi and Zakura," Julian said. "What's the matter?"

"Your parents started these?"

"The willow. The cherry tree belonged to Simon Hadaka Fowler, the nisei who first owned the Kudzu Shop."

"Tagomi used a bonsai display as the basis of a lecture. Interconnectedness was the point. Ever since, I've been seeing ghosts, revenants from my own past and the pasts of people I don't even know."

"We know everybody," Julian said. "But it's easier to pretend we don't." What did that mean? Margot seemed to understand him. She came to him, and he embraced her.

Trippi, ignored, began miaowing in a piteous and grating voice. To escape the cat Julian tried to lead Margot into the hothouse. It was an awkward dance. Kittens dropped off Trippi's dugs like soft, tiny bombs as the cat sought to follow them. Her miaowing was relentless. She weaved in and out of Margot and Julian's feet like a calliope tune.

Under the counter in the customer area Margot saw Menny's painted and varnished billy. She picked it up and handed it to Julian. "What's this?"

" 'The symbol of membership in an association of stevedores,' says Menny. That's all I know."

"It looks like a billy club."

"It's a red stick, Menny says. Just a red stick."

Margot replaced the billy and Julian opened the door to the street for her. He had to hold Trippi inside with his foot.

XLIII

THAT night at Steve & Dory's the other Red Sticks attacked Menny for his decision to attend the commencement exercises of the seminary. They accused him of cowardice, of selling them out. Shortly after they had begun arguing someone rapped hollowly on their boxcar's door. Arjuna drew it back, and for a moment the Japanese lanterns hanging in the beer garden looked like bright, swollen fruit or a flotilla of substitute moons.

"We close at one tonight," the headwaiter announced. "It's Christmas. Just fifteen more minutes, please."

Arjuna closed the door on the little man, and Menny, standing alone in the middle of the car, glanced around at his interrogators.

"You think I'm afraid to do what Shabazz, Clara, and Lou are going to do?"

"Are you?" Jastertree asked.

"We don't *need* four people in that car," Menny said, his elbow cocked out behind him. "And three people in the point are plenty, too. Jastertree on the control gantry, Nessim and Arjuna on the ground. Glom won't even be there tomorrow." The shadows etching out the faces of Menny's friends gave every one of them a ratlike rapacity and meanness. A false impression, a trick of the light. They just didn't understand what he was up to. "I've found my own way to die," he said finally. "You do what you need to and let me do what I need to, okay?"

"Menny," Nessim said, "you've gone off the crazy leap."

"The whole pootin' bidness is crazy, anyhow," Shabazz-Brown said. "Let him go to his graduation."

Just as if he'd downed too many win-a-gins and needed an escort, Nessim tried to walk Menny home. Menny waved him off. Then he came back and kissed Nessim on the forehead. Steve & Dory's Japanese lanterns were winking out in grave synchrony.

"You've got a tribe to watch over. Don't worry, Nessim. We'll meet again next cycle." He turned and walked to a station several blocks from the one the other stevedores ordinarily used.

It was Christmas. Menny's Red Sticks had volunteered to work a shift other than their own. Since most of the stevedores on the morning-shift were Ortho-Urbanists, despite their unenfranchised condition, the arrangement seemed to benefit everyone. Menny's group had filed their requests with Glom long before anyone else had thought to do so and had thereby taken all the positions allotted for the abbreviated Christmas work force. In fact, Menny had begged Glom to authorize two more such positions, from five to seven, and Glom had finally relented.

Now Menny had no intention of reporting for work the next morning. Glom would fire him, this time for sure. Thinking that, Menny stared at his wide, grinning face in the window of the pneumato-train carrying him back into the city. After tomorrow he wouldn't need a job. . . .

At one forty-five he entered the Kudzu Shop and went through the greenhouse to the patio. Trippi met him halfway, very nearly tripping him in the dark. He shook two handfuls of Kat Krispies into her dish and nodded brusquely at Aoyagi and Zakura. He ought to water them. Maybe the gods upstairs would make it rain.

"Jesus Armstrong Custer," Menny said aloud. "Three lies in one Person, Perfect Trinity." For a long time now he had believed Christ, Neil Armstrong, and General Custer separate personalities of the same unifying karmic ego. Just why, he had no clear idea.

From a clay pot on one of the shelves Menny lifted out and set aside a clump of soil. Exposed in the bottom of the pot was a plastic bag containing a tangled clot of sphagnum moss. Menny opened the lips of this bag and pulled the moss out in two easily separable clumps. He lay the clumps on the shelf, where they rested like a pair of unkempt toupees.

The object now visible in the plastic bag was a hand laser.

Newlyn Yates, the leader of the last resources-reclamation team Menny had gone out with, had given him the weapon on the very morning that Yates himself defected. Menny and Cleo returned to the Urban Nucleus in the cab of Jonah Trap's pickup while Yates stayed on at the Phoenix Plantation; presumably he'd later gone back to Scandipol with Nettlinger, on one of the cocky little physicist's alien-running excursions to New Free Europe. He had been a man much in love with the stars, and finally they had seduced him. Menny had always wondered why and how. The stars were only river pearls in a gorget of conch shells on the chest of the Cherokee's mightiest priest, and only this great physician/priest of all the *Adawehi* could ever hope to know their secrets. . . . In any case, Yates had given Menny the laser as a way of renouncing the city and smoothing over their own past disagreements. . . .

Menny took the hand laser out of the bag. No one at the debriefings had suspected him of having the weapon and so he had therefore not turned it in. . . . What would the old Cherokee have done with a weapon like this? Thrown it away, more than likely. When they needed food all they had to do was sing the songs the bears had taught them, and the bears would docilely give themselves up to the Cherokee's arrows. And why not? The *Yanu*, the bears, were Cherokee themselves; originally they had been of the *Ani-Tsaguhi* clan, people who had wearied of tribal life, retired to the woods, and grown hair all over their bodies as a result of the berries and roots upon which they fed. The Cherokee and the Yanu were related. You didn't use hand lasers on your relations.

"Nipples," Menny said, looking across the patio at Trippi. "It's all a question of nipples." He slept with the hand laser.

XLIV

Margot and her classmates, all in lavender gowns and mortarboards, stood in three columns under the central portal of Grant Field, waiting for the processional to summon them onto the lawn. Folding chairs had been set up in front of the stand from which the commencement address would be delivered and diplomas handed out. . . . Were Julian and Menny in the stands yet? An UrNu-sanctioned Dixieland band was playing Christmas carols somewhere above them, and that made it hard to think. The stable off to her left didn't help much, either; a ventilator fan wafted to them the odor of horse droppings, and in their nervousness the horses in the stalls under the A-section kept up a constant whinnying and stomping. Seven or eight stalls down, Margot thought she saw a tiny figure with ragged hair observing the graduating seniors suspiciously.

"Eddie!" she called. "Eddie! It's Margot!"

The figure ducked into a stall two thirds of the way back and disappeared, and her classmates turned their eyes on Margot as if she had committed a grave faux pas. Put out with their inflexibility and the delay they were all being made to suffer, she pertly faced forward.

The Dixieland band stopped playing, and an orpianoogla on the speakers' platform swung into "Come to the Church in the Wild Wood," not "Pomp and Circumstance" as they had rehearsed yesterday afternoon. What was going on? . . .

Acetate gowns snapping, the seniors began moving out of the entrance tunnel in their alphabetical columns. As they came out from the concrete overhang, Margot saw that it was Lileplagak playing the processional. Already seated on the platform were Saganella Ruth Lesser, the Church's five lieutenant bishops, and the six other Cygnostikoi to be ordained with Pal Lily. Overhead, balloons were floating, and on the opposite sideline a great many pigeons were cooing in capture-crates. In grandstand sections A and B stadium employees were hawking doughnuts and iced tea. These things, along with the bobbing lavender shoulders of her classmates, caused Margot to feel faintly seasick. Tonsured Billy and Alvar Caballero were several people ahead of her, and behind her she could hear Fredelle Fowles cackling at someone's whispered joke.

Where were Julian and Menny?

Pal Lily stopped playing. The graduating seniors stood in front of their chairs facing the commencement stand. Looking down the line of gowns to her left, Margot tried to find Julian and Menny in the two spectator sections looming above the field like immense, flag-strung staircases. It was impossible. They were lost in the general maelstrom. Finally everyone sat, and you could hear throats being cleared, pigeons cooing, tunics and dresses rustling, the occasional soft *blat* of a waterhorn among the Dixielanders.

Queasy and disoriented, Margot tilted her head back and watched the balloons sweep out of Grant Field in pied bunches. . . . If you were in a girder-car could you dome-dive into an ascending bouquet of balloons and thereby save your life? What happens once they—?

To the strains of Pal Lily's keyboard bugling, Bishop Holman came galloping onto the field astride a white Arabian stallion. But for his white leather boots and sacramental gold ribbons he was dressed all in canonical black. Long hair silkenly afloat, the High Bishop stood tall in the stirrups and inscribed a huge figure eight around the speakers' stand and the rows of chairs facing it. One winged sleeve fluttered madly as he hailed everyone in the stadium. And as a single person, everyone came whooshingly to his feet, including Councilor Lesser and the six Cygnostikoi beside her. The starmen got up like lawn chairs being unfolded.

At the platform Holman dismounted and dropped his horse's reins on the artificial turf. (The horse, who'd surely been out there before, tried bewilderedly for a few minutes to graze.) Then he vaulted up the stairs and positioned himself in front of a microphone pickup on the platform's draped guard railing. The rustling of his black gown, when he raised his arms, was communicated throughout the stadium in staticky crackles. Lowering his arms, he invited everyone to sit.

"This is the most important Christmas in the history of the world since the birth of Our Savior!" The stadium echoed his words, filled with applause, and then rumbled again with echoes. "Creation and the birth of Our Savior aside, of course, you may today be witnessing the most important event in cosmic history. On this eighty-fifth

day of Autumn we are marrying with our spiritual equals in an
interstellar fellowship.

"Moreover," he said after a pause, "your sons and daughters are
graduating today and will soon be ordained as deacons in the
Church." Then Holman introduced the dignitaries on the commencement stand. He introduced the Cygnostikoi as "Clarence,
Peter, Barry, Snowden, Justin, Quint, and our orpianooglist Lind-
ley." He called them "our brethren, peers, and teachers from 61
Cygni A."

Teachers. . . . Margot wondered if Mz Bitler was in the stands. If
she and Nettlinger were in the stands, though, as proud parents to
the starmen, it would be just as hard to find them as to locate Julian
and Menny.

Then Holman delivered his commencement address. He ap-
pealed for a cryptic "assault on the City of God by today's graduates
and our Cygnostik allies in spiritual sentience." (Whew.) He spoke
of converging on the breastworks of the Celestial City in two
ascending, parallel phalanxes under the generalship of the Second
Person of the Trinity. He hinted at the apotheosis of every Christian
soldier once this ascent was complete. He used a puzzling metaphor
whose terms were the potential (or the Becoming) of Atlanta, City
of the Phoenix, and the eviternal and perfect stasis (or Being) of the
City of God. He also said something about the evolution of the many
varieties of awareness toward enfranchisement in a celestial community. . . .

Margot could tell that no one knew what Holman was talking
about. The best thing about his address was that it was over in eight
or ten minutes. Six crates of pigeons were released into the air, and
Holman's audience, apprehending this as a sign, at last began to
applaud.

"And now," said Holman, tapping the microphone pickup,
"Councilor Lesser will present our graduates' diplomas."

Stunningly cadaverous, Saganella Ruth proceeded to a table near
the front of the platform and, assisted by a lieutenant bishop, handed
out the diplomas to the students who crossed behind her as Lileplagak played "Upward for Aye on Wings" and the High Bishop
called the roll.

"Abner . . . Adelbert . . . Agee . . . Aquaviva . . ."

In twenty minutes the presentations were over, and the deacon-
candidates, laminated scrolls in hand, sat in their nine rows of
folding chairs awaiting the last rare item on the morning's program.

"Today," said Holman, static crackling off his vestments, "we
ordain as priests in the covenant of the Ortho-Urban Church seven
Cygnusians. . . ." Margot, determined to overcome her own resent-

ment, kept her eyes straight ahead, her hands folded in her lap. Even so, it was hard not to dwell on the discrepancy between her situation and that of the Cygnostikoi. Diploma in hand, she still had to wait six more days before she could truly consider herself a deacon in the Church, whereas . . . whereas . . . She put it from her mind.

The seven Cygnostikoi came forward and knelt at the commencement stand's railing while Bishop Holman spoke from memory the words of ordination and investment. (Today's investment, however, was metaphorical.) It was the most Spartan ceremony Margot could recall attending. At its end Bishop Holman passed behind each starman to touch his crested head in final certification and blessing.

An animallike bellow sounded from the spectator sections. Margot, as did everyone else, turned to look.

And then she saw Menny—despite the distance she could tell it was Menny—standing ten or twelve rows up in the A-section waving something in his hand.

"Do you know what you're doing?" he bellowed, taking a step or two down the central aisle, holding the stadium at bay with the thing in his hand. *"Do you?"* He swayed like a bear in halt-chains.

From seven or eight rows up Margot heard Julian call Menny's name. On the speakers' platform the First Councilor was promptly surrounded by security personnel. The Cygnostikoi rose whirringly, and Bishop Holman tried to squeeze between them to reach the microphone.

"Enfranchisement!" Menny shouted. "If you can ordain them, you can give me my citizenship!"

Margot saw Councilor Lesser nod her head. Below the A-section a number of uniformed men and women began converging on the central aisle. Menny's position was such that they apparently feared to fire upon him. . . . It struck Margot that twenty years ago Asbury Holman would have been called upon in a situation like this.

"We don't want what they can teach us!" Menny was shouting now. "We don't want what they know! We don't want their wisdom!"

Behind Menny a man—it was Julian!—came hurtling down the steps. Menny, swaying back, saw him coming and also became aware of the guards clustering up from below and forcing their way across the grandstand tiers from the section's other two aisles. Treed . . .

Almost reflexively Menny leveled the thing in his hand and fired. A thread of light burned from his fist to the platform, where something intercepted the thread and wound it into itself. . . . People were screaming, and Margot suddenly couldn't see Menny any longer, or Julian, or what had happened on the commencement stand. Panic and astonishment were being broadcast through her ganglia, and she forgot even to pray.

Then the jostling backs of her classmates parted, and through this opening she watched as Bishop Holman vaulted to the back of his Arabian and spurred it toward the melee on the eastern sideline. The crowd continued to scream, and Margot wondered what the High Bishop thought he could do once he got over there. She sprinted past several toppled chairs and saw him urging his horse into a sea of spectators in front of the stadium's main tunnel.

"Everyone will please sit down!" a shrill voice said over the public address system. "Everyone is *requested* to sit down!" The voice belonged to the First Councilor and, amazingly, as soon as she had spoken, the chaos on the field and in the grandstands seemed to subside.

"Margot," Tonsured Billy said, appearing beside her out of the commotion; "look, Margot, one of the starmen!"

She turned and saw Lileplagak sprawled on the speakers' platform, almost obscured by the legs of the First Councilor's guards. Although his head was tilted forward and up by the circle of his halo-crest, he was certainly dead. Already his eye patches looked dry and papery. The other six Cygnostikoi had returned to their chairs and were taking in the comedy of human beings in either violent terror or rabid pursuit of one another. They might as well have been watching a ping-pong match.

A woman in the security service came dogtrotting to the platform from the grandstands and spoke to Councilor Lesser, who announced over the P.A. system that the assassin had been captured.

Captured, Margot told herself. Not killed.

"Will each of you please rise and remove any hat or head covering you happen to be wearing?" Councilor Lesser said, and over in the A-section the Dixielanders discordantly began to play. Saganella Ruth waved her arms in time and doughtily sang. Even though almost everyone joined in, even semicynical Tonsured Billy, Margot could only grip her sides and stare in mute bafflement at the ground.

> I'm a ramblin' wreck from Georgia Tech
> And a helluvan engineer.
> Like all jolly good fellows
> I drink my whis—

An explosion deafened Margot. A domequake shook the Urban Nucelus from one end to the other. Margot felt as if her heart had shut down all its operations. The city's integument grumbled and split. A thousand pigeons seemed to be flying. Her feet were pressed against an undulating green treadmill, her ears throbbed with the continuing concussion. Then, looking up and turning toward the west, Margot saw debris showering down upon the Peachtree Complex from an unbelievable height.

High above the city, in the rent this mysterious explosion had made, there already shone a triangle of pale, forgiving blue.

XLV

"WHO is it, Em?" Fiona asked when a man in a synthasuade jacket lumbered out of his seat and down the central aisle of the A-section, and turning to her Emory read premonition and a certain drained resignation in her face. She already knew who it was in the aisle— not the man's name, nor the precise set of his face, nor the personal criteria by which he defined his own existence, but the terrible identity by which the world would choose to remember him.

"Do you know what you're doing?" the man shouted. "*Do you?*"

People began to stand up, Fiona with them, and off to their left, rising from the same row the angry man had just come from, another figure got out of his seat and scrambled down the steps.

"Menny!" this person called. "MENNEEEEY!"

"Enfranchisement! If you can ordain them, you can give me my citizenship!"

Fiona's face was taut, and Emory saw in it a death mask. Her hands were moving away from her body like mottled brown manta rays, swimming into another dimension, and he wanted to catch them before they got away.

Meanwhile, the grandstands seemed to topple slowly forward, as if ready to spill all the people struggling within them onto the green below. The madman in the aisle shouted something about not wanting wisdom and Emory could feel a searing diagonal slashing of his retinas as the madman changed himself from human being into an event.

"Sit down with me," Fiona said. "Em, sit down with me." She put her wavering hands against his chest, where they had no place to dock. He grasped them. Then she slumped, and he had to catch her about the waist. She didn't say anything else, and they couldn't sit down because the people behind them, in order to get a better view of the aisleway, were standing on their seats. The P.A. system blared out something, but Emory didn't hear it because he was talking nonstop to Fiona, urging her to look at him.

Then things were all at once quieter. A scuffle of some sort was still going on in the A-section's center aisle, however, and no one paid Fiona and him any mind. When he was at last able to sit down with her she sprawled away and he barely had the strength to recover her. No one paid them any mind. Did everyone think Fiona a stone-out, a tetra-lush? Was that it? All right, all right, let them think what they would? Maybe they weren't thinking anything. . . .

Contemptuous of them, Emory kept talking to Fiona in a steady, controlled, hopeless whisper.

The P.A. system gargled again, people stood up, and suddenly he and Fiona were in a cove of legs and buttocks while the First Councilor's moronic soprano vibrated over the crowd. He was grateful that Fiona heard none of it.

Nor did she jump against him and cry out when the girder-car above the Peachtree Complex exploded and scattered its wreckage into the streets of downtown Atlanta. Nor did she have time to see that tiny bit of blue left behind in the rent up there. . . .

XLVI

CLARA stood on the girder-car's running board, her hands hooked inside the door, surveying the city laid out beneath her like a circuit diagram. Three meters overhead the shell of the Dome pressed down with its blinding batteries of solar lamps and its immense polygonal frame. There was no wind. Almost directly below, the saucer of the Regency Hyatt House stared up at her with its blue pupilless eye; the tower of the seventy-story Plaza Hotel rose above the Regency's eye like a spike. These were terrible things to behold.

Even though Lou, Shabazz-Brown, and she planned to freefall from the girder-car and then float to safety on the Domediving 'chutes Arjuna had stolen from a packing crew of the Atlanta Meteors, Clara felt like a Christmas-day kamikaze. Would they really get down before the debris from the blast came tearing through them like shrapnel? Was there really going to be any coming back? . . .

"Lordy, lordy!" Shabazz shouted from inside; "in fiftee minutes we gonna zip the top off this tin can!"

But what for? To what end? A gesture. Over there, where the stadium's artificial turf shone like billiard-table felt under hot light, Menny was preparing to die for a gesture of his own. . . . It just didn't seem very much like his description of the Battle of Horseshoe Bend, even taking into account the terrific odds against them, latter-day Red Sticks that they were. Him down there, us up here, we're all of us crazier than Menny's Crazy War Hunter ever was. . . .

How could you jump from such a height? Clara wondered if she would have the will to let go, once the time came. Why, a fall like this could . . . could kill you.

Two hours ago the Red Sticks had proved that a fall could kill by slinging the pilot of their girder-car to the receiving point's gantry and from there to the asphalt of the yard. Crimsonly splayed and crumpled, the pilot had given shocking testimony of the fatality of such a fall. . . .

The dynamite Shabazz was setting now was from one of the McAlpine Company's demolition units. The Red Sticks had pooled their salaries and bribed a McAlpine foreman to give them the explosives and to disguise the sale as the remaindering and disposal of defective goods. On Christmas, then, they had exchanged their billies for fascicles of dynamite.

"Now these are *real* red sticks," Shabazz said as Clara and Lou waited for him to finish and join them. "They gonna make some noise and wrack, yeah, lordy, they sholy will."

"Get on with it," Lou said curtly.

"Ready, Skyhook. Let's go."

Like a perverse and insistent lover urging her toward a concussive orgasm with the city, Shabazz-Brown was behind her now. Lou was on the opposite running board. . . . No. No, he wasn't.

To Clara's surprise and instruction Lou was falling away from the girder-car at a speed maddening to contemplate, a spreadeagled scrap of life with a hump on its back and a shiny blue cask on its head. Down, down, down, spiraling away until . . . *poof!* a huge orchid bloomed on his back and its weird petals began silkily rotating.

"If you don't go soon, sister," Shabazz-Brown was saying, "you and me gonna fly down docked."

She threw herself out into the vacancy below the car. A gesture; a loony gesture. Watching the buildings and p-courts rush up at her like mortuary slabs, she was pretty sure they were all going to die, anyway. Well, let it be glorious, let it be grandiose and asinine. What else had the Nucleus given her? Falling, she decided that she would try to land right in the middle of Peachtree Street, right in front of the Regency. . . .

XLVII

MENNY pushed his weapon's safety into place and dropped the pistol at his feet. He stopped swaying. Julian's arms slithered around his neck from behind, forcing him to lean back to relieve the pressure. A shrug would have dislodged the boy, but he couldn't summon the will to summon the strength.

"Oh, Menny, Menny," Julian was whispering into his ear, clinging to him, "what'd you go and do that for?"

Hadn't he told everyone? Wasn't it evident? . . . Seeing Menny corraled from behind, the converging security personnel fell upon him from every side. They pushed Julian out of the way in order to secure the big man for their own. Then, jerking and prodding, they bullied him down the steps to the stadium's walk.

Menny kept his head up, partly because he didn't want to hang it, partly because the guard at his back was tugging on the hair at his nape like a rein. A woman's voice reverberated over the stadium, but Menny couldn't discriminate among the individual words she said. Somebody's spittle was on his cheek, and he was remembering the way, just a brief while ago, his three fellow stevedores had disappeared into the canyons of the city under huge, twirling parachutes.

"Dammit, you oafy shit," the guard at his back said, "*move!*"

On the walk connecting the various sections of the stadium bodies streamed like water. Some of these, up ahead, ebbed aside to let

Bishop Holman and his Arabian stallion push through.

Bridling his balky horse and turning it in a tight half-circle, the High Bishop waited for Menny and his guards to approach him. Menny, head tugged back, caught his adversary's eye and stared at him indifferently. Holman, restraining the skittish Crusader, told the guards he was going to try to lead them to the court beyond the main tunnel.

Outside the stadium a paddyroller van was waiting for Menny. It carried him to the police station in downtown Atlanta, and even though it was Christmas, Menny was interrogated that afternoon as relentlessly as he had been five years ago upon his return from Toombsboro. He told his interrogators almost nothing.

That evening he was placed in a detention area in the basement of the station house: a volume of space defined by one concrete and three continuously generated air walls designed to render a murderous localized shock if penetrated. Three or four "cells" away, a heavyset black man wearing only a loincloth sang plantation blues in a voice like a woman's.

The following morning a detective from the homicide division, a deceptively benign, doe-eyed Negro named Thrailkill, told Menny that although one of the Cygnostikoi had in fact died, the others were all safely ordained as priests. Menny stared at the chlorine-green walls in the interrogation room and pretended that Thrailkill didn't exist. The detective said that the people who had parachuted from the hijacked girder-car hadn't done particularly well. He called them "terrorists."

"One bad landing," Thrailkill said. "One defective 'chute. The one that survived tells us you planned the whole kersmoosh, Mr Guest. If it hadn't been Christmas, you'd've had more people outside and a bigger kill. As it was, you injured a few with falling debris, knocked out some windows, collapsed a tenement building or two. Too bad."

Then, rolling his eyes like chocolate bonbons, Thrailkill asked Menny if there was anything he wanted before the second round of interrogations began. Any request within reason. Having already prepared himself psychologically to die, Menny decided to make legal preparations too. He asked Thrailkill for pen and paper.

My last will and testament, he thought. Painstakingly he wrote out instructions for the disposition of the few personal goods and items of property he'd acquired, without benefit of suffrage, in a half century of city life. Thrailkill took the list from him and vowed that he'd execute everything just as Menny wished.

That afternoon, and five more mornings after that, the grilling went on, maddeningly repetitious and mundane—until on the morning of Year Day he was transported in a closed van from his basement detention area to a strange, oddly furnished suite in the Human Development Towers. The room smelled as if someone had once used it for cutting up spoiled kidneys and serving them to randy cats. Thrailkill escorted Menny in and told him that an official in the Ortho-Urban hierarchy had recommended these accommodations. "Thinks you can maybe be rehabilitated," the detective explained. "Who knows?"

But no one came to see him that day, and he spent most of his time pacing. On one wall was a hologramic window reproducing in animated detail the Japanese gardens in the Urban Nucleus of San Francisco. Finally Menny sat down in front of it and watched the people come and go. Their clothing suggested that the projection had been made twenty to twenty-five years ago. He was watching a slice of the past unfold in tedious, three-dimensional verisimilitude. It was Spring in San Francisco. . . .

After a while Menny's vision began to take its clues from internal rather than external stimuli. He understood, a little, what was happening, but he was powerless to reverse the process. His heart began beating violently. The Japanese bridge flattened into a dry plain, the flowers lost their color and elongated into cottonwoods. The cottonwoods, in turn, leaned from the window into the very foveae of his eyes, and the blight afflicting the trees was transmitted through his optical nerves to his blood.

Menny felt feverish. His hands shook. It's cholera, he told himself. They've given me cholera.

No one came that day, and he hoped that he could survive the disease long enough for someone to remember his presence in the suite and embark him upon a course of treatment. Even though the sickness besetting him wasn't cholera, wasn't anything at all but the fever of his imagination, no one came. No one came. . . .

XLVIII

On Monday, the eighty-sixth, Saganella Ruth Lesser declared martial law in Atlanta, reimposing the curfew that had been in effect a week before Christmas and banning all assemblies that weren't related to either the city's religious life or its commercial well-being. "You may shop or pray," she said, "but in places proper to these activities."

Throughout the week Weather Control pled technical difficulties and refused to assume the blame for the Nucleus's drafty, germy weather. People gathered in the streets to look at the sky, and girder-cars approached the almost triangular hole through which the sky was visible and parked around it like a convention of gigantic scarab beetles. Men in magnetized boots and gloves worked inchmeal to close up the rent.

On Tuesday, the eighty-seventh, Fiona Bitler was eulogized in a private ceremony in the Carlo Bitler Memorial Chapel. Her remains were committed to a waste converter on Level 9. Two days later Dr Nettlinger left the city to accompany Lileplagak's body back to Scandipol. Yetunde Trap, Fiona's cousin, went with him only as far as Toombsboro, where her grandfather and parents lived. No one else, of course, would be permitted to enter or leave the city without the express permission of the First Councilor.

On Friday, the ninetieth, Councilor Lesser announced that the city's police force, in conjunction with the UrNu B.I. and security personnel, had arrested and quarantined the members of a revolutionary organization called the Red Sticks. It was dedicated, she reported, to the destruction of Ortho-Urban democracy and the Dome itself. Their leader, Alexander Guest, was the same man who had assassinated the Cygnostik Lileplagak during the commencement exercises of the King Theological Complex. Guest was now being held in solitary confinement at an undisclosed location.

On the ninety-first, a Saturday, the final day of both Autumn and the year itself, Julian attended the formal ordination of Margot and her classmates in the main sanctuary of the Worship Center. Asbury Holman presided. The six Cygnostikoi priests, busy preparing for their first full day as ministers, were elsewhere. . . . At the end of the ceremony Julian put his hands on Margot's waist, lifted her into the air, and whirled her about in the sanctuary's main aisle. Smiling, she spread her arms and turned in the stained-glass gloom like an angel of benediction. For Julian the moment was precious; in it he could very nearly forget the nightmare of the Christmas season they had all just survived. . . .

XLIX

UNDER the mahogany effigy of Christ in the Bitler Memorial Chapel, Margot and Julian were married. Despite the traumatic and trying events of the previous week, the ceremony took place on Year Day as scheduled. Tybourn was present for the wedding and filed a report.

EASTWIN-CAWTHON VOWS EXCHANGED

. . . No rings were exchanged, and by mutual agreement the marriage vows departed from Ortho-Urban tradition. Mr Cawthon, for instance, answered *nolo contendere* to an inquiry as to the status of his faith, but offered the presiding minister three character witnesses and a notarized pledge to respect his wife's beliefs. Deacon Eastwin entered in the transcript a promise not to try to proselytize her husband.

The Biblical text was 1 Corinthians 13.

The Eastwin-Cawthon wedding was the first at which a Cygnostik priest has presided. "Father" Kee Wig was appointed to officiate at this exchange of vows by the High Bishop Asbury Holman, who also intervened to permit the couple special use of the Bitler Memorial Chapel. . . .

The wedding party itself was small. The groom's best man was Nicholas Tybourn of the *Jour/Con* newstapes. The bride's maid-of-honor was Deacon Emma Gosling of the Littlest Angel Care Center. Giving the bride away was Karl Tagomi, a professor of divinity as well as a respected horticulturist. Others in attendance were Deacon William Björkman, Father Roland Flinders, Deacon Jack Russick, Bishop Holman, and the five Cygnostikoi recently ordained with the presiding minister.

An interesting feature of this wedding was that "Father" Kee Wig prerecorded his ministerial challenges as well as the orpianoogla program selected by the bride. During the ceremony he synchronized his lip movements to the tapes he had made beforehand. The Ortho-Urbanist *Register and Fact Book* contains no report of any other minister's having ever used this procedure. . . .

Refreshments were served at a post-ceremony reception in the lounge of the Littlest Angel, downstairs. On display here were the wedding gifts the couple had received. Among the most unusual of these were two lovely dwarf trees given by an unidentified friend who was unable to attend the service. The couple are now honeymooning in a provisionally assigned Level 3 cubicle.

Sitting in the lotus position on their bed, her smell tantalizingly female, Margot was holding a photo-repro of the article. The story itself wouldn't appear until the next day, and, having it in hand, they felt like keepers of privileged information. They had been married exactly eight hours and twenty-two minutes.

Julian lay with his arms behind his head, his feet on a pillow next to Margot's head. Blissful or empty, which was he supposed to feel? He experienced both emotions together.

"What's the matter?" Margot asked. "Second thoughts?"

He propped himself up. "The week's catching up with me. Being here with you seems criminal, a dereliction of duty. . . . What about you?"

"I don't feel criminal or derelict, Julian. But I know what you're talking about. Angst."

"Look over there. On the bureau." Without looking Margot knew that he was pointing to Tybourn's gift, the photographs of the septigamoklan members taken by Zoe Breedlove. Six fetching old faces. All Margot could see from the bed, though, was the photograph of Parthena Cawthon. Julian had placed it on the bureau as if establishing a shrine. Unframed, the other five old folks had been temporarily shuffled together and stacked in a drawer. . . . Tybourn had not mentioned his gift in his account of the wedding.

"Julian—" Margot began, wanting to dispel his melancholy mood.

"Margot," he said.

"Julian—" she attempted again.

"Margot," he said. Then he yawped with delight at this exchange and made her laugh with him. She scrambled the length of the bed to his mouth, and in mid-kiss the Sillies carried them off again. He smelled Lime Mime and she smelled herself in Julian's breath, an incense they'd made together. At last they stopped laughing.

"We both believe in ghosts," Julian said, referring obliquely to the photographs, "and in their power. Maybe we're both afraid of who or what'll be behind our door when it suddenly gets knocked on."

"Curious. Not frightened."

There was a knock on the door.

Despite what Margot had just said, each could see a flare-up of fear in the other's eyes. Why not? It was nearly eleven P.M., and only the UrNu Housing Authority was supposed to know where they were. . . . Margot remained in bed while Julian pulled on a dressing gown and went into the main living area to answer the door. Don't open, a rational corner of his mind advised. But acting on a light-headed suspicion Julian ignored the communicator and let the door slide back.

In the doorway was a wholly unfamiliar starman humbling him with its towering presence and its chrome-and-mahogany fixtures. . . . Wait, that's wrong. You *have* seen him before.

The Cygnostik was carrying a shopping bag and its eye patches were a feeble, glowing lemon in color. It was Lileplagak! It was Lileplagak in the body of Dragsted's statue from the Promenade of Universal Amity!

"Lily? Lily, is that really you?"

Lileplagak flapped his shopping bag, nodded his noggin.

Clutching her robe at throat and navel Margot padded into the living area, recognized the statue, and somehow identified the intelligence inhabiting it as Lily's. Certainly it was. She knew him. Despite having found his way unassisted to their cubicle Lileplagak looked harried and disoriented. His eye patches had a touch of jaundice, his halo-crest had an eleven-o'clock droop, his whirr was raspy.

"Julian, let him in! And take the sack. He's not trick 'r treating, he's got something for you."

Lileplagak, his B-bulbs dilating, edged gratefully into the room, and to make up for his stunned rudeness at the door Julian led him to the sofa and made him sit. Then he looked in Lily's shopping bag and extracted a pale brown folder. A binding like vellum . . .

"It's a wedding present, isn't it?" Margot said.

Whirr, said the resurrected Lileplagak.

Julian exhaled and turned the silky cover back. The folder contained only two pages, each of a vellum somewhat lighter in weight than that of the cover. Forearm flesh? Maybe. Anyhow, the text on these pages was set in neat, perfectly justified triple columns. He read a bit of it. It was his short story "No Other Gods," the one Saba Dearborn had embarrassed him with on his birthday, the one containing the names the Cygnostikoi had so arcanely appropriated for their own!

Lily, Margot noticed, looked better already. His eyes were brighter, his purrings perkier, his features a good deal more fierce than was altogether comfortable. The starman, apparently wanting to embrace them, opened his arms . . . and Margot and Julian retreated, until a recollection of their manners halted them and drew them back. Lileplagak didn't seem to care. He examined furniture, bric-a-brac, and wall hangings. Then, uninvited, he hitched and jiggled into their sleeper-cove, where there was very little to look at but their unmade marriage bed.

Embarrassed, Julian and Margot followed him.

His attention suddenly captured by the photograph of Parthena, Lileplagak paused at their bureau. His pupils were now so large that his eye patches were obliterated, only a little lemon light showing around the bulbs. Then his A-bulbs contracted so rapidly that Julian was sure the starman had turned off the current energizing them; they became dots when a moment before they had been snifter bowls. Margot and Julian were both shocked when Lileplagak picked up the framed photograph of Parthena and rudely turned it face downward. *Wham!*

"Hey," Julian said, stepping forward.

The starman held up a hand to stop the former katzenappler and then brought both hands to his head from behind and hooked his fingers over the forward edge of his halo. This was a touching posture somehow, but a pretzely one. Meanwhile, Lileplagak's body shuddered like a fuselage of a pneumato-train.

"What's the matter, Lily?" Margot asked him. She understood that the photograph had moved him. Resisting an impulse to hysteria, he was trying valiantly to compose himself.

He wiggled a few of his fingers toward the bed.

"You want to lie down?"

Uh-uh; Pal Lily shook off this suggestion. He untangled and pointed at Julian and Margot, indicating that it was *they* who ought to lie down. Then, ignoring the absence of a chair, he assumed a seated posture at the foot of their bed. A voyeur's posture, it seemed to Julian.

"Margot, I don't think I'm—"

"Hush. Come on." Margot crawled across the bed and stretched out next to the wall. She patted the hollow beside her. "Don't you want to find out everything you can about your employers?"

"*Ex*-employers." But he relented and lay down. He experienced a moment of *déjà vu*: a Cygnostik beside his bed, a vinegary dream, a frail woman holding him on her lap. . . .

"Hush," Margot said, touching his lips. Even though he had said nothing, she wanted to forestall new surfacings of Julian's anxiety. It was a wonder *she* could be so calm. Now Lileplagak had his arms outstretched, a "wingspan" almost wall-to-wall, and he had drifted into a homeostatic trance. Just think what a "nap" initiated in this way had done to Jeremy R. Downson. . . .

At their feet, beyond their toes, Lileplagak loomed terrifyingly. They each had one look, then no more. Their eyes shut of themselves, and they lay side by side asleep.

They were asleep but their consciousnesses flowed together so that Margot didn't know which part of her was Julian and Julian didn't know which part of him was Margot. Each was aware of the physical parts—hair, toenails, stomach panels, genitals—lying outside this fluid merging, aware of the continuing separateness of their fingertip-touching bodies—but none of *this* separateness mattered anymore because in their sleep each was the other, each dreamt what the other dreamt, each felt what the other felt. And their joined consciousnesses sat up out of their sleeping bodies to converse with the resurrected Cygnostik, Lileplagak.

—*I never got to see you when you was jes' a li'l chap,* Pal Lily said, *'cause I done died the year you was bo'n. You Georgia's chap, Julie, and I see her in you, I really do. . . . Ain' it crim'nal what I got ɩɔ do to talk to you? Put both you and yo' new missus asleep ɑnd climb out on top o' this body what I got now. Seconds I'm takin', seconds. It ain' what I s'pected, Julie. Hardly ever is, you 'wanna know the truth. I thought I'd get waterhorns and orpacycles right on up to God's throne . . . but the universe don' work that way, it wasn' to be. We in one profoun' state of ig'runce, Julie, and even up here, where I am now, we got a long way to go. It heartbreakin' how far we got, and no way to 'scape tryin' to get there, neither. Die and you jes' come back, a bit futhah on if you lucky and done made a li'l progress in yo' soul. . . . But it's slow, Julie, it's mighty, mighty slow. . . .*

Superimposed on Lileplagak's statuesque form was the wavering image of a frail, bemused black woman. Seated, she brought her

arms into her midriff and quietly folded them. Lileplagak's body
was her chair, but she was so much a plasmic aura, so little an
elemental substance, that even without a chair she could have
floated forever at the foot of their bed.

—*Yes, it's true. After dyin' here, I went out—jes' a streamin'—
to someplace that wasn' noplace, really. And when I woke I wasn'
me but the critter you see me sittin' on . . . only I knew who I'd been
befo', you see, ever so far back, all umpity-thousand of myse'fs, all
the way back to when we got spun out o' nuthin' by a 'God' who
wasn' himse'f nuthin' but a chip off'n the True One. . . . You
comin' to it too, you two, you comin' to a death what's gonna lif'
you out o' this dungeon—'cause that's what it is, the bottomest
dungeon of 'em all—and put you in bodies like what I'm wearin'
now. A body what makes it easy to see The Light inside yo'se'f so's
you can unnerstan' that the main thing you gotta do is go up another
notch, and then another one, and then one more, jes' as far as you
can go—till the las' pit's been 'scaped and you all the way back to
The Beginnin'. That's when the universe gets blown out like a
match and we all of us at las' together in the True God. . . . .Shoot,
we all of us gonna be the True God, you see.*

—*Ah, but we got other bodies and other dungeons to get
through, Julie, and we don' even know what they like. We in one
profoun' state of ig'runce. And you folk, people folk, you was worse
off than us till we come down here to you from Out There. Julie, we
tryin' to he'p you skip a step, that's what we hopin' to do, that's
what-for we come. . . .*

The etheric essence inhabiting this new Lileplagak had once
inhabited Julian's great-grandmother, and she—no, *it*—was speaking to them from that previous incarnation, apprising them in
Plantation Patois of ontological truths so staggering that the Margot
/Julian consciousness recoiled, fell back in metaphysical disarray,
hovering in its mirth and panic on the edge of what it was ex-
periencing.

If Lileplagak had once been Parthena and Parthena had once been
others, then Margot and Julian had also had previous aspects,
identities, personalities. Avatars, one could say. Must they therefore believe that one day—how many incarnations hence?—they
would tenant the same sort of cybergamic shells as did the Cygnostikoi? Could this really be a step up, this vile dependence on alley
cats and apples? How much better to believe in the possibility of
enlightenment, or salvation, or mystical union in the "Omega
Point." How much better to believe than to know. . . .

—*Course you don' like it. It's jes' like stoopin' down to a li'l
chap, a poor lovin' chile, and sayin', 'You ain' ever gonna grow
up, honey, you jes' gonna turn into a whole bunch o' different*

*bogey-monsters.' . . . It's a turrible thing, this what I gotta tell you.
But evvybody the same in it, ain' nobody better off'n the next un. . . .
Fiona and Emory, they was tryin' to say that, sorter, in all their talk
'bout takin' down the Domes. They unnerstood this here 'Phoenix
City' was jes' another dungeon in a dungeon.*

*—You two jes' the same as them, even 'f you don' believe it yet.
That's why the critter I'm scooterpoopin' aroun' in done some
matchmakin' to get you to hitch. Fiona dead, The Light in her still
skyin' aroun' somewheres, and Em gone off to Scandipol again.
You a smart boy, Julie, I don' have to write out what you and
Margot oughta be doin' with all this info I give you. Jes' start,
mainly. Nobody don' ever get too far, that's the truth, but you still
gotta start. You sholy got to start. . . .*

Sleeping, dreaming, Margot/Julian realized they had just been
privy to a revelation and a charge. In a way what they had just heard,
or dreamt, or absorbed through spiritual osmosis, was a contradiction of what each of their waking selves believed. Margot's faith
was mocked, and Julian's absolute agnosticism, his Know-Nothing
stance in the face of cosmic politics, was undermined by too exact a
knowledge. . . . *We've been fed answers to questions we didn't
know to ask,* the Margot/Julian consciousness reflected numbly.
*We've been given answers we would rather have remained ignorant
of. For what, what really, can we do? . . .*

Parthena Cawthon faded. In her place was only the great chrome
and mahogany statue that Lileplagak's soul had just that morning
entered, the corpse of a Cygnostik who had perhaps found the
gateway to the next prison-keep on the spirit's forced march to God.
How long, O Lord, how long?

The statue brought in its arms, eased itself out of its seated
posture, and stared down at the sleeping bodies of Julian and
Margot.

They awoke, and Pal Lily's A-bulbs dilated to a size equal to that
of his shrinking outer pupils. Margot drew up her knees and
clutched them. Julian swung his feet to the floor and then went to the
starman to embrace him, impulsively oblivious of the artificial
barrier of his great-grandmother's body. What did these housings
matter? Of what importance were they in the communion of kindred
souls?

And all souls, Margot thought, watching them, are kindred. She
envisioned Tagomi's shy, smiling face as he led her to the altar.
What would *he* do with a revelation like the one she had just
received.

"The Cygnostikoi are going to need a new katzenappler, Julian," she said aloud. "And Lily's been away from the cold too
long. Why don't you walk him back to the Regency—your grand-

mother, I mean—and see what sort of arrangements they've got now that Nettlinger and Yetunde have left? . . . We might be able to persuade Bishop Holman to assign us to the Regency, if you could stand living there again. He'd probably be agreeable to whatever's best for the Cygnostikoi.''

After what they'd just been told, Julian wondered how Margot could think so pragmatically about things. My ignorance has merely been dispelled, after all, but Margot has to cope with the overwhelming possibility that her belief system is a lie. Why isn't she overwhelmed? Why aren't we both despondent, crushed by the weight of our prisons?

"Gramma, let me get dressed,'' he said to Lileplagak, kissing him on the chin. ''Then I'll go surfaceside with you, okay?''

Lileplagak—Parthena—retreated to the living area, and Julian dressed. Pulling on his leggings he asked Margot, ''How do you feel?''

''Empty,'' she said. ''And elated.''

''What Parthena's just told us destroys the significance of Or—'' He stopped. ''Of most human religions. Only the Hindus among us believe in reincarnation, but I don't think they believe in it like *this*, the way Parthena's explained it.''

''No,'' Margot said.

''Are you all right?''

''I'm not destroyed, Julian.''

''We're recipients of revelation. Like Saint John, like Muhammed, like Joseph Smith. I don't know how to react . . . what do do.''

''Revelation doesn't change who we are. We still have our lives and personalities, Julian. I don't feel like a prophet. I didn't feel like a prophet when I found little Moses—Jeremy Downson—in the parcel locker. I don't think I can undergo a second metamorphosis. I don't see why I should. Or why you should, either.''

Margot's serenity was intimidating. Had her faith prepared her even for its own demolition? So many things were crumbling, so many suppositions coming unstuck and unstrung. As an adolescent, bereaved and bitter, he had often wished for just such a denouement. Now, with his great-grandmother awaiting him in the guise of a masterfully disney'd entity from 61 Cygni, the irony of his own unpreparedness struck him. He had wanted people to be so much more than they were, and he himself was so much less than he could be. . . .

''It *was* a revelation, Margot. Or don't you believe what we've been told.''

''I'm an agno on that, Julian. What else can I be? How do we attain to knowledge without faith? Every epistemology requires that, finally.''

Margot watched Julian dress. He wore a melon-striped overshirt and a pair of cantaloupe-colored slippers. She had prommed for these at Consolidated Rich's, and she thought he looked good in them. . . . What could she tell him, though? That not everyone accepts every revelation? That Julian was himself still wobbling between alternatives? Two thousand years from now (if Judgment Day hadn't come, either at God's behest or humanity's) people might still be worshipping the "True God" of the Cygnostikoi.

But there would still be heretics, even against the evidence of other men's revelations. And, perhaps, their own. People were joined by their intransigence in this matter of joining together, and few, so very few, recognized the bond. . . . Maybe the Tagomis of the future would succeed in illuminating the several strands of the universal web so that one day, canted to the light, it would glint like a gong of silk and summon everyone to its witness. And even then, gloriously human, some would choose to be blind. . . .

"The smell of you is an epipsychidion call," Julian said. He put his knuckles on the bed and leaned forward to kiss her. Ultimate Reality mattered, he knew, but you had to be a fanatic or a madman to commit yourself utterly to the Truth . . . even if it was, in fact, The Truth, The Whole Truth, and Nothing But The Truth. After all, you didn't spend your entire life on the witness stand. . . .

"You'd better go," Margot said. (In the other room Pal Lily, or Parthena Cawthon, was jiggling nervously about, waiting.) "I'll be here when you get back. Just be careful."

Out in the Level 3 corridor a paraplegic beggar/guard, one of MeeJee Stone's brothers-in-arms, was holding his submachine gun above the heads of a crowd of revelers. In the red light they advanced toward Julian and Lileplagak in a straggle of loose legs and lank arms. Their joy, although almost completely unfocused, was uncompromising. Their teeth gleamed ferociously, and their feet, Julian noticed, were bare. Somewhere a computer clock had just struck midnight. It was the New Year. . . .

CHRONOLOGY

On November 4, Old Calendar Designation, Parthena Cawthon is born in Madison, Georgia.   1964

Apollo 17, final American manned flight to the moon.   1972

Maynard Jackson, first black mayor of the city of Atlanta; on January 8 (O.C.), Zoe Breedlove, nee Stevens, is born in Winder, Georgia.   1973

Celebration of American Bicentennial; Vikings I & II put down on Mars.   1976

Domes of the twenty-five Urban Nuclei are constructed; formation of the Urban Federation and collapse of the United States as a discrete political entity.   1994-2004

First Evacuation Lottery, during which many citizens of the old political unit called Georgia enter Atlanta on the basis of random computer-selection.   1995

Second Evacuation Lottery.   1998

Third Evacuation Lottery; Fiona Bitler, nee Foe, aged six months, enters with her family from an enclave near Toombsboro, Georgia.   2001

Dome is completed; Fourth Evacuation Lottery.   2004

Fiona Foe marries the young evangelist-reformer Carlo Bitler.	2119
A joint project involving Europeans, Eurasians, and Japanese establishes Amity Base on the moon.	2023
Emory Nettlinger (later adopted by a man named Coleman) is born in the Atlanta Nucleus.	2025
Political disturbances, social ferment; Carlo Bitler becomes spokesman for the city's disenfranchised.	2025-2029
Tyler Kosturko, son of a prominent ward representative, and Georgia Cawthon, granddaughter of Parthena Cawthon, are born.	2028
Gerard Nettlinger (Emory Coleman's biological father) assassinates Carlo Bitler.	2029
Disappearance of Fiona Bitler and her Van-Ed student Emory Coleman from the Atlanta Nucelus.	2034
Urban Council and Conclave of Ward Representatives pass the Retrenchment Edicts; covenant ceremony of the original Phoenix septigamoklan takes place.	2035
After death of Yuichi Kurimoto, Zoe Breedlove becomes a member of the Phoenix septigamoklan.	2040
Light-Probe Institute in Scandipol, in conjunction with Amity Base, test-advances a spacecraft four light-years and then retrieves it in a ninety-three-day period.	2043
Margot Eastwin is born in the Atlanta Nucleus.	2044
Ty Kosturko and Georgia Cawthon, Julian Cawthon's parents, are married.	2046

Dr. Leland Tanner resigns as head of the city's
gerontological programs; the ten existing septigamoklans are dissolved.   2047

Parthena Cawthon and Zoe Breedlove die; Julian
Cawthon is born; light-probe ships go from lunar
orbit to six different, computer-selected solar
systems.   2050

"Glissador Revolt" occurs; Julian Cawthon's
parents lose their lives as a consequence.   2063

Fiona Bitler and Emory Nettlinger return from
Scandipol to the Phoenix Plantation near
Toombsboro; a resources-reclamation team is sent
to escort them back into the city.   2066

Margot Eastwin enters the King Theological Complex; Fiona Bitler and Emory Nettlinger return to
Atlanta with two visitors.   2067

Julian Cawthon finds temporary employment with
the *Jour/Con* newstapes; several alien conversions
occur; Margot Eastwin service-assists at a special
ceremony in the First Ortho-Urban Worship
Center.   2071

Revelation.   Year Day, 2071

SCIENCE FICTION BESTSELLERS
FROM BERKLEY

Frank Herbert

DUNE   (03698-7—$2.25)

DUNE MESSIAH   (03585-9—$1.75)

CHILDREN OF DUNE   (03310-4—$1.95)

Philip José Farmer

THE FABULOUS RIVERBOAT   (03378-3—$1.50)

NIGHT OF LIGHT   (03366-X—$1.50)

TO YOUR SCATTERED
BODIES GO   (03175-6—$1.75)

* * * * * * *

STRANGER IN A STRANGE
LAND   (03782-7—$2.25)
   by Robert A. Heinlein

TAU ZERO   (03210-8—$1.50)
   by Poul Anderson

THE WORD FOR WORLD
IS FOREST   (03279-5—$1.50)
   by Ursula K. Le Guin

Send for a list of all our books in print.

These books are available at your local bookstore, or send price indicated plus 30¢ per copy to cover postage and handling to Berkley Publishing Corporation
390 Murray Hill Parkway
East Rutherford, New Jersey 07073

FANTASY FROM BERKLEY

Robert E. Howard